Brother of Sin

The Blackwood Brotherhood
Book 1

Wendy Vella

ARE YOU SIGNED UP FOR DRAGONBLADE'S BLOG?

You'll get the latest news and information on exclusive giveaways, exclusive excerpts, coming releases, sales, free books, cover reveals and more.

Check out our complete list of authors, too!

No spam, no junk. That's a promise!

Sign Up Here

www.dragonbladepublishing.com

Dearest Reader;

Thank you for your support of a small press. At Dragonblade Publishing, we strive to bring you the highest quality Historical Romance from some of the best authors in the business. Without your support, there is no 'us', so we sincerely hope you adore these stories and find some new favorite authors along the way.

Happy Reading!

CEO, Dragonblade Publishing

CHAPTER ONE

L ORD HAMILTON SAT on the side of the bed to pull on his boots.

"I will be unavailable for a few days," the woman behind him said.

Anthony rose when he'd finished and glanced down at her. Lush full breasts, thick blonde curls, and a sated smile on her face. Sienna was a beauty, and he felt nothing when he looked at her. He used her, as she did him, and that was where their arrangement began and ended.

"I have a friend—"

"I need no one else." Anthony placed some money on the table beside the door when he reached it and left without another word.

Outside, he walked, feeling the cold creep back into his body now he was no longer in the throes of passion. Needing something else to indulge in, he hailed a hackney.

Twenty minutes later, he walked into Hugh's gambling establishment. Anthony felt the ebb and flow of fear and excitement around him as he studied the tables. The air held the scent of tobacco, alcohol, and desperation, and it was a fragrance more familiar to him than most. This should possibly bring with it shame, but as the emotion, like many, was a waste of his time, Anthony sat at a table and began to play.

The light was low, but enough to see which card he needed

to lay next, but not bright enough to read the faces of some of those seated farther away.

Lifting his whiskey, he threw the entire contents down his throat, enjoying the burn. Anthony enjoyed anything that made the numbness inside him ease, no matter how briefly.

Across from him, Mr. Stephens shot him a wide-eyed look before quickly lowering his eyes. He inspired that reaction in most people.

"Beaton has just lost a vast amount. We'll see his family pack up and leave London in no time," the man to his right said, glee evident in his voice. "They will be living off his brother soon, you mark my words."

He turned to face Mr. Joshua who had spoken. Anthony doubted much showed in his expression, but whatever was there made Joshua pale. It no longer surprised him how his fellow man could find joy in another's demise. He was no different.

"Just making you aware, Hamilton," Joshua muttered.

Normally he wouldn't care if a fellow nobleman lost his entire fortune and ended up sleeping in the poorhouse, but Beaton was a Blackwood boy, and they were different.

No Blackwood boy will walk alone.

"Didn't you have a large loss recently, Joshua, and your father had to pay off your debts?" Anthony asked.

"Just a run of bad luck," the man muttered.

Anthony had heard those words far too many times to care.

He played a few more hands before the murmur of voices had him raising his head to take in his surroundings once more.

"That French bastard is winning again," Mr. Dolton, also seated at Anthony's table, hissed.

Anthony turned slightly to the left to see which "French bastard" was the subject of Dolton's anger. Searching the tables, he stopped when his eyes landed on a young man with white hair. *Unnaturally white*, he thought.

"Why anyone who is not a lawyer, doctor, or old enough to remember when they were in fashion would wear a wig is

beyond me," Joshua muttered. "The man looks like a fool."
Everyone but Anthony agreed.

"Who is the French bastard?" someone queried.

"Goes by the name of Mr. Renee," Dolton said. "His play is cautious, but he wins most often and well, damn him."

"Doesn't talk unless necessary. Odd sort. Never takes a drink either," Joshua added.

As Anthony was still watching the Frenchman he saw him raise a hand to push back a strand of the blond wig in a surprisingly elegant gesture. He had a thick dark beard that covered the lower half of his face, and eyeglasses, which made him appear scholarly.

"I'm convinced that as well as the wig, the beard is fake," Dolton added. "I've wondered a time or two if he's an excellent cheat, but as yet there's been no whisper of it."

The commotion coming from Beaton drew Anthony's eyes away from the Frenchman. The man was staggering to his feet. He stared down at the table for long seconds and then stumbled from the room.

Looking at those seated around Beaton's table he noted one man in particular. Cavendish. Catching Anthony's eyes, his lips twisted into a smirk. He then nodded. Anthony showed nobody fear, especially not someone responsible for his past torment, so he raised his glass and gave him a mocking smile in return. Rage flashed across Cavendish's eyes, and it was he who turned away first.

You believe you are better than me do you, boy? That because you're an earl you are above me. I'll break you of that notion.

He remembered the words and the punishment that had been the first of many delivered by the older boys, of which Cavendish had been one. The thrashings had taken place at Blackwood Hall, where Anthony had lived for five years.

Looking down at his hand, he noted it was clenched in a fist and released it. That time had shaped him into the cold, emotionless man he was today.

Dismissing Cavendish and the memories, Anthony continued to play until he was ready to leave.

Rising from his chair, he nodded to the men at his table.

"I say, Hamilton, you can't leave now!" Sharpe cried. "I haven't had a chance to win back my money."

Anthony may have a reputation for being ruthless, with an attitude that suggested he cared about very little, but one thing he would never endanger was what kept him safe. Money. Wealth gave him power, and he would never forsake that for anything. So, he only gambled what he'd allowed himself that night, no more and no less.

He walked away without speaking to where a waiter stood. Pulling out several notes, he pressed them into his hand. After finding out what he needed about Beaton's losses he then headed toward the first door, of which there were three before he could leave the building.

Anthony stepped out of Hugh's into foggy London air. He waited for a carriage to roll by before crossing the street. The driver hunched into his heavy coat, hat pulled low. Inside, Anthony saw a couple in an embrace and felt his lip curl. No woman had made him feel the need to spend more time than was necessary with her. He enjoyed his mistress's company, as she did his, but neither wanted more.

Love, Anthony had long ago decided, was for the weak. He was not that and never would be again.

Crossing the road, he headed for his town house. Sleep wasn't something that came easily to him, so he walked a lot at night and never feared the shadows where danger could lurk. In fact, he embraced a good fight if one came his way.

A whimpering sound reached him as he neared a narrow opening.

"I'm sorry," someone whispered. "But surely this is not the way."

Anthony was not a man who involved himself in the lives of others. So, he prepared to pass the narrow opening.

"You don't understand. I have lost it all. Dear lord, I cannot continue knowing the shame I will face. Let me do this, I beg of you."

"Nothing is worth your life, Lord Beaton." At a guess he thought the heavily accented voice had to be Mr. Renee as he'd left after Beaton.

Anthony thought about walking on, but the pledge he'd made many years ago stopped him.

"Is that you, Beaton?" Anthony asked moving into the narrow opening.

"Go away." His voice was slurred.

"Help! He is going to kill himself," the Frenchman sounded desperate now.

Sighing, Anthony moved closer, damning the small sliver of honorability that raised its ugly head inside him on rare occasions.

He saw Renee's hands gripping Beaton's pistol, and Anthony could only guess he was attempting to stop the idiot from taking his life after his losses at the table.

"Move now. Leave Beaton to me." *They will never walk alone.* He cursed silently as the words filled his head.

The Frenchman didn't appear to take orders well as he continued to struggle with Beaton.

"If you have no wish to have that pistol blow out your brains, Renee, move now," Anthony said.

Releasing Beaton's hand, Renee finally rose and backed away.

He couldn't see his face now as the man stood in the shadows. "Leave," Anthony snapped.

"Oui." The Frenchman did as he was told.

Beaton raised his pistol, but Anthony wrenched it from his grasp and dropped it into his pocket.

"Let me be! The shame. I cannot continue," Beaton said in a drunken wail. "Why does a bastard like you care what I do, Hamilton?"

"I don't," Anthony said in a hard tone. "But you are a Blackwood boy. Therefore, I am doing my duty."

"I don't understand?"

"I'm sure you don't, but listen to me now, Beaton."

"I-I have lost it all," the man whispered. "The shame—"

"You are to go home to your bed. In the morning, you will rise and not say a word to anyone about what you've done."

"I have nothing—"

Anthony took a card out of the inside pocket of his jacket and handed it to Beaton. "Come to this address on Friday at 10:00 am."

"I-I don't understand?"

"You will. Now you are going home." He pulled the man to his feet.

Anthony walked and heard the slow scrape of shoe leather almost as if each step was too much effort, and yet the broken man followed. He saw the movement from the corner of his eye. The Frenchman was still watching from the shadows.

"I told you to leave."

"I was just checking you needed no further assistance." He spoke the words in French, clearly thinking Anthony could understand them.

"I need nothing from you. Do as I ordered at once, and forget what you have seen," Anthony replied in the man's tongue. "This is no place for one such as you."

He did, but only after a few muttered words Anthony translated to mean arrogant nobleman, and then Renee was gone.

"Damn fool Frenchie," Beaton rallied himself enough to say. Clearly having forgotten that were it not for Renee, the man would now be dead.

"As he was attempting to help you, I doubt he is any more a fool than you," Anthony replied.

No words were exchanged after that. They walked to a main street, and Anthony hailed a hackney as it rolled closer. Opening the door, he waved Beaton inside.

"Go home and present yourself at the address on the card on Friday. Bring your son, as he has a great deal more sense than you. This is not up for debate, my lord," Anthony added when the man opened his mouth. He then shut the carriage door, and it rolled away.

He'd done what he could. If Beaton lived long enough, they would help him because he was one of them, for better or worse.

"Got any money?" Two men stepped into his path, both looking for trouble. He would be happy to oblige them with that.

"What's he smiling about?" one asked the other.

"Maybe he's not right in the head?"

"Believe me, you couldn't be further from the truth. Let me pass, gentlemen, or pay the price," Anthony said welcoming the rush of excitement.

They ran at him. He stuck out his boot, and one tripped and fell hard on the ground. The other was faster and punched him in the jaw. Anthony tasted blood and returned the favor. They traded blows until the other man regained his feet, groggy and bleeding from his nose. Anthony finished toying with the man and landed a blow that sent him to the ground. The sting of his knuckles making him feel alive.

"Come on then," Anthony taunted the other man. Blood streamed from the brigand's nose. The man turned and fled, much to his disappointment.

Stepping over the unconscious one, Anthony continued his journey home, relishing the surge of heat inside him. For those few brief minutes, the cold was gone again. Entering his townhouse, he made his way up the stairs with lamps lighting his path. His staff were familiar with his nighttime movements.

The house was large and had been lived in by Earls of Hamilton for generations. Things left behind by his dead relatives were everywhere, including the portraits that hung in a perfect row in the gallery.

Reaching his rooms, Anthony tugged off his boots and clothes. After washing, he held the cloth to his throbbing cheek, then pulled on a dressing gown. He then stepped back out into the hallway, and across it to his study.

Lighting the lamp he kept there, he then pulled out paper and pen and wrote the notes. When that was done, he took them downstairs and placed them where his butler would find them for delivery in the morning. Only then did he retrace his steps and head for his bedroom.

Minutes later he was lying with the curtains open, watching as the gray light of dawn crept slowly over the city of London, his heart once again a cold shriveled organ.

CHAPTER TWO

T HE FOLLOWING EVENING, Miss Evangeline Spencer, not by a flicker of an eyelash allowed anyone to see the pain she suffered. If she could get her finger into her ear without someone noting, she would. The screech from the violin was giving her a headache, as was the supposed highly regarded soprano singing on the stage.

"Isn't she amazing?"

Glancing to her right, Evie looked at her sister and the delighted expression on her face.

"You are not serious?"

"Deadly. Miss Dornetto has a wonderful voice."

"It's hideous, and every dog nearby is howling."

"Oh shush," Prudence whispered.

Shorter than Evie, Prue was the softer, sweeter Spencer sister. She always had a genuine smile on her face, unlike the cynical one Evie wore. Her hair wasn't simply brown, but more cinnamon and shot through with gold streaks. Pale skin and lovely blue eyes. She wore a simple cream dress with a blue sash under the bodice, which suited her elegant figure. In short, Prudence was the epitome of what every debutante should aspire to be... unlike her older sister.

"At least father is not here tonight, so we do not have to listen to him humming or clapping," Prue said.

"A small mercy, but one nevertheless," Evie agreed.

She felt an arm brush hers on the left side, and turned to look at who was lucky enough to have arrived halfway through the performance and was now taking the empty seat. Her eyes met Lord Hamilton's, and the breath lodged in her throat as she saw the dark bruise on his jaw. It made him appear more savage than normal, which was saying something.

What was he doing here? She doubted a man with his reputation would willingly come to such an evening.

His head did a tiny dip to acknowledge her, and his lip curled as if to let her know he was about as happy to see her as she was him. She did the same and then they both looked to the stage, united in their mutual loathing of each other.

Of course, he would arrive late. Beastly man, he could do whatever he wanted. Hostesses either gushed all over him or quaked in fear. His reputation was blacker than coal, and he had the manners of a barnyard animal. Arrogant, rude, he cared little for society and its rules. Evie despised him even more than jellied eels, which was saying something.

She attempted to move to the right, so their bodies did not touch. Even through layers of clothing, she felt like his skin was in direct contact with hers. The man was far too large to be considered elegant. She could see the width of the knee closest. Encased in white breeches, it was at least twice the size of hers. His boots must be huge.

"Dear God," he muttered as the soprano hit a high note, badly.

"Perhaps if you are not enjoying the performance, you could leave, my lord?" She spoke the words in a sickly-sweet tone out of her smiling mouth, so that anyone looking would think she was being polite.

"I don't believe I asked your opinion, Miss Spencer."

His insulting drawl made Evie want to slap him. Instead, she focused on the performance, which was not easy as it was terrible.

Unlike the man next to her, she had to be polite. Evie's family did not have the status and wealth to offend. In fact, their future depended on the success of this season. Appearances were everything and while the Spencers seemed a family that could walk with ease in society, they most definitely were not. Their time in London was short, and Evie did not want to contemplate what would happen after.

"Next time you drag me to another spectacle like this, I will refuse, no matter if I win or lose," Lord Hamilton said.

Evie turned her head slightly, and out of the corner of her eye noted the crossed legs beside him. No doubt they belonged to one of the two men he seemed to keep company with, Lords Corbyn and Jamieson. Although why anyone would want this man as a friend she had no idea.

She heard the men murmuring and then a loud shushing from in front of them.

"Apologies, Lady Linley," Lord Hamilton said, much to Evie's surprise. She didn't think the man knew how to apologize.

"Don't come if you don't want to listen." Lady Linley added, now glaring at him, her many chins quivering with indignation. "What happened to your face, Hamilton?"

Evie braced herself, as surely he'd eviscerate the woman for daring to question him.

"I walked into a door," he said, which she thought was a lie.

Lady Linley huffed out a disapproving breath. "Your aunts will tell me the truth."

"Undoubtedly," he replied.

The woman wore a garish mix of colors and things in her hair that defied gravity. She also said exactly what she wanted. Evie aspired to be just like her one day.

"Is that a bearded tit in your hair, Lady Linley?" Lord Hamilton asked minutes later, drawing the woman's eyes back to his.

"No," she snapped.

"A coal tit?"

Evie swallowed her giggle. She absolutely would not let that man see her smile over something he'd said. He was a dissolute rake whom she loathed.

The first time she'd stepped into society, Miss Everland told Evie and her sister to keep their distance from Lord Hamilton, as he was a destroyer of reputations who drank and whored his way through London. Of course, Miss Everland had not mentioned the whoring, but it was implied.

"A blue tit," Lady Linley said. "Now do be quiet, Hamilton."

Again, to her surprise, he did as he was told.

Long minutes ticked by, with Miss Dornetto showing no sign of drawing breath on stage or the performance coming to an end. Evie was clenching her muscles to ensure she did not touch the dark lord at her side. Hopefully her agony was over soon.

"Not only are you clumsy, but you constantly move."

"Pardon?" She faced Lord Hamilton, and their eyes clashed like swords on a battlefield.

"Your leg, it's twitching," he snapped.

"Better?" Moving so their legs were no longer close, she faced forward once more.

He didn't answer. Horrid man. It was vastly unfair that he looked as he did and had wealth and status but the personality of a feral jungle cat, while she had to find inventive ways to ensure financial security for her family. Not to mention remain socially acceptable. One slip and they were doomed.

"Now your fingers are tapping."

She spun back to face him. Why any man should have such lovely eyes was beyond her. They were a dark shade of amber and surrounded by dark brows and lashes. She'd heard Miss Brittle say that Lord Hamilton's eyes made her swoon, and it was a shame he was such a savage, as he'd make a wonderful husband.

Evie thought they were hideous, simply because they belonged to him.

"Go away if my presence annoys you," she snapped, stopping short of insulting him further. He was after all rich, titled, and powerful for all he was a hideous person. She could not afford to insult him in a public setting.

"Unfortunately, I lost a bet," he muttered, "or I would gladly oblige, as the performance is terrible."

She wasn't sure he could be termed handsome, but she'd heard other women describe his face enthusiastically. It comprised of sharp angles and planes, with a long nose that had a slight kink to it. His hair was black, and a little long, which she thought added to his air of insolence and entitlement. He stood half a head above her, which she loathed.

"Don't be rude," Evie snapped. "Some people are enjoying it."

"I'm not sure how. However, if I must endure the performance," he added, "I'd at least like to do so without you constantly moving."

Prue always said Evie's biggest failing was her inability to shut her mouth at the right moments. She loathed bullies and fools, and especially hated when people took her to task, even if she deserved it, which in this instance she most definitely did not.

She counted slowly to five, as ten was beyond her, and told herself no good would come of her taking one of society's most notorious members to task, even if he deserved it. It didn't work. She faced him once more.

"I can stop my movements, my lord, whereas you can do very little to change your personality, which I assure you is that of an ill-mannered feral dog."

"Pardon?" His dark brows now met in the middle in a fierce frown.

"Evie." Prue hissed the word into her ear.

"Nothing," she muttered.

"Oh, that was definitely something," he said. "Don't back away now, Miss Spencer. Tell me exactly what you think of me. After all, it's likely nothing I haven't already heard."

"Then one wonders why you don't try harder to be nice," Evie snapped.

"I have no wish to be nice," he drawled. "I much prefer being bad." The smile accompanying those words could only be termed wicked, and she itched to slap it from his face.

She bared her teeth at him.

"Wonderful," Prue said rising. "The performance is finished, and the dancing shall begin. Come, sister, let us take some refreshments first."

Prue tugged her arm, and she was soon following the other guests out of their row and leaving that hideous man behind.

"We are walking a thin line in society, Evie, as you are aware. Do you think it wise to start an argument with Lord Hamilton, who with a single word could destroy both our reputations?"

"He is vile and obnoxious." Evie looked at her sister, who was rarely angry, but clearly was now.

"He is terrifying, and his reputation is blacker than midnight. Therefore, stay away from him, as he would not hesitate to ruin you, and ultimately us," Prue said. "Besides, it's not like you even know the man."

Not quite true. In fact, they'd already shared several terse words when they'd collided on her first night in society. Ever since then, until tonight, she'd kept away from him... well, at least as Miss Spencer she had.

"Miss Spencer, how lovely to see you again."

"Lady Petunia," Evie said with a genuine smile at the elderly woman before her. They'd met two nights ago and chatted over a plate of supper. The woman had a lively mind and wicked humor, and a forthright nature. Unfortunately, she was also Lord Hamilton's aunt, which could not be easy considering his reputation.

"Did you enjoy the performance?" Lady Petunia asked. The words were fired at her like hail on a windowpane. Perhaps there were some similarities between her and her nephew after all. "I saw you were seated beside my nephew."

Evie nodded. She would say nothing further because no good could come of insulting the man who shared Lady Petunia's blood.

"We loved it," Prue said before Evie could speak.

"Miss Spencer, would you allow me this dance?"

She hid the need to flee at the deep words. Instead, she smiled up at Lord Cavendish.

"Lady Petunia, Miss Prudence Spencer, if you will excuse us," he then said, before Evie had agreed to dance with him.

Hand forced, she followed him to the floor. Looking over her shoulder she saw the frown on Lady Petunia's face and wondered what had put it there?

At least it was not to be a waltz, so she could put some distance between herself and Lord Cavendish. Since entering society, he'd sought her out constantly, and she felt uncomfortable around him. What she couldn't work out was why she had found favor with him when there were plenty of other prettier woman who were younger, titled. Plus, they had dowries, which she did not.

"I would like to call upon you and take you driving, Miss Spencer," he said when the music had started, and they were dancing. "There is also a picnic I will accompany both you and your sister to."

"I am, of course, honored," Evie lied. "However, I am unsure of our movements at this stage, my lord." She scrambled for excuses.

"You will come driving with me and attend that picnic, Miss Spencer. Your beauty has bewitched me, and I will not take no for an answer."

"Lord Cavendish, I'm here to look after my sister—"

"You are too beautiful to be a chaperone." He dismissed her words, which made Evie's teeth snap together. She hated anyone doing that.

"Thank you for your kind words," she choked out.

She looked around for anything to distract him. Her eyes found Lord Hamilton's. He gave her a mocking bow, and Evie thought seriously about poking out her tongue, but knew someone other than he could see it.

"They are the truth," Lord Cavendish said as the dance finished and he led her back to where Prue stood chatting with a group of people. "I will return shortly, with some refreshment for you and your sister."

She watched him walk away from her and wondered why men always believed they knew what was best for women? Her father, of course, was the exception to that rule. He rarely knew what day it was.

Both Spencer sisters knew that one of them needed a husband, and Evie had decided Prue was their best prospect. However, Lord Cavendish was rich and titled, or so she believed, and seemed interested in her. What she couldn't understand was why? It would not do for her to insult him, but if she was honest, she had no wish to spend her life with the man if that was his intention.

Which makes you selfish, as your family needs financial security.

"Miss Spencer, how lovely to see you again."

Happy to be dragged from her thoughts, Evie turned to look at the lady standing behind her.

"Lady Agatha." Evie dipped into a curtsey. This was another of Lord Hamilton's aunts, of which there were three. It was something she could not quite reconcile with the rude lord. He had three delightful aunts, two who seemed to have soft edges and loved to gossip, and one who was forthright but equally lovely.

"Do you know my nephew well, Miss Spencer?" Lady Agatha stared hard at Evie after these words.

"I don't, my lady."

"Lovely boy. We, his aunts, dote on him, you know."

Dear lord, why?

"He is exceedingly lucky to have you, I'm sure," Evie said when nothing else came to mind. That anyone would want to dote on that man was completely beyond her.

"Excellent rider, and of course, titled and wealthy. He has all his own teeth, you know, and is admired by both men and women," she continued.

This conversation was growing odder and odder. Evie looked at Prue, but she was chatting with two young ladies and no help at all.

"He, ah, he sounds a wonderful man."

Lady Agatha beamed, all the wrinkles in her face flattening as she did so.

"His reputation does not portray him accurately you see, my dear. He is misjudged and is quite gentle when you get to know him."

Her eyes found him a short distance away, leaning against a wall, looking bored with a glass in hand. He bowed his head as two young ladies scurried past sending him fearful looks. It took clenching every muscle in Evie's body to stop from laughing hysterically. *Gentle?* She knew a sow that had the same mean disposition as him. Clearly, his aunt was not right in the head. She turned back to Lady Agatha.

"Do you like lavender, Miss Spencer?"

"It has a lovely aroma," Evie said.

"Well, let me tell you about its healing properties."

This, Evie thought, had to be the oddest conversation she'd ever had in society, but she found herself liking the woman who thought her horrid nephew was misjudged, even if she was deluded.

CHAPTER THREE

ANTHONY WOKE TO the tap on his bedroom door after achieving about four hours of sleep, which was usual for him. He'd not slept long hours at Blackwood Hall, and that had become a habit.

"What?" he bellowed.

"You have visitors, my lord."

"Who?"

"Your aunts, my lord," the voice told him through the door.

Scrubbing his face, Anthony sat on the side of the bed. Only they would dare to show up at his house at such an hour. Unlike the rest of society, they did not fear him.

"Enter, Dibley, but only if you have coffee."

The door moved and then his butler appeared with his manservant on his heels. Tall, bald, and with manners that would make any mother weep with joy, Dibley had been in Anthony's employ for ten years.

"Are they all here?"

His butler lowered the tray he carried to the nightstand, thankfully bearing coffee, while Bernard scurried to the window to open the heavy drapes. Anthony grabbed the cup and sipped, letting the hot, black, bitter taste slide down his throat.

"Yes, my lord."

"Did they offer any clue as to why?"

"As to that, Lord Hamilton, I am unsure. I believe the words, 'it is dire, Dibley, extremely so. Please wake our nephew with coffee at once,' were spoken by Lady Petunia."

Anthony didn't growl because he'd learned long ago to let no one hear or see what he felt, but it was clearly implied as his butler took a large step back and left, bowing out the door.

The room he slept in was not as grand as the rest of the house. Anthony had stripped every memory of his father from it. Changed the curtains and flooring. Removed the bed and had a new one put in. It was now plain without the fussy trimmings the late earl had adored.

"The gray will do, Bernard," Anthony said when his manservant appeared with a pale green waistcoat and black jacket.

"Your aunts—"

"Will take me as I am at such an hour," Anthony added as Bernard scurried back to replace the green for the gray waistcoat.

He pulled on his clothes and allowed Bernard to tie his neckcloth.

"I have no wish to look like a puppy; no more folds if you please." Wisely, his manservant kept his thoughts on the matter to himself, although the tightening of his lips suggested he was displeased.

Another who had been in his employ for some time, Bernard was short, immaculate, and knew a great deal about meat as his father had been a butcher, much to the delight of Anthony's cook.

He looked in the mirror and saw the bruise on his chin was now an ugly shade of burgundy, but there was little he could do about that, so he stomped his feet into boots and left the room. Stalking along the halls lined with the treasures of his ancestors, he took the stairs down and reached the parlor his aunts were in. Their conversations were never quiet, so Anthony could hear every word as he approached.

"He will have to come about, Petunia."

"There is no choice."

"We have the list now."

Anthony entered the room, bracing himself for the kissing

and touching. He'd told them he'd rather they didn't do that every time they saw him, but they'd ignored his wishes. So, he endured the fussing because he owed them that much.

"One hopes that bruise was not from a fist, Nephew!" The first to reach him was the eldest of his father's sisters, Lady Petunia. "We have an urgent matter to discuss with you." She leaned in to brush the air beside his cheek, leaving the scent of lilacs when she straightened. Large in every way, including her personality, her husband had died, leaving his entire fortune to a nephew, and thus her penniless.

"Of course not," Anthony said.

Like the other two women in the room, Aunt Petunia had silver hair styled perfectly in a bun at the back of her head, and she always wore the color of lavender no matter the season. The shade varied slightly but little else.

"Hello, darling boy." Lady Agatha was next. "That bruise looks sore." The middle sister, who Anthony thought secretly had the most sense, stepped forward. She patted his cheek with a soft hand and smiled. "Sorry to descend on you, but the matter is urgent." She had married an earl, who had died five months later, leaving no heir and all his money to his brother. Her favorite color was apricot.

"Quite urgent," the youngest sister said. Aunt Lavinia was the smallest and had little to say unless she first asked her sisters if it was appropriate to do so. She'd been the gentlest of his aunts growing up. Her favorite color was a soft sage green.

Her husband had been the third son of a baron, and they'd had fifteen years of wedded bliss before he passed. Anthony knew she still missed the man she'd loved dearly.

"Please sit," he said, waving to the sofa they always sat on when they invaded his privacy. Petunia on the right, and Agatha on the left. Lavinia wedged in the middle. His aunts were creatures of habit.

Anthony had left for school, happy, as the nephew of three doting aunts, who had stepped into his and his sister Harriet's lives when their parents died. That soon changed, and the cruelty he faced left him reeling.

"Have you heard from your sister?" Aunt Petunia demanded in that forthright way she had, sounding like the words were fired from a pistol.

"A letter arrived yesterday. I will be reading it when I take my morning meal." Harriet was married and living in the country happily with her husband. They were as close as he let anyone get, but did not see each other often.

"She's well, and happy with Simon. We also received a letter yesterday, but unlike you, have read ours."

"I know she's happy, Aunt Petunia," he said, resisting the need to rub his forehead. Conversations with these three were exhausting.

"She's excited about the child."

"I beg your pardon?"

"You should have read the letter," Aunt Aggie said stepping into the conversation.

"Child?" he said instead of repeating that he was about to read it before they invaded.

"She is with child, Anthony," Aunt Petunia snapped.

He was to be an uncle. Anthony felt a stab of something he thought could be joy, closely followed by pain that a child would be someone else he needed to watch over. Someone who could be harmed if not protected. It would also need love, but not from him. He was incapable of such things.

"You must visit her, Anthony," Aunt Petunia said.

"I will." He gave the response he always did when they asked something of him, and then usually did what he wanted, but in this they were right. He would make time to visit with his sister, now he knew she was expecting.

"Now tell me, what else has you all here at this early hour?" he added, looking pointedly at the clock on the wall behind them.

"We saw your Aunt Louise," Aunt Agatha said. "I told my brother all those years ago not to wed her, yet he would not listen. Woman is completely irrational."

"Dreadful person," Aunt Lavinia added.

"Beastly," Aunt Petunia agreed.

They always talked like this. One would start a conversation, and then the others all added their bit, until eventually someone got to the point. Anthony waited patiently, which wasn't something he excelled at.

"She said that seeing as there is no heir, it's imperative that simpering weasel Nigel, her—"

"Son," Aunt Agatha added, cutting her elder sister off, in case Anthony did not know his cousin's name.

"I know who Nigel is," he said.

"Yes, well," Aunt Petunia continued. "Your Aunt Louise said that Nigel should learn how to run the earldom, seeing as he is the one who will be inheriting it!"

After speaking, his aunt waved a hand in front of her face, upset, and her sisters clucked their comfort to her. It was for his benefit, as Aunt Petunia had the constitution of a bull.

The door opened and in staggered Dibley with the tea tray.

"Oh, Dibley, you have arrived just in time!" Aunt Lavinia said. "My sister is quite overcome. I hope you brought the honey?"

"I did, my lady."

There followed ten minutes of teapot turning to the left and right, and cups eventually filled with the beverage, and liberally doused with honey until everyone was happy. Dibley handed Anthony another cup of coffee.

"I'm not sure why you drink that sludge," Aunt Aggie said.

"And yet we digress," Anthony said with the practiced ease of a man who had dealt with these three for years.

If society saw him now, he thought, they'd never believe he could exercise so much patience.

"We are here, nephew," Aunt Petunia said after they all exchanged looks, "to tell you it is time for you to marry. You need an heir. That sniveling weasel—"

"For the purposes of expediting this conversation, shall we call him Nigel?" Anthony asked.

"You cannot allow us to be thrust into his unscrupulous hands if you die, Anthony," Aunt Agatha said dramatically. "We shall be tossed onto the streets."

"Not that we want you to die," Aunt Lavinia added quickly.

Anthony wasn't worried about death—it would come when it did—and he doubted anyone but the six closest to him would miss him. In fact, they'd probably rejoice. But he was worried about what would happen to these three if it came prematurely. He may appear to care about very little, but he took his responsibilities to his aunts seriously.

Thrust into the role of earl at a young age, he'd worked hard to repair the damage his father had left behind after his death. The late Lord Hamilton had believed money magically appeared, even when you spent more of it than you had. He was like many from that generation and loathed the thought of actually investing in your future, to ensure those you supported were cared for.

"I will ensure you are not left destitute should I die tomorrow. I have things already in place with my lawyers. You need not worry about your futures."

"We've made a list," Aunt Petunia said pulling something from the small bag she always carried around her wrist. "All nice young ladies and will be suitable applicants for your countess."

"I beg your pardon?"

"List, nephew. You've shown no inclination to get yourself a wife, so we thought to hurry the matter along," Aunt Agatha said, taking the note and bringing it to him. "There are only three, as we had no wish to overwhelm you. But should none of these women interest you, we have a secondary list of possible brides. Of course, that horrid Miss Beasley is not on it. The woman is convinced you will choose her this season and has been putting it about the place."

He stared at the paper in his hand. "You cannot be serious?"

"Oh, we are, dear," Aunt Lavinia added, thinking he was talking about Miss Beasley and not the note. "I heard from Lady Baldwood, and Mrs. Smythe, that Miss Beasley has decided you will be her husband, and none other will do."

Anthony actually shook his head to clear it. "I've never spoken to her. I don't speak to young ladies. They tend to faint."

"Pooh to that. We know you're nothing like you appear." Aunt Petunia waved a hand about, as if the matter of his reputation was a trifling thing he would in time grow out of.

Anthony had never understood why they didn't chastise him over his behavior. They always patted his cheek and hugged him, as if he were not one of society's most notorious bachelors.

"Miss Beasley's mother, you understand, is behind the entire thing. Cynthia hunted her husband, poor man, until she caught him, and she's urging her daughter to do the same with you," Aunt Petunia added.

"A very calculating woman, that one," Aunt Aggie said.

Anthony took a large mouthful of coffee. "It's too early for this," he muttered after swallowing.

"Now, back to the lists. I have memorized both. As you know, reading is not something I do well."

Aunt Petunia had made up stories when he was a child because she struggled to read. Some had teased her for that, but not him. Anthony and Harriet had loved her stories.

"I am not marrying anyone," he said slowly and firmly so they understood. "If I do, it will be years from now."

"It is time. We cannot have that sniveling weasel as the next Earl of Hamilton. It's not right," Aunt Petunia said getting to her feet. Not as agile as the others, it took a few attempts. "We'll leave this with you and call again next week to see how things are progressing."

"I don't want to marry," Anthony said with more force as he too rose. "This discussion is over," he added in his society voice. None of them so much as flinched.

This was the problem when people had seen you in the cradle.

Aunt Lavinia was the first to reach him. She patted his cheek with a soft, sad smile. "It's time, nephew. You need someone to care for other than us. Now the last name on the list we only met this season, but she had a great deal to say on the healing properties of lavender and seemed a sensible girl."

"Oh yes, lovely gal. I chatted with her at the musical. A little older, which could suit you, Anthony, and did not appear to be someone who giggles all the time and says silly things like some of the new crop of debutantes. I will dig some more there, but she's on the list until we say otherwise," Aunt Petunia said.

And then they were gone, leaving the familiar blend of their scents behind. Anthony sat again and out of curiosity unfolded the piece of paper clenched in his fist.

You need someone to care for other than us.

No, he did not. He dismissed Aunt Lavinia's words. Anthony cared for his aunts out of duty; there was no more to it than that. He had nothing left for anyone else.

He tried to imagine sitting across the breakfast table from Lady Hester, who was the first name, and remembered her penchant for laughing like a goose. The second was Miss Amelia Leighton, who ran in the other direction if he so much as glanced her way.

The last name was Miss Evangeline Spencer. Anthony shuddered, remembering their encounter at the musical Jamie had forced him to attend. But their irritation of each other had started before that.

Miss Spencer had been walking out of a door, and Anthony had been walking through it, the night of the Shepperton soiree. He'd not been looking and collided with her, sending her backward and a glass of champagne flying. He'd staggered, attempting to right them and fallen, landing on top of her.

They'd stared at each other briefly, shocked. She'd regained her composure first and shrieked, "get off me at once!" Anthony had complied, lifting her to her feet. She'd called him a clumsy fool. He'd said she needed eyeglasses and to look where she was going in the future. They'd both then turned and walked in opposite directions, fuming. Their interactions since had done little to endear either of them to each other.

Shrew.

No one got a reaction out of Anthony, but she had... did.

Rising, he walked to the small desk in the corner and took out his pen. Dipping it in the ink pot, he then drew a dark line through her name.

CHAPTER FOUR

"EVIE, HAVE MERCY. Must we walk home yet again from the dressmakers?"

"If we are to dress as young ladies should, then indeed we must, and a hackney costs money. We are saving our funds for when appearances suggest we need to ride in one. Besides, a walk in the sunshine will lighten your foul mood."

"My mood is just fine, and I think it deuced unfair that father may sit about the place and we are walking everywhere, when all this is his fault. He even went to his club today, can you believe? As if he'd not a care in the world."

She looked at Prudence. There were only five years between them, but sometimes she felt like it was ten. Evie had aged considerably since her father walked into their front parlor one evening many months ago, while they were still mourning the death of their mother, and stated they were in dun territory. No funds were available, and they would likely end up in the poorhouse as his investment in a gold mine had failed.

One would expect this news to be delivered in a somber tone, with a lot of hand wringing. Not the case at all. Lord Heathcliff Spencer, first son of the late Baron Spencer, was smiling. In fact, that was the look he wore most often, even a year after the passing of his beloved wife.

Not that he was mean spirited or even enjoyed telling his two daughters that he'd ruined their life. No, it was just his way. Their father was a simpleton, but one his daughters loved very much, even when they were angry with him, which they both were.

"If we are to keep up appearances, then father must still go to his club," Evie said looking up at the late afternoon sky, which seemed darker with the threat of rain that had not been there when they left the house earlier.

The Spencers had carefully planned what events they would attend this season. Tonight they were to stay home, which suited Evie perfectly. Her feet hurt, as did her jaw from all the smiling, and she relished the idea of a night seated in a chair reading. Of course, there was always the option to slip out and make some money too, but she'd think about that later.

"I still question why he didn't speak up. Perhaps then we could have saved ourselves from this drudgery," Prue said as they trudged up the street.

"You are going out to balls and society functions most evenings. Surely that is not drudgery," Evie protested.

"The rest of it is drudgery. The charade of being wealthy, and yet living a frugal life."

"Hardly that when compared to those that clean out chimneys or scavenge the Thames or sewers for their survival. Maids who clean chamber pots and—"

"This again." Prue sighed.

"Yes, that again. We are the lucky ones, Prue. Never forget that. And when you marry someone, then our life will change again, unlike those who will continue to live a truly horrible existence."

Prue's face scrunched into distaste, but she wisely did not speak again.

"I think you will marry first," Prue said suddenly. "That man, Lord Cavendish seems quite taken with you."

Evie couldn't hide the shudder. There was just something off with the man that she couldn't put her finger on. She felt like he was watching her closely, and he never missed the opportunity to touch her intimately, which was usually followed with an apology, as if it had been an accident.

"We've discussed this. You are our best chance at achieving a marriage. I also have no wish to wed Lord Cavendish," Evie said. "I know I should, as he is wealthy, but I don't like him, Prue."

"Then you will not marry him, Evie. We both agreed, we must at least like our future husbands."

"Yes." Evie yawned.

"You are always tired."

"We stay out late."

"You also stay up reading by candlelight, Evie."

If her sister actually knew what she was doing, she'd be horrified.

Their father was with them in London, for appearance's sake. In fact, everything the Spencers did was for that, but all those things took money, of which they did not have a great deal. She was taking steps to ease the financial burden, but the risk could far outweigh the reward.

Evie tamped down the fear that was her constant companion. They were all right, and would achieve what they needed to this season, she had to keep telling herself.

"Oooh, look at that bonnet!" Prue cried suddenly. She then hurried to press her face to the glass of the shop window.

Evie allowed her sister to dream as she stayed near the road.

New lace and trimmings were added to repurpose old bonnets in the Spencer family. Running through what they had, she thought about how to rework one that would make Prue smile. Perhaps they could afford some ribbon?

Oblivious to people milling about around her, Evie continued working through things in her head.

"Watch out, Miss Spencer!"

She looked down the street at the words and saw the riderless horse galloping her way. Before Evie could flee, someone hurled more words at her.

"Move, you fool!"

Hands grabbed Evie, yanking her out of harm's way. She was

spun, and the thud of hooves sounded close and then galloped away.

Evie's heart thudded as she became aware of the hard body holding her. Arms banded tight around her waist from behind.

"Are you all right?" someone rasped in her right ear.

"Yes. Th-thank you," Evie said, stepping forward when the arms released her. Turning, she encountered a pair of amber eyes. *Why him of all people?* "I assure you I was moving out of the way, my lord. There was no need for you to grab me."

"Not quickly enough, Miss Spencer," Lord Hamilton snapped. "One would think by now you would have learned your lesson and looked where you were going."

His bruise was fading now, but it simply added to the picture of a dissolute rake as far as she was concerned. Other than the night of the musical, she'd done her best to avoid him.

"You ran into me when first we met, Lord Hamilton. I concede I was in part to blame, but I will not take all of it."

Unlike her, he looked his usual immaculate self, except his hair that was too long. Evie cursed herself for wearing one of her old dresses with a hem that was too short and worn boots. She should always be prepared to run into someone from society.

"Perhaps, if I may offer a suggestion, Miss Spencer?"

"I am, of course, all ears, Lord Hamilton. To receive advice from one such as you is surely an honor," Evie said with zero sincerity, but a fake smile on her face.

"You are a mouthy woman." His eyes narrowed.

"Forgive me," Evie added quickly, realizing how churlish she was being. "Allow me to thank you for rescuing me, my lord."

"Those words sounded like they were forced through a sieve," he said, glaring down at her.

Evie slowly counted to ten before answering. She could be the better person here.

"Are you counting in your head, Miss Spencer?"

"I have apologized, my lord. Perhaps you could simply accept that and not question the delivery?" Evie gritted out, her smile strained. "After all, I'm sure there have been times in your life when you've apologized, considering how you live it?"

"And how do I live it?" His amber eyes were narrowed to mere slits now.

"I'm quite sure I don't need to tell you," Evie said and then sighed. "I have apologized, Lord Hamilton, and now I think we should continue to ignore each other."

"Yet I question its sincerity."

"Now, who is being petty?" Evie muttered, looking around her. She spotted Lord Hamilton's hat just in time to watch a carriage wheel roll over it.

"Children are petty, as are silly young ladies. I am not." The words came out a growl.

"Oh dear. It seems your manservant will have his work cut out for him, my lord," Evie then added.

His eyes followed hers to where the black hat now lay flattened. A gust of wind had his thick dark curls ruffling in the cool London air. He returned his glacial gaze to Evie once again. She saw him then as others did. The dark lord many feared. A man who could crush her if he chose to do so.

"Evie!" Prue arrived before Lord Hamilton could speak, and she had to say she was relieved about that.

"I'm all right, Prue," she said.

"Lord Hamilton saved you," Prue added. "Thank you, my lord. It was a brave thing to do." Her sister followed these words with a pretty smile, which made Lord Hamilton's eyes narrow suspiciously.

Rat. How dare he look anything but pleased to see Prue. After all, she was the sweet Spencer. But then he rarely smiled at anyone.

"Miss Prudence Spencer." He gave an insultingly shallow bow.

"My lord." Prue curtsied, and Evie stayed upright, unmoving. He raised a single brow slightly at her. She dipped, with great reluctance, realizing that anyone could be watching and it would not do for the murmurs of Evie's ill manners to circulate through the ton. His ill manners, however, were accepted, which was deuced unfair.

"'Tis a lovely day for a walk," Prue said, doing what she did best. Putting people at ease.

"Miss Spencer!" The words came from behind her and had Evie's back stiffening. "Is there a problem I can aid you with?"

If Evie hadn't been looking at Lord Hamilton, she would not have seen the flash of rage that was quickly masked with his usual insolent expression at Lord Cavendish's words.

"I need no help, thank you, Lord Cavendish," Evie said when the man moved to her side and stood far too close.

"I saw the entire thing. That horse should be whipped for running at you."

"The horse bolted, Cavendish. I fail to see how it could be his fault," Lord Hamilton said with that mocking smile Evie loathed. He then walked away without another word.

"Stay away from that man, Miss Spencer," Lord Cavendish ordered.

"I beg your pardon?" Evie said. The man's lips were now twisted in an angry snarl, his eyes on Lord Hamilton's back.

"He is dangerous with a black reputation. I insist you keep your distance from him."

"You insist?" Evie said slowly. No one insisted anything of her, and especially not a man she barely knew. "You have no say in what I—"

"I like you, Miss Spencer, very much. I watch over the people I like." The words sounded like a threat to Evie.

"I don't need anyone watching over me, my lord, and I will thank you to remember that."

He leaned in closer. It was an intimate gesture to anyone looking. As if he would kiss her.

"You are a lady who deserves to be worshipped and cosseted, Miss Spencer. It's my hopes that one day—"

"No," Evie said quickly. "I-ah, I'm not looking—"

"Oh, look at the time. We are due at an appointment, Lord Cavendish. Terribly sorry, but we must leave. Good day to you," Prue said, sliding her hand through Evie's arm.

Evie saw Lord Cavendish's eyes narrow, but at least he straightened, putting distance between them again.

"I will see you at the next society event, Miss Spencer. We will waltz together and continue with this conversation."

Evie felt frustration rise inside her. Lord Cavendish had all but outright declared his intentions toward her, and it was selfish of her to hate that... him. Her family needed the safety of such a match, and all she could think about was that married life with him would be hell.

"Evie, I thought he may make you a good husband, but I've changed my mind. He makes my skin crawl, and you shall not marry him."

"He revolts me," Evie said bluntly. "I would rather marry a rat."

"Yes, but both he and Lord Hamilton are important men, and a single word from either would harm your reputation... our reputation. You must tread carefully."

Evie exhaled loudly, in a very unladylike manner. "I will have to dissuade Lord Cavendish's attentions without insulting him. That will not be easy. Lord Hamilton is not a problem, however, as he dislikes me as much as I dislike him."

"There is certainly something between you when he is near," Prue said.

"It's called animosity at first sight."

"Very likely. He is a man with a dark reputation, but I don't feel he is as horrid as Lord Cavendish," Prue added. "Rude, arrogant, but not mean. I do not feel that in him."

"Oh please," Evie scoffed. "You cannot know that. He is feared by everyone and drinks and does other things that rakes do."

"He has nice aunts, however."

"You can hardly credit him for that. He was born with them,"

Evie said.

Prue let out a loud sigh. "Perhaps you are right. Playing ladies is not easy, Evie, but we have only a single season to do so, or end our days in poverty, living in a stable back in Chipping Nodbury."

"Hardly that," Evie said. "We are not done in yet."

"Perhaps that is an exaggeration, but our lodgings will be small, and we will both have to find employment. You will tutor spoiled young ladies on etiquette, and I will look after horrid young children or take in sewing."

She shot her sister a look. "You've given this a lot of thought clearly."

"Of course. It is important to have a second option, should the first not work."

"Always good to be prepared, but why is it you get to be with the children, and I take the young ladies?"

"They will respect you more due to your age."

"Thank you for that, but we are not that far apart."

"Five years is a lot by society standards," Prue said unhelpfully.

"And there was me thinking I could treat you to a fruit pie—"

"Oh, please do!" Prue shrieked.

"Very well, let us find somewhere that sells them."

As they walked, she came up with ideas to dissuade Lord Cavendish. She had to say something that did not offend but convinced him she would not be a suitable wife, because life with that man would be horrible. There was much Evie would sacrifice for her family, but she hoped it did not come to that.

CHAPTER FIVE

G LANCING BEHIND HIM, Anthony noted the Spencers were no longer speaking with the loathsome Cavendish. Miss Spencer was standing before a shop window now, looking around her, while her sister studied it.

The woman irritated him far more than she should. Now there was also something else about her to contend with. When he'd held her and felt those soft curves pressed into his body, Anthony wanted to tighten his grip and keep her close, which had been enough of a reason to release her.

She'd left him with her soft scent and a longing for more, which shocked him. Anthony felt nothing but lust for women, usually.

The mouthy baggage had told him his personality was like a feral dog and then had the audacity to smirk after a carriage wheel flattened his hat. He'd wanted to shake her.

She was trouble, so he was avoiding her from now on, which shouldn't be hard as she was a debutante, and they were usually terrified of him... except she wasn't.

His aunts had put her name on the list of prospective brides for him to consider. Anthony was glad he'd crossed her off because she was about as comfortable as a hedgehog. If and when he married, which he knew was expected of him, it would not be to a woman like Evangeline Spencer.

He shot a final look in her direction as he prepared to turn left. She stood with her shoulders back, chin slightly raised, as if daring anyone to approach.

That horse would have hurt her, and possibly worse, if he'd not pulled her out of the way. Anthony's skin felt prickly just looking at her. Damn her for not heeding his warning when he'd yelled it, because now he'd touched her, and he knew exactly what she felt like in his arms.

His eyes swept down her one last time, noting the hem of her dress did not brush her boots, but was several inches higher. He wondered what the Spencers' situation was, and then instantly dismissed that thought. They were of no interest to him.

She stood on one foot, like a stalk, with the toes of one boot resting on the other. It was an odd stance for anyone, but for a society miss out in public, even more so.

She turned her head, as if sensing him, and their eyes collided. Anthony nodded his head, and she did the same, and then they both looked away.

His chest felt tight, and he had an urge to run. Instead, he moved out of her line of sight. Only then did Anthony draw in a deep breath and slowly release it.

It took him a further twenty minutes to reach his destination, in which time he'd dismissed Miss Spencer from his mind. Taking the six steps up to the townhouse, he arrived at the front door. Raising the brass knocker, Anthony let it drop. Seconds later, it opened.

"Good afternoon, Lord Hamilton."

"Chadders, are they both here?"

"They are." The door was opened wider, and he stepped inside.

"Lord Beaton and his son will arrive shortly. Have them wait in a parlor and then notify us, please, Chadders."

"Of course, my lord."

Short, solid, and somber, John Chadderly had been the son of the cook at Blackwood Hall. Those who considered themselves above him treated him terribly. It had been Anthony and his friends who protected him. Ever since, he had worked for one or the other of them, and eventually became Toby's butler.

Handing over his hat, Anthony then walked to the stairs that would take him up to the next floor.

The interior of Toby's house was elegant and grand. He was the last in a long line of viscounts who had simply added to the family coffers over the centuries. Huge portraits hung in gilded frames. Two lions symbolizing the bravery of past viscounts flanked the Corbyn coat of arms. Anthony's feet sank into plush carpets as he climbed to where he knew his friend would be.

Reaching the top, he turned right, and then stopped before a door. Knocking, he entered and found two of the six people he trusted most in the world.

Lord Tobias Corbyn and Lord Jamieson Stafford. They'd met when they moved into accommodations at Blackwood Hall, and their friendship had strengthened over the following years of abuse. Their ranks had not saved them. In fact, nothing but unity and Anthony's aunts had done that.

"And here he is, society's most infamous rake," Toby said. He lounged in a chair with his booted feet resting on his antique desk. The shortest of them but only by half an inch, he was the largest, with arms that rivaled tree branches. He had brown hair and eyes, with a wit only he understood.

Society saw him as a charming gentleman who was happy being one of their most eligible bachelors. A man with everything he wanted at his fingertips, and with few worries. They were wrong.

It was rare he let the polite facade slip, but the few times Anthony had seen it, he'd known, that like him, Toby suffered from their past. He was just better at hiding his darkness.

"He's scowling, which is never a good sign," the other man in the room said.

The Marquess of Stafford was tall and carried no spare weight on his body. He rarely sat still, and if he wasn't boxing, he was fencing with someone. Dark-haired with green eyes, women flocked to him. Little did they know the demons the man carried beneath that wicked smile.

"Why have you called us together?" Toby asked.

"I was at Hugh's the other night—"

"Again? Good God, man, learn to sleep like the rest of us," Jamie said.

"But then, how would he maintain his reputation?" Toby added.

"If I may finish?"

Jamie waved a hand at him to continue.

"Beaton lost everything at the tables," Anthony added. "I found him with a pistol when I was walking home. A Frenchman called Mr. Renee was with him, attempting to stop the idiot from putting a bullet through his skull."

Toby swore loudly but Anthony knew that like Jamie, the words, *they will never walk alone,* would run through their heads.

"He is one of us, even if the man is a fool," Anthony added.

"And his son is a good man, but this will destroy his reputation and that of his two sisters, who are a great deal younger and as yet have not entered society." Toby spoke the words slowly while that fertile mind of his worked through the problem with which they were now faced.

"Did he lose everything?"

"Enough to make him want to leave the mess he'd created to his son," Anthony said, disgusted. "They will arrive in an hour, so we must work through what is to be done before then."

"Noblemen," Jamie sighed. "Lord, save us from them."

They spent the next hour outlining a plan which Beaton would have to implement, even if he didn't like it. Only then would he be able to repay the debt and not destroy his family's legacy. It would take time to rebuild what he had recklessly lost in a single evening, but it could be done.

Anthony began investing years ago with the help of his man of affairs. Toby and Jamie had followed suit. Their wealth had steadily grown because of it, and now they could help others do so, if they wished to listen. He hoped Beaton would.

"I just saw Cavendish," Anthony said when they had finished.

"We see that revolting excuse for a man most evenings. What is different about today?" Toby asked.

A vision of Cavendish standing over him with a whip flashed through Anthony's head. He dismissed it. That man could no longer hurt any of them.

The three of them had entered that place on the same day excited about what the future held. Eager to experience what their fathers had. They soon realized they'd been sent to hell.

Theirs had been a sharp initiation into understanding that a title and wealth did not give you anything when away from those who protected you. Together, they'd learned to survive, and when they were older, they'd sought retribution.

"Anthony?" Jamie asked. "Did you and Cavendish have an altercation?"

Swirling the brandy around his glass, he said, "We did at Hugh's." He went on to explain what had happened.

"And that is where you got the bruise, from the fight on the way home?" Jamie added.

"Yes."

"You can't keep doing this," Toby said solemnly. "The gambling, the drinking and whoring—"

"We all fight our demons our own way," Anthony said.

"And likely they will one day be the end of us," Toby said softly.

"I rescued Miss Spencer from being run down by a horse earlier, and Cavendish arrived after the fact and asked if she was all right," Anthony said changing the subject. He had no wish to delve into what drove him to do what he did, just as his friends didn't.

"Miss Spencer," Jamie said taking his lead. "Nice lady. Articulate and witty, unlike her father who is the simplest soul I have ever met."

"Heathcliff," Toby added. "Yes, jovial fellow, but completely brainless."

"Miss Spencer is definitely not brainless," Jamie said. "In fact, quite the opposite. I know little about the younger one, however."

"Miss Spencer is a mouthy woman who is far too ready with her opinions," Anthony said. He instantly had his friends' attention. "What?" he asked when they said nothing but continued to stare at him.

"You never speak about a woman in such a way," Toby said.

"Anyway, if we are honest, I've never so much as heard you mention one is pretty or whey faced," Jamie said. "You just bed them and leave."

"You make me sound like a rakehell," Anthony protested.

"Which is exactly what you are," Toby said with no remorse.

"Are you both finished with the assassination of my character?" he said, temper now tweaked.

"For now," Toby added. "But back to Miss Spencer."

"She annoys me," Anthony said. "The woman has far too much to say for herself."

"I like that about her," Jamie said.

"I heard a rumor about Heathcliff," Toby said scrunching his face which meant he was thinking.

"You're a viscount. You really shouldn't look like that when you think. It makes you appear simple," Jamie said.

"Or constipated," Anthony added, pleased they'd moved on from him.

Not much insulted Toby; he simply smiled. He then clicked his fingers.

"I remember now. I heard he had gone into a consortium of some sort, a gold mine somewhere, I believe. Apparently, it was all a hoax to fleece noblemen from their money."

"Which is easy," Anthony said. "And it can't have taken all his funds because the man has brought his daughters to London for the season."

"It was just a rumor, and we all know how many of them are

swirling about society on any given day," Toby added.

"Both Spencer sisters seem nice, although the youngest is a bit silly. All smiles and giggles," Jamie said.

"Deuced glad we don't have to do what they do," Toby added.

"What?" Anthony asked shaking his head to remove the imagine of Evangeline Spencer's nicely rounded backside pressed to his groin.

"Marriage mart. They have to look their best at all times and show their good sides to impress would-be husbands. I would hate that."

"That's because you don't have a good side," Jamie told Toby.

"It must be hell though," Anthony agreed. "We can do what we like, and they have to watch their every step. I was glad when Harriet met Simon and stepped away from society."

"How is Harriet?" Jamie asked.

"My aunts called this morning. It seems I am to be an uncle."

"Now, that is exciting news," Toby said.

"A little person for Uncle Anthony to dote on," Jamie added.

He didn't tell them he wasn't capable of doting on anyone.

"As you can imagine, my aunts are excessively happy."

"I love your aunts," Jamie added.

"Me too," Toby said.

"That was not the only reason they called early to see me," Anthony said. "My Aunt Louise told them that seeing as it was not likely I could produce an heir, her son will become the next earl. Aunt Petunia then said, and I quote, 'it's imperative that simpering weasel Nigel is never the Earl of Hamilton'."

"She's not wrong," Toby said. "And your aunt isn't a very nice woman."

"All true," Jamie said raising his glass. "Your aunts will be terrified she'll cut off their funds and leave them penniless and living on the streets if you died."

"Exactly right," Anthony added.

"I bet they are going to apply the pressure for you to wed and come up with lists." Jamie said.

Anthony looked at him.

"Lord, they've already done so. Tell us at once who is on it?" Jamie said.

"No." Anthony took another sip.

"It is not like we are not getting the same pressure. Lists have not yet been formed, but it's only a matter of time," Toby added.

"I have no wish to discuss this further."

"We could just sit on him. Between us we're larger," Jamie said.

"Get Chadders. He's excellent at getting things out of people," Toby said.

"Lady Hester, Miss Amelia Leighton, and Miss Evangeline Spencer," Anthony said because they'd keep at him until he told them. He should have just kept his mouth closed.

"All good prospects," Jamie said.

"Miss Evangeline Spencer? The woman is prickly and opinionated, and we can barely tolerate each other," Anthony protested. "In fact, we dislike each other excessively. I crossed her off the list."

"I didn't know you had spent that much time together to form these opinions," Toby said.

"I haven't."

"But you did save her today, and there is that reaction you have to her—"

"There is no reaction," Anthony lied.

"I've always found her an excellent conversationalist," Jamie said.

"Then you marry her."

"I don't have to marry like you. One day, of course, but there is no urgency at this point," Jamie said smugly.

"I don't have to marry either, as I don't plan on dying," Anthony said.

"But your aunts count on you," Jamie said.

"As your sisters count on you."

"But my sisters will wed and have others to provide for them."

Anthony didn't answer that because all three of them knew the words for the truth. Still, he was not marrying anyone and especially not Evangeline Spencer. The woman was the least comfortable person he knew.

"Lord Beaton and his son have arrived," Chadders said from the doorway.

"Bring them here, Chadders," Toby added.

The men were ushered in minutes later. Faces solemn, they sat and the hard talking began.

Lord Beaton took two hours to be convinced that his finances could be saved. Humbled and surprised, he and his son left the house with renewed hope and the knowledge that in fact he had not destroyed his family's future, but there was work to be done before he was out of danger.

After the Beatons left, Anthony and his friends talked for hours, like they often did since becoming friends all those years ago. They drank brandy, ate a meal, and discussed a variety of things. These were the only men he let see the true Anthony, as they did him. It was late by the time he walked out Toby's front door, but as he was not ready to return to his home, he headed in another direction, seeking a different form of entertainment to keep the cold inside him at bay, no matter how briefly.

CHAPTER SIX

E VIE SLIPPED OUT of the bed she shared with Prue, biting back the yelp as her toes touched the cold wood floor. She then tiptoed to the door, and out, closing it softly behind her.

Taking the stairs down, she stepped off the second from the bottom, as the first creaked. Heading into the parlor, she lit the candle on the narrow side table.

In the middle of the room was a chest, over which Evie had draped a large, thick blanket, she'd said, to give the room a more cheerful look. On top were stacked an array of things, including books, her father's pipe, a length of ribbon, and sewing supplies. Removing them all, Evie pulled aside the blanket and opened the old wooden lid. She'd decided this was the best hiding place for her disguise, as it looked like a pile of clothing that possibly needed darning.

"So you're going out again?"

Evie muffled her squeak at the words and spun to find one of the two servants they'd employed upon arriving in London.

"Humphrey, you will be the death of me," Evie whispered, clutching her chest. "Go back to bed."

"You'll come trouble, you will." He had his large beefy arms folded and was giving her a hard look.

"We've discussed this, and I am taking no risks."

The first night she'd been just about to leave the house dressed as a man, he'd walked into the room scaring her half to death.

Humphrey needed little sleep apparently and liked to get a start on the next day's chores after the Spencers retired for the evening. He'd asked what was going on, and she'd had to tell him. He'd voiced his displeasure many times since. But he had kept her secret from her father and sister.

"Just leaving the house dressed as a man is a risk for a young lady such as yourself. What if you are hurt? Or someone tries to rob you and realizes—"

"I am quite safe. I never lurk in the shadows, and stride everywhere so no one can grab me—"

"You are a lady, and as such should be upstairs in your bed." He scowled at her. "I could come with you," Humphrey offered, as he had every time he'd caught her.

"I will get in a hackney from here to my location, and then return in one," Evie said. Actually, she only took one on the return journey if her winnings were good enough.

He gave her a hard look before leaving the room, his disapproval clear.

Evie took the man's clothing out of the trunk and dressed. She'd borrowed them from her father, without his knowledge, and he'd never even known anything was missing. After a few alterations, she was able to dress as the Frenchman, Mr. Renee.

The idea for her foray into gambling establishments came from her father. They often played cards together, and he'd once commented that it was a damned shame Evie wasn't a man, as she would stand to make a great deal of money with her skills.

Deftly she dressed and then stood before the small, speckled mirror to fold the cravat. She fixed the beard she'd purchased from an advertisement in the newspaper. It had wires that molded it to her face and then hooked around her ears.

To her eyes, she looked good… manly even. Of course, she had no one to test that theory on, but every time she'd gambled there had been no awkward moments. But then, most were just worried about winning, or not losing all their money as that fool Lord Beaton had.

Lord Hamilton had helped him that night, and while she loathed the man, she had to admit that was kind of him. She'd watched from the shadows as he'd helped Lord Beaton into a hackney, after handing him his card. Evie could not hear the words they'd exchanged, however, which had been annoying, but still, at least the man was still alive, so she was grateful to Lord Hamilton for that much.

Tweaking her cravat, she hoped tonight's winnings were good. It made their lives so much easier having a little extra money.

Upon arriving in London, Evie had started her investigations into the places gentlemen gambled. She'd found two locations that would take anyone who knocked on their door.

The last thing she donned was the blond wig she'd found in her mother's possessions when cleaning out her things after her death. It was comforting in a small way to have something of hers. She'd been a wonderful woman, who often made sense of things when Evie couldn't. Kind and generous, but also practical, something their father was not.

Evie swung the overcoat hanging by the front door around her shoulders and let herself out into the cold night air. Taking out the spectacles she'd also removed from her father's possession, she put them on, pushing them to the end of her nose, so she didn't end up walking into something.

Heathcliff Spencer was luckily slender like Evie, but he was a great deal taller, so she had to hold up the hem of his overcoat so she didn't trip on it.

She'd so far gambled in two different locations. Both places had terrible lighting, which suited her. She never talked to anyone, just entered, gambled, and then left.

She'd worked out she could walk fast, and no one approached her. Head high, stride long and confident, she swung her cane like she was out for a promenade in the park.

Should anyone approach, Evie ignored them and walked on. So far, she'd been safe. Was she scared? Yes, terrified actually. But this had to be done if they were to get through the entire season living in that house and keeping up appearances.

The walk took her thirty minutes, as she knew the route well now. Reaching the gray stone building, she saw no one lurking about outside. The facade didn't look like much, but she knew that inside fortunes would be won and lost, and some on this very night.

Tapping the head of her cane on the front door, Evie waited. A small opening at eye level had two eyes appearing.

"Mr. Renee," she said in heavily accented English, having practiced deepening her voice for hours.

The door opened, and the man waved Evie inside. He closed and locked it before leading her to the next one.

She did not know the big and burly man's name, only that he was the perfect person to squelch trouble before it escalated. One of those beefy fists could inflict a lot of damage.

He unlocked another door and waved her through. After the third one, she was inside the hellhole that was Hugh's gambling establishment. The doors, she guessed, were to make it hard to get in, and equally hard to leave. She handed over her father's coat, hat, and cane. Then Evie made her way down a hallway, to yet another door. Opening it, she stepped into a room thick with cigar smoke and the reek of desperation.

Shutting out the niggles of doubt that she always got entering a place like this, she focused on what needed to be done. Evie played to win, and then left without making eye contact, which was easy as she couldn't see anything because the lighting in here was terrible.

Thick curtains covered the windows, and the entire atmosphere aimed to make a person forget about the world outside Hugh's. Time for those in here passed without their knowledge as they focused on one thing: winning.

"Sit," someone growled, as Evie apparently took too long to do so.

She sat slowly, like she'd practiced, in a manly way. Evie then played as she did most things, with determination. Two hours later, people had come and gone, but she had stayed, as the goddess of luck was on her side tonight.

"Brandy," a voice to her left said, and every hair on the back of her neck rose.

She didn't look his way but knew that voice. Damn the man, he was turning up everywhere.

"I-ah, I need to go," the man opposite said, his eyes on Lord Hamilton. Clearly very aware of the lord's reputation, he had no wish to play cards with him.

Evie didn't look up as the dealer dealt. *Relax. Lord Hamilton can't tell who is sitting next to him.* There was not much he cared about from what she'd gathered, other than doing exactly what he wanted to excess.

Exhaling slowly, she pushed her glasses farther up her nose. *I am wearing a wig, and a beard. He will never recognize me.*

The game was whist, which Evie was good at, as she could keep track of cards and what her opponents were doing. Shutting out the fact that Lord Hamilton was beside her, she focused.

He drank brandy, others whiskey or whatever suited them, and Evie touched nothing. She loathed spirits, or alcohol of any sort. At society events, she would take a sip of whatever was offered, but she rarely drank much. It was important to always keep a clear head when you were constantly one step away from social ruin.

"Bloody Frenchie, I say you're cheating," the man across from her said suddenly, his words slurred, when Evie won another trick. She battled over what to say, not wanting to draw attention to herself, but she must say something.

"Unless you have proof, Moore, I suggest you retract those words," Lord Hamilton said before Evie could speak. "Losing because you are drunk does not allow you to insult another because they are winning clearheaded."

"H-How dare you speak to me like that?" Moore staggered to his feet. "You of all people. A man with no morals, and a—"

"I would not continue that sentence were I you," Lord Hamilton said. His words came out like the crack of a whip. "How I live my life is my business."

"That Frenchie—"

"Apologize at once, Moore," Lord Hamilton demanded.

Considering his reputation, it was a surprise he was demanding an apology on her behalf... well not her, but still.

Whatever Moore saw in Lord Hamilton's face had him uttering an apology, and then he was stumbling toward the door.

"My thanks," Evie said.

"I'd advise you to stand up for yourself, Renee. Being a weak-kneed simpleton will get you stomped on," Lord Hamilton advised.

And suddenly, any softening she may have felt for this man was gone. How dare he call her a weak-kneed simpleton.

"Well now, it seems this seat is vacant." Evie's entire body tensed at the nasal draw. Not only was she at a table with Lord Hamilton, but now Lord Cavendish had joined them.

CHAPTER SEVEN

A NTHONY DIDN'T LOOK at Cavendish. Instead, he nodded for the dealer to begin a new game. He'd been enjoying the play until Moore had called Renee a cheat. The Frenchman was a skilled player, if a coward for not standing up to Moore, but now that Cavendish had arrived the game had lost its appeal.

"How is the luck tonight, Hamilton?"

"I don't believe in luck," Anthony replied to Cavendish. "Winning takes skill, which I have."

They both knew what had happened all those years ago, and that the tables of power had turned between them. Anthony no longer feared this man, and Cavendish knew it, even as he tried to intimidate him. Cavendish was now the weaker of the two of them.

There had been times over the years Anthony, Jamie, and Toby had made life extremely uncomfortable for the men who had treated them no better than animals.

"Lady Luck is always with me, Hamilton," Cavendish drawled.

"Please accept my condolences, Cavendish. I hear your investment did not show the expected returns," Anthony said with no sympathy. "I believe one of the larger investors pulled out."

"How did you hear about that?" Cavendish snapped, laying a card which had him losing the trick, and Renee winning.

The Frenchman spoke little and instead concentrated on

winning, which he was doing a great deal of this evening.

Anthony smiled, knowing it would not reach his eyes. "Nothing goes on in London relating to business opportunities that I do not know about. It would pay you to remember that."

Cavendish's lips drew into a hard line, and the hand he had rested on the table fisted. "You?" He scoffed. "All you care about are whores and alcohol."

"That is not very nice," Renee said in halting English.

"Who are you to speak to me that way?" Cavendish snarled, turning his attention from Anthony to the Frenchman, seeing an easier quarry to argue with. "What is your name?" Cavendish demanded.

"Mr. Renee," the man said in French.

"Speak English!" Cavendish snapped. "Can't abide foreigners who come to my country and don't speak the language."

Renee uttered a few words in French, which Anthony interpreted loosely to mean Cavendish was a fool with low intelligence, to which he replied "Oui" in total agreement.

"What did you just say?" Cavendish demanded. Clearly his French was not good.

"I wish to be an Englishman," Renee lied.

More drinks arrived then, and the dealer dealt the cards. Anthony watched Cavendish's anger grow as Renee won more hands. Anthony, too, held his own.

He felt the Frenchman's tension climb every time Cavendish thumped his fist on the table or swore loudly. Renee wore glasses perched on the end of his narrow nose and this close, Anthony could see the beard and wig were indeed fake.

Why would anyone want a fake beard and wig if you were not deliberately hiding your identity?

The more he observed the Frenchman, the more something felt off about him. *But what?*

"I said I wanted a whiskey!" Cavendish snapped, slamming the empty tumbler down on the edge of the table.

Anthony knew many things about Cavendish. Like the fact he

drank too much and flew into fits of rage easily. That his mistress was called Jasmine, and she thought him a selfish lover, but put up with him as he showered her with gifts. He also knew the man mistreated his staff terribly.

Know thy enemy.

"*Je quitte la table maintenant,*" Renee said softly.

The Frenchman had just said he was leaving the table, and Anthony was sure that was due to Cavendish's behavior. Odd, considering he was in a gambling hell, where men behaved badly constantly.

"What did he say?" Cavendish demanded. "English, man!"

"He is French, Cavendish. I'm sure when you visit his country, those within its borders do not demand you speak their language," Anthony said.

"Can't abide the French."

"I'm sure there are plenty who feel the same about the English."

"I doubt that, Hamilton. We are far superior in every way," Cavendish boasted.

"Thank you," Renee said, and Anthony had a feeling he was deliberately misunderstanding Cavendish.

"Idiot can't even understand me," Cavendish said loudly, which had others around them sniggering.

"*Imbécile d'esprit petit.*"

"*Oui,*" Anthony said, because Cavendish was a small-minded fool.

"Did you just insult me?" Cavendish demanded.

"French is a difficult language to grasp...for some," Anthony drawled.

"It's not an important language. English is all I need. Now I demand you tell me what he said, Hamilton. I heard him utter the word imbecile."

Renee called him a strutting peacock this time, which made Anthony snort. The Frenchman clearly had a sense of humor.

"I never forget someone who offends me," Cavendish

snapped, now glaring at Renee.

"There must be an excessively long list by now," Anthony added.

"Meaning what, Hamilton?"

"I'm quite sure you understood exactly what I said, Cavendish."

The angry look on Cavendish's face slid away suddenly, to be replaced by a smirk.

"I do hope dear Miss Spencer does not interest you, Hamilton? After all I did see you with her the other day, and you seemed quite chatty."

He ignored the man and continued to play.

"Because I have plans for her, so keep your distance," Cavendish persisted.

"I'm not sure what gave you the idea I care about your interests, Cavendish, but let me dissuade you of that notion. You have never, and will never, feature in my thoughts. You are of no consequence to me."

Fiery red filled Cavendish's cheeks at the insult.

"And I'm sure Miss Spencer will do as she wishes," Anthony added.

Renee, who hadn't left as he'd said he was, made a noise low in his throat that sounded like a growl. Anthony shot him a look, but with that beard and the thick glasses, he couldn't tell what the man was thinking.

"She will do exactly as I wish. One of my strengths is discipline after all," Cavendish added, recovering from the insult Anthony had given him.

He and Cavendish had never outright discussed what had taken place in Blackwood Hall, but the man across from him had alluded to it a few times. Anthony had not engaged until now.

"I'm sure I'll break her spirit as I have done others," Cavendish continued. Anthony knew all too well, *like you*, was what he wanted to add. "She is a woman, after all."

"*Il est indigne de votre colère, mon seigneur, car c'est un lâche,*"

Renee said softly.

He is unworthy of your anger, my lord, as he is a coward.

"What I've always found," Anthony said, in total agreement with Renee, "is that bullies pick on those they see as weaker than them because stronger opponents would turn them into sniveling cowards, which invariably they are."

Cavendish rose from his chair, bracing his hands on the table and leaning in to glare at Anthony.

"I am no coward!"

"I don't believe I mentioned your name," Anthony said, rising and doing the same. Beside him Renee rose too. "But of course if my description fits you, then—"

"I will break you as I have done so before, Hamilton. Never forget that!" Cavendish roared, eyes blazing with rage now.

Anthony smiled but knew it would not reach his eyes. "I would be very careful who you threaten, Cavendish. It will not go well for you." He leaned in closer until their eyes met. "This time you are the weak one, and I can destroy you with ease. Watch your back, my lord, and your purse, because both are in danger. Especially if you ever speak to me again as you just have."

Cavendish spluttered, and Anthony smiled at the flash of fear he saw in his eyes.

"How dare a man like you threaten me!"

"Oh, I dare, and I can and will harm you if need be," Anthony said softly. "Remember my words."

He left before Cavendish spoke again. Renee was walking through the last door as Anthony reached it. He followed him to where they left their outer clothing.

Any encounter with Cavendish left a sour taste in Anthony's throat, and tonight he'd showed his hand. Before now, he'd just tolerated the man, but no longer. He also now knew Cavendish had plans for Miss Spencer, and while she vexed him excessively, he would not wish a life with that monster upon anyone.

"Be careful of him, Renee," Anthony said, because the man needed the warning. It did not take much to make an enemy of

Cavendish, and he thought tonight that may have happened. "He will not forget your insults, even if he did not understand them all."

The man shrugged as he slid his arms into his overcoat, and Anthony thought he had done what he could. It was not usually his way to intervene, but he'd felt the need. If the Frenchman had no wish to heed his warnings, then so be it.

He watched Renee raise the back of his wig to straighten the collar of his overcoat. Even in the dim light, he clearly saw the two small dark marks, before he lowered it again.

Had he seen those marks before?

CHAPTER EIGHT

"A N ICE? WE are to go to Gunter's, Evie? Really?" Prue followed these words with a little bounce on the balls of her feet.

"Well, there is the small matter of a walk through the park first we are about to undertake. It is everything to be seen as you know, sister dear," Evie said, smiling at her excitement.

"But an ice." Prue sighed. "I've so longed for one." She lifted her face to the sun. "It's a beautiful day to savor a Gunter's ice," she sang.

"You sound like a child."

"And happy to be so rather than a curmudgeonly old woman like you," her sister said, poking out her tongue.

She'd won well three nights ago. For all, it had been the most uncomfortable evening she'd spent so far at the tables. If Evie could choose to never see two men again, it would be Lords Hamilton and Cavendish. Yet, that night, she'd sat with both, gambling with social disgrace, dressed as a Frenchman, and won well, while they shot arrows of displeasure at each other and exchanged cutting words.

"Why can we spend frivolously on ices today, when a few days ago we could not?" Prue asked.

"Because I worked through our finances again, and things are not as dire as I'd first thought." In fact, what she'd earned had eased the financial burden greatly. They still needed to show caution, but an ice was now within the budget.

"Goody," Prue said, sounding five years old.

They entered the park through a gate no one from society used. The walks were a trifle overgrown, but the Spencer sisters had found it not long after their arrival in London. Here they could walk in solitude before they frequented the more socially acceptable areas.

"I danced with a man last night who seemed very nice, Evie. We talked on a great many topics."

"Did you? Well, I'm glad to hear it." Evie knew who her sister meant but waited to have it confirmed.

"Mr. Landon. He has a very nice smile and is charming."

"Excellent."

She often thought about what would happen when Prue married and Evie was left alone with her father. She would miss her sister dearly, as they shared everything, but if Prue was happy, that was all she could ask for.

"What is happening over there, do you think?" Prue pointed to the left to a line of trees.

"I have no idea, but there appears to be a group of people beyond them. It is hard to tell what they are doing from here."

"Then we must investigate," Prue said.

"Must we? We are walking and then going to Gunter's. Why do we care what a group of people we likely do not know are doing?"

"Yes, we must," Prue said walking in that direction.

"Perhaps they want to be left alone?" Evie followed.

"If they wanted to be left alone, they would do so in a more private setting."

"They're behind some trees in an area of the park hardly anyone uses," Evie protested.

"I just want to see what they are about, Evie. They could be murdering someone."

"Yes, and of course if they are we would simply introduce ourselves and say, stop, don't do that? Come, this is not for us to investigate," Evie said. Before she could leave, a man she met most evenings in society ballrooms walked through the trees toward them.

"Miss Spencer, Miss Prudence Spencer," Lord Corbyn said bowing. "How lovely to see you." His smile seemed genuine, and not that of someone with murder on their mind.

"Apologies, my lord, we were just leaving," Evie said.

"Why are you apologizing?"

Prue turned to look at her, as if to say, yes, Evie, what are you apologizing for?

"I can see you are… have something—"

"Archery," he said cutting her off, as clearly she had no idea what to say next. "We play here once a month. If you would care to watch, then by all means do."

"Oh no—"

"We would love to, Lord Corbyn. My sister is an exceptionally skilled archer," Prue said.

"Is she? Well then, come along." He walked back through the row of trees.

"I don't want to go with him, and why did you tell him I was good at archery?" Evie hissed.

"Because you crow loudly when we play at home about how easy it is to beat me." Prue followed Lord Corbyn. Evie stood there for two seconds, then hissed out a breath and did the same.

"I do not crow," she said when they'd stepped through the trees. Evie looked at the people gathered and felt her stomach plunge to her toes. She'd known these men were often seen together but hoped that was not the case today.

Lord Jamieson and Lord Hamilton. The man was appearing far too frequently in her life as far as Evie was concerned. Her opinion of him may be changing, slightly, after his protection of Mr. Renee and clear dislike of the revolting Lord Cavendish, but still, she had no wish to encounter him too often. Besides, she doubted he could ever change his wild ways, and she and Prue should not associate with such a man.

"Look who was lurking in the trees," Lord Corbyn said much to Evie's embarrassment. "Miss Spencer and Miss Prudence Spencer."

Lord Hamilton's head turned so fast it was amazing it didn't do permanent damage. He impaled her with a look of absolute displeasure. Evie almost smiled. Instead, she looked around for any women present. There were none. Their reputation would be ruined if anyone saw them, which was a good reason to leave.

"We will leave you gentlemen to your archery," Evie said.

"Damned grass everywhere!"

These words came from behind Evie and Prue. They turned in time to see Lord Hamilton's three aunts making their way through the trees. Three footmen were with them, carrying chairs. Another a picnic basket large enough to hold a body.

"Well now!" Lady Petunia said, seeing Evie and Prue. "Isn't this grand? How wonderful that you ladies are joining us! We shall have a picnic while these fools see who can best the other. We are here to referee, you see. They are extremely competitive and have been since they were boys."

"We were just leaving," Evie said.

"Lovely," Prue said at the same time. "I do enjoy a picnic."

"What are you doing? I have no wish to be here," Evie hissed in her sister's ear.

"You told me this very morning you are bored with society, so this could be fun and alleviate that," Prue said watching the elderly ladies make their way to where the footmen were placing chairs.

"I do not class being here fun in any way. Especially if he is here."

Prue looked around Evie at Lord Hamilton.

"Stop it."

Her sister had that mischievous look in her eyes that usually meant trouble for Evie.

"Come along, ladies," Lady Petunia called to them.

"There really is no need to leave," Lord Corbyn said. "You

could keep my friend's aunts company, and stop them heckling us."

"We have no wish to intrude on something that is clearly an intimate gathering," Evie said stiffly.

"Let Miss Spencer leave, if that is her wish," a deep voice said that she instantly knew was Lord Hamilton.

"We shall stay, but only for a few minutes," Evie said far too quickly.

Lord Corbyn smirked at her words. "He has that effect on most people. Now, go and sit with the aunts, who are wonderful ladies. It will be entertaining, I promise you," he said before walking away.

"This is fun," Prue said moving toward the three women.

"No, it's not."

"Stop being so stuffy."

"We are in the company of one of society's most... most—"

"Rakish rakes?" Prue supplied.

Without telling Prue what had happened between them, she couldn't explain why she felt as she did around that man. As Renee, she was grateful to him—when he wasn't insulting her that was as Evangeline Spencer. She thought him a horrid man... *who saved you from being trampled by a horse.*

She sighed, silently. Evie moved to stand behind the party of women, who were all settling in chairs, like nesting hens around a blanket that Prue had lowered herself to.

Evie could say with complete honesty she would rather be anywhere but here. Even listening to Father Colin's long, monotonous sermons in Chipping Nodbury's church that made her fall asleep.

"We come every month," Lady Petunia said. "Our nephew excels at archery."

Evie only just managed not to roll her eyes.

"My sister is a superb archer," Prue said, shooting a look over her shoulder at Evie.

"Prudence is fond of embellishing," Evie said with a smile

that did not reach her eyes. "I am below average at best."

"Nonsense. You were Chipping Nodbury area champion three years running."

The look Evie sent her sibling should have reduced her to ash. Sadly, it did not.

"Three years, you say?" Lady Petunia said. "Anthony!" Lord Hamilton turned at his aunt's call. "Come here at once."

He looked like he'd rather walk over hot coals but did as she asked.

"You bellowed?" He shot Evie a look and frowned.

Yes, well, it's not my wish to be here either.

He'd removed his jacket and wore only his shirt and waistcoat. The others had put on their jackets, but not him. The arrogant lord never did anything he didn't want to.

Seeing him dressed so informally made her stomach feel odd. Or perhaps the eggs she'd eaten for her morning meal were not sitting right. Evie felt a desperate need to leave here at once.

"Prue, we need to—"

"Miss Spencer was the three times Chipping Nodbury area champion for archery, nephew," Lady Petunia said before she could finish the sentence.

"Allow her to play, Anthony," Lady Agatha added, much to Evie's horror.

"Absolutely not," he said, just as Evie said, "I don't want to play."

"Are you afraid she will beat you?" Lady Agatha asked.

"No, Aunt Aggie, I am not afraid," he said through his teeth.

He called his aunt, Aunt Aggie? Why did that seem ridiculously sweet coming from a man like him? Evie thought. "Come, Prue, we have that...thing to attend to."

"I hate it when a thing gets in the way of doing what I love," Lord Jamieson said, arriving to stand beside his now fuming friend.

"How do you know I love archery?" Evie found herself saying.

"Because you are a three times Chipping Nodbury champion. I doubt you won because you loathed archery and did not practice."

Drat. She should have put more thought into that question.

"Let Miss Spencer leave. She has something that needs her attention," Lord Hamilton said glaring at her, which she was sure was meant to prompt her to do just that.

"What's the problem here, nephew? Are you scared she will beat you?" Lady Petunia asked with a glint in her eyes which suggested she knew exactly how to annoy him.

"No," he snapped. "But we never let anyone else participate on these days."

"Well," Lord Jamieson said. "There is no time like the present to change that."

Small daggers of anger fired her way from Lord Hamilton's eyes.

"Excellent. I'm glad that's settled," Lord Jamieson said, clapping his friend on the shoulder.

"Perhaps she is not comfortable competing against men?"

Lord Hamilton had given her a way out and may not have intentionally meant the words as a challenge, but Evie took them that way.

"I will compete," she heard herself saying seconds later.

"Evie is extremely competitive," Prue said. "I'm sorry to say I am not."

Evie followed the men back to where Lord Corbyn now stood, watching everything unfold. His smirk matched Lord Jamieson's.

"Well, give her a bloody bow then," Lord Hamilton snapped.

"Tsk tsk," Lord Jamieson said, a look passing between him and Lord Corbyn that she had no idea how to interpret. "There is no need for bad manners, Anthony."

"Indeed," Evie added, because she knew it would annoy Lord Hamilton, and they disliked each other already, so why not annoy him more.

He closed his eyes briefly, and when he opened them he was smiling. It was forced and would terrify small children.

"One hopes your prowess is not exaggerated, Miss Spencer. I would not want you to leave here weeping piteously after losing to me."

Bastard.

CHAPTER NINE

"I'M NOT SURE why you are needling me, both of you," Anthony said to Jamie and Toby when Miss Spencer went to inspect the bows. "But desist, or I shall make you pay."

"He is excellent at revenge," Toby said. "Do you remember that time he—"

"God's blood, you two are trying," Anthony snapped.

"Come now, she is three times Chipping Nodbury champion. Surely you can allow her to compete with us?"

Jamie's face was all innocence, but when you knew someone as well as you knew yourself, you understood when you were being played.

"She's a lovely woman and would make you an—"

The words finished on a wheezing sound as Anthony elbowed Toby hard in the stomach.

"Right, then," Jamie said, grinning because he hadn't received the jab. "Have you selected a bow that would suit you, Miss Spencer?"

When Anthony had turned to find Miss Spencer standing there with her sister, he'd thought seriously about leaving. Just picking up his bow and disappearing into the trees. But as his aunts were due to arrive, he couldn't.

The woman made him feel like he had an itch he couldn't quite reach, and then there was the fact that she was on the list his aunts had written, about which he seriously regretted telling his friends, even if he'd crossed her name off. Plus, now he knew the plans Cavendish had in place for her, and that unsettled him.

Miss Evangeline Spencer got under his skin, and no one did that. He couldn't understand why her, of all women?

It certainly wasn't her fashion sense. Today's bonnet had a wide brim that looked like it was more poor design than deliberate, and under her chin was a fat blue silk bow. The long ends trailed down her chest to a simple white dress with no lace or frills. At least the hem reached her footwear this time.

"I will use this one if I may," she said, holding up a bow for them to see. It was the one Anthony always brought in case his aunts wanted to participate.

"Off you go then, or we will be here all day."

She glared at him.

"Take a step forward, Miss Spencer, as women's targets are usually a great deal closer."

She looked at him, her brown eyes narrowed, suggesting she would like to tell him exactly what to do with his words.

"There is no need for that." She stomped into place.

"Well, I fear the animosity is not yours alone, my friend," Toby whispered.

Ignoring him, Anthony watched as she prepared to fire her first arrow. Clearly, if she was a three times champion, she had some ability, but he did question her competitors. Her shoulders rose as she inhaled and lowered as she released the breath.

The thought of Cavendish breaking her spirit made him want to warn her off. She had to be told what that man was capable of. Not by him, but perhaps by Jamie or Toby?

He watched as she released the arrow, and, much to his annoyance, hit the target dead center.

His friends clapped loudly, as did his aunts and Miss Prudence Spencer. Anthony said nothing.

Miss Spencer gave them a small smile and stepped back out of the way.

"Right then, I'm next," Toby said, looking far too happy.

He shot close to the center, as did Jamie, and Anthony, who had always been better than his friends, as he practiced regularly, having set up targets in the garden of his townhouse, hit dead center also, just beside hers.

"Oh, well done!" Aunt Aggie cried.

"Excellent shot, my lord," Miss Spencer said in a tight voice that suggested she did not think it excellent at all.

Anthony fought his smile. It seemed he was not the only competitive person present.

They shot three more rounds, and she'd got the closest to him, but not close enough, Anthony was pleased to say.

"You have excellent aim, Miss Spencer," Toby said. "It seems you are worthy of your title."

She gave him a tight smile. Clearly she was still as uncomfortable as he in being here, even if he'd seen the spark of excitement when she moved to fire her arrows.

Anthony stepped back as she prepared to fire her last one.

Cavendish would dictate her every move if he married her. Anthony knew Miss Spencer. She would fight back, but it would not last. Cavendish would break her. The thought left a foul taste in his mouth. He would use Miss Spencer and discard her.

"I fear I will get frostbite if you two continue with this rigid politeness," Toby said pulling Anthony from his thoughts.

"It's like watching two wary dogs circling each other. Neither wants to attack first," Jamie added.

"What are you talking about? We are being exactly as two people who barely know each other should be."

"If you insist," Toby said.

"But I think she's wonderful and would make you a—" This time it was Jamie who received the elbow.

"Another word, and I'll follow that up with a punch," Anthony snarled. Jamie simply laughed.

His eyes went back to Miss Spencer. Back straight, feet shoulder-distance apart, and her knees slightly bent. Arm straight to prevent her muscles tiring. Anthony wondered who had tutored her, as she was good. She released the arrow, and he watched its flight all the way to the center of the target.

"Well done," Jamie said clapping loudly. "You are indeed an excellent archer, Miss Spencer. No one has bested Anthony in years, but it seems you may do it."

She nodded, but there was no smile as she retreated. His friends didn't get close to her arrow, and then it was Anthony's last turn.

"Down to you now, Anthony!" Aunt Lavinia called as he prepared to fire. He focused on the target and Miss Spencer's arrow. Releasing it, he watched it hit hers, dislodging it.

Loud clapping ensued, with his aunts congratulating him. He turned to face Miss Spencer, who to his surprise was clapping too.

"Well done, my lord. That was excellent aim."

He nodded his head. "As was yours," he said reluctantly.

"Thank you for allowing me to intrude on your private time. I am grateful." He knew those words had been spoken with reluctance. Dropping into a curtsey, she then walked back to her sister. Anthony watched as she hauled Miss Prudence Spencer to her feet.

"I'm enjoying myself," the youngest Spencer protested.

"But we are intruding, so it is time to go," Miss Spencer added as he and his friends approached.

"Oh, but now we are to picnic," his Aunt Petunia said.

Anthony knew what his aunts were about. They had Miss Spencer here, and she was on the list, so this was the perfect time for Anthony to spend time with her.

"We have a... thing," Miss Spencer said as she had earlier. Clearly, she did not excel at lying like some he knew. He watched as she nudged her sister in the side.

"Oh right, that thing," Miss Prudence Spencer said.

"Good day to you all, and enjoy your picnic," they said together.

"And thank you for the entertainment and lovely biscuits," Prudence Spencer added.

"Lovely girls," Aunt Lavinia said watching the Spencers leave. "So well mannered."

"I'm now doubly pleased to have put Miss Spencer's name on the list, Anthony, as she is your equal in archery," Aunt Petunia added.

"Both girls are indeed sweet natured," Aunt Aggie said.

"Are we talking about the Spencers?" Anthony said, no longer able to keep quiet. "Because there is no way that older one could be termed sweet natured. She would be the last person I could ever marry."

"Funny how she's like that with you," Toby said dropping down beside Aunt Aggie's chair to forage through the picnic basket. "With the rest of us she's exceedingly sweet natured."

"That is interesting." Aunt Petunia got a look on her face that told him she was more than happy with the thought that Miss Spencer was only irritated when Anthony was near. "How intriguing."

"Not intriguing," Anthony snapped. He then bent to take a biscuit and bit into it, so he couldn't speak again.

His friends and family then proceeded to list the merits of the three women on the list, much to his frustration. Anthony's reputation was fierce with anyone but this lot, and now Miss Spencer had infiltrated that part of his life. He was not happy about that... not happy at all.

"Well now, Miss Spencer has more merits than others, so I think we have the future Lady Hamilton," Toby said. Anthony threw his half-eaten biscuit at him.

CHAPTER TEN

O NE WEEK AFTER the archery contest, Evie and her family
entered the Bailey ball.

"Smile, daughter, there is so much to enjoy at these events."

"Sorry, father." Evie forced her lips upward.

She'd faked an illness and avoided taking a carriage ride with
Lord Cavendish after he'd sent word he would collect her. Prue
had answered the door and told him she was in bed with a sore
throat. He'd not been happy. This Evie knew as she'd listened.

She'd then had to stay in the house for three days, which if
she was honest had been a relief. This polite pretense they were
forced to maintain—well, she was forced, her father and sister
seemed to actually enjoy society—was stretching her nerves to
breaking point.

The words Cavendish had said at the Hugh's club were constantly inside her head. She would rather live on the streets than
be subjected to life with that man, but how did she dissuade him?

"Of course, there is much to enjoy," Prue said when Evie
remained silent.

"Exactly," Heathcliff Spencer said, beaming. Their father
never understood the subtleties of sarcasm, which, unfortunately
for him, his daughters excelled at.

"That painting is larger than the wall in our bedroom," Prue
whispered, looking up.

Following her sister's eyes she took in the artwork. The huge, gilded frame had a gentleman dressed in severe black glaring down his long nose at them. At his side was a spaniel with long floppy ears.

"Clearly the dog was his favorite, as there is no sign of a wife or children," Prue added.

"I can understand that as most people are fools," Evie said.

The entrance was lined with servants waiting to take outer clothing and assist in any way they could.

Evie would need to keep her eyes open tonight so there was no possibility of running into Lord Cavendish. Lord Hamilton was not a problem because they disliked each other, so he'd never seek her out. But he had stood up for both her identities in small ways, so she could be polite at the very least if she saw him. Plus, there was that bond they shared of hatred for Lord Cavendish.

"It is the grandest house we have visited so far," Prue said.

"It is."

Their father smiled and waved to people he knew. After all, he was a baron and had been in and out of society for years.

"Do you think people wonder why they have never seen us until this season?" Prue asked.

"No. You're the perfect age for a debutante and I'm old and jaded, and here to chaperone you."

"But do you think they wonder why you didn't have a season before, Evie?" she persisted.

"We were in mourning, Prue. They may wonder, but we have an excellent reason to be presented at the same time." Even if money had a lot to do with it.

"I miss her," she whispered.

"So do I, but Mother would be proud of us for doing this and taking care of Father," Evie said squeezing her sister's fingers.

Their mother had died unexpectedly four years ago, leaving her family reeling with grief and shock. Heathcliff Spencer had loved his wife deeply, as had they, and mourned for her, and Evie believed still did.

What the Spencer sisters hadn't realized until it was too late was that it had been their mother who had kept the household on track by doing the bookkeeping. Evie often cursed herself over the fact she hadn't been more aware of what was going on around her.

"Imagine living here?" Prue whispered.

"It's certainly large," Evie added.

The walls were pea green, and a line of gold and cream trim ran around the center. The floor was tiled black and white, and the furniture elegant and, she guessed, expensive. A mirror allowed new arrivals to ensure they were just so, and then they were heading to the huge sweeping staircase.

Placing a foot on the first red and gold carpeted step, she took her father's arm, while Prue stepped to his other side.

This was not about her, she reminded herself. So she could avoid two men and ensure her sister did what was needed to secure a happy future with a man she respected.

They walked behind the other guests, climbing the stairs slowly. The woman before them wore pale gold that seemed to float around her. Hair the color of midnight piled high on her head, with tiny sparkling diamond pins holding it all in place.

Looking down at the skirts of her own dress, Evie wondered if it was too simple? It was pale rose with bows on the bands of each sleeve. She looked at Prue. Her dress was cream with an overskirt of sheer apricot that opened at the front with apricot silk binding. Her sister looked wonderful, and in no way out of place, and that was all that mattered.

"Good evening."

Evie hadn't even realized they'd stopped until she heard that greeting and looked at the beautiful woman before her in the gold dress. Of course, she knew who she was, but they'd never conversed.

"Good evening," Evie said dropping into a deep curtsey. Rising, she studied the stunning woman, who was on the arm of a man who suited her perfectly. Tall, dark, with graying hair, he was chatting with Evie's father and Prue.

"Are you enjoying the season?" the woman asked.

"Yes, thank you. Very much," she added.

"It can be excessively boring at times, and wonderful at others. The trick is to find humor in every situation."

"Is it?"

"Oh yes. Take that old windbag Captain Williams. The end of his nose moves when he talks. I find if I watch that, I can count how many times it twitches until the conversation ends, and it makes him think I'm interested in every word he speaks...which I assure you I am not."

Evie laughed.

"My name is Dimity," she said, and her smile, if possible, increased her beauty.

"Evangeline, Miss Spencer," Evie added.

"Enjoy your evening, Evangeline, and remember humor will make it easier."

They moved on then. After greeting the hosts, the Spencers walked into the ballroom.

"Do you know who that was?" Prue asked her.

"Who?" Evie looked around.

"The woman you were talking to dressed in gold. That was the Countess of Raine."

"Of course, I know who she is. I remember names, as my memory is far better than yours."

Prue waved her words away. "Lord and Lady Raine are two of society's most popular members."

"So not everyone who is wealthy is a snob then. Excellent," Evie said.

"What are you both whispering about?"

"Nothing, Father," both daughters said together.

"Well, I see some of my friends over there. Come and get me should you require my presence for any reason." He then wandered off without a backward glance.

"I sometimes wonder if there is anything inside that head of his but an empty space," Evie said. "Can he not see this is hard on us? Can he not see we could do with his support?"

"If we asked, he would have stayed," Prue said. "But we have not done so before now, so he thinks we are more than happy being out in society at such an occasion."

"I know you're right, but it would not hurt him to be a little more aware," Evie added.

To their right a group of four young ladies waggled their fingers at Prue. She waved back.

"Come, we will talk with your friends," Evie said.

They moved closer, and soon Prue was chatting, and Evie had stepped back and out of the group to stand behind. Not exactly a chaperone but close to it. She was happy with that. The nuances of society were complex and exhausting. She was constantly on her guard to ensure she was saying the right words instead of the wrong ones, which were usually what was on the tip of her tongue.

Evie watched the group of chatting young ladies from a safe distance, her eyes doing the occasional sweep of the room, and then returning to them. This time, on her return glance she found three men had infiltrated their ranks. One in particular was speaking with Prue, with a smile on his face. Mr. Landon.

It was moments like this she wished she knew more about society and its members, or at the very least had someone close who did. She had no wish for her sister to fall prey to some man who would not treat her well. Moving closer so she could overhear what was being said, she caught her sister's eye.

"Mr. Landon, allow me to introduce you to my sister, Miss Spencer," Prue said.

The man turned and offered her a smile. He then bowed deeply, and Evie curtseyed.

"I have claimed your sister for her first dance, Miss Spencer, if you will excuse us."

Prue looked happy about that, and as she knew nothing about Mr. Landon, she couldn't stop her. So, she nodded and stepped back once again, this time retreating farther to the wall.

She watched Mr. Landon lead her sister to the dance floor. Perhaps her father had heard the man's name, or could casually ask someone about him?

"Miss Spencer, now you have arrived my night is complete."

Evie stiffened at the nasal drawl. Damn, she had not seen him coming or she would have hidden. Lord Cavendish had spoken about Evie that night at Hugh's like she was a horse that needed breaking.

"It is time for our dance, Miss Spencer."

Looking at her dance card that was empty, she said, "I seem to be busy for this dance, my lord."

"And yet I wish to dance with you." He simply took her hand and walked, and she would not make a scene, so allowed it.

"I like you, Miss Spencer," he whispered, leading her onto the dance floor.

"Thank you, my lord, that is most kind." She forced the words out of her mouth through a tight smile.

He pulled her too close as the waltz began. Had he known this was the next dance?

"Please observe the correct distance, Lord Cavendish." He relented, but only slightly, and put a small amount of space between them.

"I've decided that this season I will select a wife," he said.

Dear God, she knew where this conversation was going but did not know how to stop it.

"When I find something or someone that interests me, Evangeline, I watch them closely, and you interested me from the first time I met you."

Evie was scared. How was she to stop him from courting her? Surely, it would not go well for the Spencer family, in the eyes of society, if she tried. "I did not give you leave to call me, Evangeline, my lord."

He laughed at that. "But we are to be husband and wife, Evangeline, so there need be no formality between us."

"But I—"

"I like to know everything there is about the people who will be in my life, Evangeline."

"I don't understand why you're speaking to me like this, Lord Cavendish?" She had to at least try to dissuade him. "I am not here to marry this season, merely watch over my sister."

"Listen carefully, Evangeline, and I will explain it to you. I have watched foolish men pass you by for younger women. Women who are sweet natured and spoiled. You are neither. You have fire, and that will suit my needs."

She remained silent, her eyes on those dancing beside them as her mind whirled with thoughts, desperate to find a way out of his plans for her.

"It is time for me to marry, Evangeline, and I've decided it will be you."

"No," the word came out a hoarse whisper. "I am, of course, honored, my lord." She recovered quickly as it would not do to make an enemy of this man. "But I have chosen not to marry."

"Come now, I can give you so much, Evangeline. Further to that I can support your family. Surely that alone will change your mind?"

She looked up at him, and while he wore a polite smile, those eyes were narrowed and the mean glint in them made her shiver.

"I want children, and you are healthy, intelligent, and will suit my needs and care for them. It is the perfect solution for all concerned."

Her eyes shot left and then right to see if anyone had overheard their conversation.

"Your offer is flattering and extremely generous, Lord Cavendish," Evie began, swallowing down the fear that clawed at her throat. He was offering her family a chance. Offering her a life she'd never thought to have. Why then would she rather choose one of poverty over one with him?

Think of Prue and father.

"I had hoped you would simply concede, my dear, but I can see I must offer more persuasion," Lord Cavendish added as he steered her around the floor. "A rumor reached me before the season started. A rumor about your father losing all his money. I sent someone to investigate, and it turns out the Spencer family are completely without funds. In fact, I'm not sure how you were able to have a season, but one word from me and you would be ruined."

"H-how dare you." She felt the color drain from her face.

"I don't need your money, my dear. I simply want you to have my children. So, we shall marry, and it will work out well for all concerned."

"No." Evie shook her head.

"Yes, and you don't want to cross me, Evangeline. I can make your family's life extremely difficult."

"I have no dowry." Evie grasped for anything to change his mind.

"Yes, these are not the normal actions of a man such as I," he bragged. "But I want you and must have you. You have good bloodlines, and I do not need another mistress. I need a wife. Therefore, I am willing to overlook your family's fall from grace."

"Please allow me time to think about your offer, my lord," Evie said as meekly as she could, scrabbling to come up with a way to get out of this mess.

"Of course, but remember, my dear, I am not a patient man. If I think you need further persuasion, I will not hesitate to offer it."

Evie heard the threat behind those words. She tried to pull from his arms, but his hands gripped her tighter, his fingers crushing hers painfully.

"You and I will have a long and happy life together, my dear, as long as you understand it is I who have all the control."

He released her when the music finished and then led her back to Prue. She watched him walk away with nausea swirling in her belly.

Dear lord, how could she refuse him?

CHAPTER ELEVEN

"W HO ARE YOU searching for?"

The words were spoken by Jamie, who had stepped into Anthony's path as they circumnavigated the ballroom.

"You've been prowling the perimeters since you arrived. This I know as Toby and I have been watching you. It is not your normal behavior. Usually, you are leaning against a wall drinking and scaring young ladies with your devil may care attitude."

"Where is Toby?" Anthony asked instead of answering his friend's question.

"That way, dancing with Miss Hyde."

"Why?" Anthony asked. "Miss Hyde is the daughter of the innocuous Mr. Hyde, who if he gets a single sniff of interest from Toby, then will move heaven and earth to see him wed to his daughter."

Jamie smiled. "I doubt anyone could make Toby do anything he had no wish to."

"True, but Miss Hyde could lure him somewhere and compromise him," Anthony said.

"Not all women are set on tricking us surely, Anthony? Even you are not that cynical."

"Perhaps," he said looking around him.

"Who are you looking for?"

"Aunt Louise has arrived in London, and sent word she and

Nigel would attend this ball. My cousin is barely old enough to enter society, but she feels it's important to acquaint him with what his future will hold."

"Unless they murder you, I can't see why you are avoiding them, other than the fact your aunt is a crashing bore."

"I'm not avoiding them, but the note stated quite clearly Aunt Louise wants me to do my duty and teach her son how to become my heir, as clearly I will never have one."

Jamie winced. "I've often wondered what it would be like to be without a title and work as a lawyer or doctor?"

"You hate the sight of blood. But I could see you in one of those wigs," Anthony added. A memory of the one he'd seen Mr. Renee wearing the other night slipped into his head. Decidedly odd, that a man of his age would wear such a thing, and the beard.

"But we would not have the complications that come from—"

"Being ridiculously wealthy with everything we want?"

"Thank you for putting me in my place."

"Any time."

"So, your aunt has yet to arrive, and you think that if you keep moving she will not track you down?"

"It was a faint hope at best," Anthony said.

"Have you danced with Miss Spencer yet?" Jamie asked.

"Why would I dance with her?"

"She's on your aunts' list, so the least you can do is appease them by showing interest." Jamie was smirking now.

"Very amusing."

"And there is that mutual love of archery you both share," his friend continued.

"Shut up, Jamie."

"I have danced with her, as has Toby," Jamie added.

He knew that, because he'd seen them.

"I fear all is not well with Miss Spencer," Jamie continued. "She barely spoke a word, and to me looked pale and nervous."

"And you know her character well enough to know that's not

normal?" Anthony mocked his friend, while searching for Miss Spencer before he could stop himself. He located her sister in a gaggle of men and women, but not her.

"I am an excellent judge of character," Jamie said. "Ask anyone."

"Your sisters don't count."

"I asked Miss Spencer if she was well, and she assured me she was—"

"There you are then."

"Cavendish danced with her before me, and I think it was he who upset her."

Just the mention of that man's name made him tense. He remembered the conversation about Miss Spencer they'd had while gambling last week.

"I met him in a gambling hell a few nights ago."

"Cavendish?" Jamie asked.

Nodding, Anthony went on to explain. "Do you know a Frenchman called Mr. Renee?"

"I don't believe so. Why?"

"He was gambling also, and then Cavendish joined us. He warned me to stay away from Miss Spencer. From what I gather, he has decided she will be his future wife. Once he's broken her spirit, that is."

"Dear God, the poor woman. Let's just hope she doesn't have to accept anything he offers. But then there was that rumor about her family's circumstances, so perhaps she will," Jamie added.

"You need to warn her away from him," Anthony said.

"I thought you and she disliked each other?"

"We do, but I would not wish my worst enemy to endure what Cavendish will do to her. Plus, thwarting him—"

"Enough said. I will see what I can do." Jamie walked away.

Miss Spencer was no match for someone as evil as Cavendish. He'd done the right thing in asking Jamie to warn her.

Feeling restless, Anthony left the ballroom and walked with no particular destination in mind. Reaching stairs, he descended.

"May I be of assistance?" The Bailey butler appeared.

"What's through there?" Anthony pointed behind the man to where there were two large double doors.

"Lord Bailey's exotic plants, Lord Hamilton."

Without asking permission, Anthony opened the door and let himself in, closing them behind him.

Warm, humid air settled around him like a heavy blanket, as did the earthy scent. He headed down the first path. Discreet lamps cast shadows from the plants around the walls, and Anthony drew a deep breath at the blissful silence.

Pulling off his gloves, he plucked a leaf off a tree and crushed it. Raising it to his nose, he stood and inhaled the fresh scent.

Perhaps it was time to visit Harriet? His aunts were hounding him to wed someone. Plus, his aunt and cousin were in London, and then there was Miss Spencer whom he disliked and yet couldn't stop thinking about. The city was suddenly filling up with people he wished to avoid.

And you're Lord Hamilton and care nothing for anyone or anything.

"Botheration."

The word came from behind a row of plants. Moving quietly forward, he looked through the leaves.

"What to do. What to do."

Miss Spencer was there, pacing up and down the next path. She'd not heard him approach as she was muttering to herself.

Before he could retreat, she said, "Blast! That man is a horrid, pernicious toad."

Anthony wondered for a moment if she was talking about him. He continued to watch as she paced away from him and back again. Then she stopped, and her shoulders lowered, and shook. Was she weeping? Anthony took a step back, his boot crunching on a leaf, and her head lifted, looking his way.

"Who is there?" she demanded and then sniffed loudly.

"It is I, Lord Hamilton."

"Go away," she said.

"Are you all right, Miss Spencer?" he said through the leaves.

"Yes."

Anthony kept his distance from people for a reason, to keep himself safe.

"Go away, my lord. Please," she added. "I-I wish to be alone."

He should do what she said. It was the sensible course of action. He found himself walking down the row, turning at the bottom, and then making his way to where Miss Spencer now stood.

Her eyes were dry, so she wasn't crying but Jamie was right, something was very wrong with her. She was pale and clutching a handkerchief in both hands.

"Is there any way I can assist you?"

"No."

"Allow me to take you back to your sister then."

Anthony could feel her desperation, even from a few feet away. He'd never seen her anything but bored or cutting, which were two things he excelled at. What he did not excel at was dealing with a woman who was not herself.

"I believe Lord Bailey has twenty species of ferns growing in here," Anthony said when nothing else came to mind.

He could feel her eyes on him.

"Apparently he spends up to four hours a day tending them, according to his wife, who is a friend of my aunts."

"I met her," Miss Spencer said quietly. "She is... ah, very nice."

He snorted at her hesitation. Bailey's wife was a woman who could talk from sunrise to sunset.

She fell silent.

"Miss Spencer, can I help you in any way?" he asked again.

"Why?"

"Why what?"

"Why do you want to help me when we dislike each other?"

"At least look at me when you are arguing," he said.

She did then, lifting her head slowly until their eyes met. The turmoil in the depths spoke of her utter devastation.

"Perhaps I can see you are not yourself and have ceased hostilities briefly, until you are once again prickly and antagonistic."

That didn't produce a smile either.

"It is hardly my fault I am that when there are so many fools up there." She pointed above her head. "Besides, with your reputation I fear you are not one to talk, my lord."

"There is that. However, it's my hope I am not one of those fools?"

"If I say you are, then will you leave me alone?"

"Come, let me escort you back, Miss Spencer."

She sighed, and it was a sad sound.

"Would you like me to collect your father or sister?"

She shook her head before speaking. "We cannot be seen in here together, my lord. Alone like this would be disastrous, and my family can ill afford that kind of scandal considering..." Her words fell away.

"Considering?"

"Considering you are who you are, and I am who I am. I'm sure you understand."

Of course he did. He could get away with his behavior due to his title and the fact he was a man.

"Why are you down here alone and not upstairs watching your sister?"

"She is fine and surrounded by people." Miss Spencer then waved a hand about dismissing his words.

A heavy, tense silence settled between them as Anthony weighed the words he would speak next.

"Is your current predicament, which you will not share with me, anything to do with Lord Cavendish?"

Her shoulders jerked, and she stumbled back a step. Anthony grabbed her arm as she tripped on the edging of the garden behind her. He pulled her upright and closer to his body. Looking into her eyes, he felt it again, that rush of expectation he always got when she was close.

"Why would you ask me that?" she whispered.

"Because you danced with him before Lord Jamieson, and he said you appeared upset."

She pulled her arm from his grip and turned away. Delicate shoulders rising and falling as she looked, but he was sure didn't see the fat, shiny-leafed plant directly before her.

His eyes traveled up the rigid line of her spine and then the pale skin above the line of her dress. Anthony felt the urge to lean in and place his lips there. He stepped back, out of range. Her hair was piled high, with several soft curls trailing down her spine.

She bent her head slightly, and his eyes followed the elegant curve of her neck, and stopped.

Surely not? Leaning in, he studied the two dark dots. Did more than one person have marks like that on their neck? Because the alternative was not something he could contemplate.

"I must return to my sister, my lord. Good evening."

She walked away and he let her, because he knew that Miss Evangeline Spencer was capable of anything, even dressing as a man and leaving the house to gamble in a place where, if anyone found out, she would be ruined and forced to leave London.

CHAPTER TWELVE

H IS BUTLER CAME into the dining parlor looking harried as Anthony, Jamie, and Toby sat down for their evening meal before heading to their club.

"What is it, Dibley?"

"Your aunts have arrived, my lord."

"All of them?"

His butler nodded.

"Have three more places set," Toby said, looking happy. "I wonder if they have further women to add to your prospective brides list?"

"Entertainment with our meal. How wonderful," Jamie added.

Anthony sighed. "What I want to know," he wondered after his butler had left, "is how they are always aware of my movements?"

Jamie looked down at his empty plate.

"What?" Anthony demanded.

"Nothing," he said far too quickly.

"Oh, come on, Anthony, you are normally awake to everything. Surely you must see someone here is feeding them that information?" Toby said.

The thought that a member of his staff would do such a thing silenced him.

"Also, they are devilishly good at getting information out of us," Toby added. "They are constantly and subtly pumping us for our movements. Ergo, they know where you are going."

Anthony was busy running through his staff to ascertain who would betray him and came up with his housekeeper and cook. Dibley was far too loyal. He knew there were others, but those two were the most likely in his opinion.

Dibley reappeared in the doorway and announced his aunts, who all then sailed into the room like royalty.

"Aunts," Anthony said rising and bracing himself for the onslaught of kisses and cheek pats. They had no respect for his reputation. "What has you here at such an hour and not preparing for your night's entertainment?"

"We merely wished to discuss the list and how things are progressing," Aunt Aggie said not meeting his eye.

"We will not stay, Dibley. This is merely a stop on the way to the Brambleberry soiree," Aunt Petunia added.

"We should have let him know we were calling," Aunt Lavinia said.

"Nonsense. He's your nephew; you can call on him anytime," Toby said kissing paper-thin cheeks.

"Exactly right," Jamie added, following his friend and greeting the women.

"Such manners," Aunt Lavinia said patting Toby's cheek. "Anthony, you could learn much from these two."

"It's a wonder you two aren't married," Aunt Petunia added.

"It is a wonder," Anthony drawled. "Perhaps you could write a list of prospective brides for them also?"

His friends shot him a glare.

"Focus on Anthony first," Toby said. "After all, his need is greater. We must secure an heir, so the perfidious Nigel and his mother have no say in your futures."

"We will be forced out of our home," Aunt Petunia said as Anthony thought about how to seek retribution on his friends for encouraging his aunts. "To live in a one-bedroom house and eat gruel."

"I agree," Aunt Aggie said. Aunt Lavinia nodded her agreement.

"No one is putting you out of your home," Anthony said battling the frustration. "As I have already told you, there are plans put in place to ensure that doesn't happen."

"But if he is the heir, surely he can overrule your plans?" Aunt Aggie asked.

"Your nephew is a very astute man, ladies," Toby said. "He will have prepared for all eventualities, and never forget that you have Jamie and me also. We will always be there to look after you should anything happen to Anthony and the perfidious Nigel tosses you from your beds."

Aunt Lavinia made a noise between a sob and a shriek and hurried to hug Toby again.

"So now you know you have nothing to fear, perhaps we can throw out the list of prospective brides," Anthony said.

His aunts all looked at him then.

"But, nephew, it is our fondest wish to hold your babe in our arms before we die. We are of an age that it could happen at any time," Aunt Lavinia said.

"Any time," Aunt Aggie agreed.

"So we have decided to renew our efforts to help you find a suitable bride," Aunt Petunia said. "We're thinking you should host a ball. Plans are already in motion, and invitations will be sent out shortly."

"I don't—"

"Not another word. We want to do this for you, dear," she added. "Now who have you taken a liking to on the list?"

"Miss Spencer," Toby said. "She's quite lovely and would make Anthony an excellent wife."

"Shut up," Anthony snapped.

"I find I am partial to Miss Amelia Leighton," Jamie said looking smug. "She has such a way about her when it comes to home decor."

"Oh indeed. Both excellent candidates for your future countess, nephew," Aunt Petunia said.

"I don't want to marry or host a ball," Anthony said deciding it was time to be blunt. "My reputation is blacker than hell, and no woman would want to wed a man like that."

"Rubbish," Aunt Petunia said. "That's just an act on your part, and besides any woman would be lucky to have a man as handsome and wealthy as you."

The other two women agreed loudly.

"Well," Aunt Petunia added. "I'm quite sure we will have this wrapped up before the season's end. We are not giving up until you are married to the perfect woman, Anthony. Expect regular visits to strategize the ball. Come along. We will leave these men to their meal, ladies."

Anthony then watched his three aunts walk out the door. "It's like they don't hear me."

"I always feel as if I've been run over by a dozen carthorses towing a plough when I'm in their company, no matter how brief," Toby said collapsing back into his seat. "I'm not sure where they get their boundless energy from, but I would like some."

"And you're not even related to them," Anthony added. "But thank you both for easing their minds over what would happen should my death be premature, even if you were absolutely no help with anything else. A ball." He sighed.

"We have known them since we were young boys, Anthony. They are important to us, especially as their intervention changed our lives," Toby said.

"Agreed," Jamie added.

"Now, about this list," Toby said. "Which women do you favor?"

"Hilarious," Anthony said. "My life is going to be hell for the rest of the season."

Thinking of the list brought Miss Spencer to mind. He'd spent the last seven days watching her when she was near. She was always moving, and he knew that was because she feared Cavendish.

Last night, Anthony had intercepted her before Cavendish could. He'd then told her they were dancing, to which she'd replied it was customary to ask. They'd then danced in silence until the music had stopped, and he returned her to her sister.

He'd also frequented Hugh's. So far, he... she'd not returned. Had he been wrong there?

"I need to tell you both something," Jamie said, dragging Anthony from his thoughts. "Two nights ago, a young lady by the name of Molly Allsopp went missing. Now, normally I would not be aware of something like this, but she is my housekeeper's niece, so my butler brought it to my attention. When I spoke to her, she told me her niece was the third woman to go missing in the area where the family live. There have been two from Brawley, and one from the next village."

"Three?" Toby said slowly. "That is cause for alarm surely?"

"Greville has an estate five miles away from Brawley," Jamie added.

The words were chilling to all three men. Greville, Cavendish, and Calthorpe were at Blackwood when they were there, and took their lead from the Housemaster, who had been a man to whom cruelty was a sport.

"We believed that Blackwood Hall concealed something more sinister than just the beatings and the hell we endured. Six women went missing there over the time we were at school. Only one of them was ever found, floating in a nearby river, dead," Jamie said.

"What are you saying?" Anthony asked.

His friend ran a hand through his hair. "I don't know, but I know that my housekeeper's family are distraught, just as I know something is not right when three girls go missing without a trace."

"It could be a coincidence that Greville has an estate nearby," Anthony said. "Everything that happened at Blackwood Hall was many years ago."

"I know, but there is one more thing," Jamie said. "A local farmer found a young man with his horse and cart when he was checking his stock. He was naked, with a red satanic symbol on his chest. The farmer said he appeared drunk and was rambling. He took him back to Brawley. The lad was the nephew of the tavern owner there."

"What kind of symbol?" Toby shot Anthony a look.

"I don't know."

The vision slid into his head even as he battled to keep it at bay. His hands bound and being forced to drink something vile.

"Anthony?" Jamie said.

"I'm all right." But his hand was shaking under the table. His friends had found him in his bed one morning, with a red symbol painted on his chest. They'd said his speech was slurred.

"I am going to visit Brawley," Jamie said.

"We will come with you," Toby said.

After that they finished the meal in silence, all lost in the past. His friends left. Twenty minutes later, Anthony put on his hat and coat and did the same. He knew only one way to rid himself of his demons.

⤖⤜

"I BELIEVE A seat has come free, Lord Hamilton, if you will follow me," a servant said as he entered the gaming room of Hugh's.

Searching the gloom, he found Mr. Renee and was soon seated at the table next to his, and facing the Frenchman, which would allow him to observe the man…if he was a man.

He then played hand after hand and watched the Frenchman. He won more than he lost, much to the annoyance of those seated with him, but like Anthony, he didn't interact with anyone.

Could she really be that foolish or desperate? He observed as Renee touched his wig. It was a gesture many women did each night, securing a pin. In this light the disguise was a good one but would not withstand scrutiny in daylight hours.

A commotion broke out at a table and Anthony watched two staff members approach. At the same time, Mr. Renee got out of his chair. Bowing, he walked from the room. Anthony rose and did the same.

He caught up with the Frenchman as he waited for his things to be retrieved. He was leaning his weight on his right leg, and the left boot was resting on the right one.

If he needed further confirmation that this was Miss Evangeline Spencer, he had it. But he would not approach her here, where anyone could overhear their conversation.

She left, buttoning up the too large overcoat. Outside, he watched as she hurried away from the club, then when she was a few feet in front of him, he followed. Only when he was sure they were alone did he speak. "Miss Spencer."

She spun to look at him. Then realizing her mistake, she turned back and kept walking.

"Too late," Anthony said, moving closer. He then grabbed her arm. "I can't work out if you are a fool or to be commended for your audacity."

"Unhand me," she demanded in French.

"The game is up, Miss Spencer. I saw the two brown marks on your neck here last time, and then at the Bailey ball. I know it is you under that wig and beard."

She wrenched her arm free and asked if he had lost his mind in a flurry of French.

He moved fast and tugged the beard down her chin. She tried to stop him, but Anthony was stronger. The wires gave and he faced a very angry Miss Evangeline Spencer.

"How dare you!" She attempted to rally. "What I do is my business."

He wanted to admire her courage, but he was too angry.

"You," he said slowly, tamping down his rage, "are an idiot to take such a risk."

He waited for her to speak, watching the emotion chasing across her pretty face. Instead, she surprised him by fleeing.

CHAPTER THIRTEEN

*R*UN, *EVIE!*
This was the only thought she had. Flee and get to her house where she could think about her next move before Lord Hamilton told everyone she was dressing as a Frenchman to gamble.

She would return to the country and stay there for the remainder of the season, while Prue and her father stayed in London and hoped to achieve a match.

But they could not do that if Lord Hamilton exposed her for the fraud she was.

Nausea roiled in her belly as she ran, trying to find a place to hide. Eyes going left and right, she saw no convenient narrow opening or dark space.

Everything she'd done. Everything she'd fought to achieve for her family would all come to nothing because he would expose her, and everyone would believe him.

"Stop!"

The bellow from behind spurred her on, as did the thud of his large feet. It was certainly a great deal easier to run in trousers and not hampered by skirts. Evie heard him gaining on her. Finally, she saw an opening, and she ducked down it.

He was larger and faster, but she was nimble. It was dark down here, which was a good thing. Evie knew she could not outrun him. She had to hide.

Removing the spectacles, she searched for somewhere to wait him out, and then she would go home and rouse Prue. Together they would decide the next steps to take.

Dear lord, she'd have to tell her sister what she'd been up to. The thought was almost as terrifying as facing Lord Hamilton. Prue could be fierce when riled.

Moving quietly along the buildings, she found what she was looking for. Slipping through the opening, she took the stairs down below the ground. Evie then huddled behind a wood box. She wasn't game to climb in because of the bugs that would be inside, but she could hide here.

She curled into a ball and lowered her head between her knees, then listened. There were no footsteps which was a good thing. Perhaps he would give up after a quick search? *Please give up.*

London was a noisy city, but right then it felt like everyone had taken a vow of silence. She heard no roll of carriage wheels or clop of hooves. No dog howled or cats yowled. There was just Evie, alone with her loud breathing. She tried to calm down. Tried to inhale and exhale slowly.

"I know you're here," she heard him say. "I'm not leaving, Miss Spencer. You may as well come out."

Why was he bothering with her? The man was a womanizing gambler who drank too much and cared nothing about anyone or anything... except maybe his aunts and two friends. He was a cold-hearted scoundrel, so why did he care what she did?

She could hide here all night, or she could show herself. But what then? What would he do to her? Plunge her family into ruin? And yet couldn't he do that anyway? Would he blackmail her into doing something she had no wish to do?

"I'm waiting, Miss Spencer. You may as well just come out. After all, I know your secret."

She didn't want to come out. She wanted to stay curled behind that dirty wood box forever.

Why had everything become complicated? First Lord Cavendish's attentions and now this. Lifting her head, she saw no sign of him but knew he was close.

I must get out of here and get back to the townhouse.

"I'm sure my current situation is far more comfortable than yours, Miss Spencer."

She heard the scrape of something and realized he had a flask with him and was likely drinking from it.

"I am standing in the entrance way. There is nowhere for you to go," he added in that deep drawl she loathed.

Evie realized he was right. She couldn't escape. Regaining her feet, she climbed back up to the lane.

He stood there, waiting for her. Evie said nothing, simply walked past him and back out to the street. He fell into step beside her.

The clop of hooves had her moving to the left, but large fingers clamped around her upper arm, and then she was being tugged into the road.

Was he going to throw her under a carriage?

He raised a hand, and the hackney slowed.

"What is your address?"

"I will walk," Evie said.

"No, you will not," he replied. "Address. Now, or I will tell everyone you dress in men's clothes and gamble."

"You will do that, anyway," she said, trying not to let the fear she felt show in her voice.

"Now, Miss Spencer," he said, looking as malleable as a one-hundred-year-old oak tree.

Defeated, Evie told him. The game was up, but perhaps if she promised to never again dress like Mr. Renee, he would tell no one? The hope was faint at best, considering his reputation. Why would he care about the Spencers? They were nothing to him.

Before she could climb into the hackney, Lord Hamilton had picked her up and tossed Evie inside. She landed on a seat, bracing her hands to right herself. He then climbed in and shut the door with enough force to have it rocking on its chases.

The carriage started rolling as he sat across from her. Dragging her eyes from him she looked out the window. Her family's fate was in his hands, and that did not sit well with Evie.

"Why are you taking such risks, Miss Spencer?"

"Because I must."

"Why must you?"

She watched the streetlamps cast shadows on the buildings as they passed and felt her desperation climb. How was she to get out of this? How would she stop him from exposing her and ruining any chance Prue had of happiness? Evie fixed things, but this was beyond her.

"Because I must." She heard the defeat in her words.

"That does not answer my question, and considering you are seated across from me dressed as a man and I could ruin you for it, I suggest you do so."

"Will you?" She faced him.

"Ruin you?" His amber eyes held hers.

Evie nodded. "We do not like each other, so I know there is no reason you would keep my secrets, but if I must, I will beg." The thought actually left a foul taste in her mouth. This man was the last person she would ever want to beg for anything.

"Watching you beg would, I admit, be entertaining."

Evie bit back the words she wanted to hurl at him.

"But that will not be necessary," he added. "However, I do want the truth."

"Why?"

He simply stared at Evie. Unlike her he was relaxed. His large body rested against the seat, hands on his thighs. Big and imposing, which she guessed helped him intimidate people when required. Well, she was not one of those. Evie's back was to the wall, and she was out of options, but she would never show this man weakness, even if she felt the sting of tears. Those she would keep at bay until she was alone, if it killed her.

"What I do is no concern of yours, Lord Hamilton."

"Just tell me your reasons, Miss Spencer."

"I don't want to," she snapped, which made his lips twitch.

"You're extremely strong willed, aren't you?"

"You make that sound like a fault, my lord."

"I'm sure in some situations it is."

"As I am a woman, Lord Hamilton, I must be meek and agreeable?"

"I did not say that, Miss Spencer." He raised a hand as she opened her mouth. "Tell me why you were in that gambling hell dressed as a man?"

Evie gave up then. It was done. He had seen her and could destroy her family with just a few words. He held all the cards. She would have to swallow her pride and tell him her story.

"We have no money, and this season will be our one and only."

"And you want a wealthy husband to rescue your family?"

"You make me sound shallow, when all I want is to settle my father and sister in comfort."

"And that will not happen if you do not marry well?"

"Not me, my sister," she said. "I want that for her. I am more than happy to go back to the country with my father."

"Presumably with your sister's husband's money to live on?"

"Don't you dare mock me," Evie snapped. "You live in your bloody grand town house with staff to run hither and yon after you. Never, not once in your life, have you worried where your next meal would come from, or how you will provide for your family," Evie said, desperation making her angry. "You have no right to stand judgment on me for doing what I must."

Evie could hear the rasp of her agitated breathing in the sudden silence.

"I was not judging you, so please do not presume to know me or my motives." His face held no mockery.

Evie returned her eyes to the window, unsure what to say next.

"So, you are gambling to keep your family afloat while you are here in London for the season?"

She nodded.

"Miss Spencer, I want to ask you another question, something I asked you the evening I found you in Lord Bailey's conservatory."

"I have no wish to answer any more questions, my lord. I have told you why I did what I have done. If you choose to ruin me and my family, there is little I can do about that."

"Were you distressed at the Bailey ball because of something Lord Cavendish said to you?"

"Yes," Evie whispered.

"What did he say to you, Miss Spencer?"

"He wishes me to be his wife and told me he knows of my family's circumstances," she whispered.

"He is going to blackmail you into marrying him?"

"I fear that is exactly what he will do."

"And you have no wish to marry a man of his circumstance and wealth?" The words were cool. "It would surely solve all your problems?"

Evie looked down at her gloved hands clenched in her lap.

"I hate that man, Lord Hamilton. I would rather marry a rodent."

He studied her. "You are an astute judge of character, Miss Spencer. Never trust Lord Cavendish. He is ruthless and without morals. He will not hesitate to destroy anyone who stands in his way."

"Why do you dislike him?" Evie asked.

"How do you know I dislike him?"

"I watched you that night at Hugh's."

He nodded. "You're right. I do." His honesty surprised her.

They stared at each other, and then he spoke.

"Miss Spencer, I think we can help each other out if you will allow it."

"In what way, Lord Hamilton?" Evie wasn't sure what to expect, but she clenched her hands tighter in her lap.

"I need a fiancée to deter my aunts from their pursuit to

marry me off this season, and you need a fiancé to deter Cavendish and allow your younger sister to find a husband."

"You are not serious?"

"Deadly. We will become engaged, then you will retire to the country at the end of the season, calling off our engagement, which will be my fault entirely, thereby casting no cloud over your family or you."

She opened her mouth, but he continued talking.

"But there will be no more Mr. Renee, Miss Spencer. I cannot allow you to take such risks again."

"But—"

"I must insist on this."

"I need the money," she said bluntly. "I am exceptionally good at gambling, and it really has nothing to do with you what I do."

He smiled at that. "Ah, but as my fiancée I must argue that point." He leaned forward, which put him suddenly a great deal closer to Evie. "You will never again dress as that man and leave your house."

The carriage rolled to a stop as she was formulating another reply. Lord Hamilton opened the carriage door.

"I will call on you tomorrow, and we shall discuss the matter further. Good evening, Miss Spencer."

"Oh, but—"

"Tomorrow," he said urging her out the door. He then closed it, and the hackney rolled away, leaving her standing on the street.

"This can't be happening," Evie muttered as she headed up the path to the front door of her family's lodgings. It wasn't until she was in her night dress and lying next to a slumbering Prue that she allowed herself to think about what he'd proposed.

A fake engagement until the end of the season. Could she? It would deter Lord Cavendish, but then it would also deter anyone else from making her an offer. But wouldn't her engagement to Lord Hamilton promote Prue up the favorable ranks of debutantes in the eyes of men?

He was a rogue, but still titled.

Could she do it?

Her eyelids began to close, and Evie thought that tomorrow was soon enough to make sense of the mess she'd made of her life.

CHAPTER FOURTEEN

A FTER SNATCHING A few hours of sleep, Anthony rose and dressed, all the while wondering what the hell he had been about proposing what he had to Miss Spencer.

Calling for his horse, he was soon trotting through the streets of London, wondering if he was losing his mind, even as he knew that what he'd proposed would benefit them both. If they could pull it off.

But her, of all people. Prickly, opinionated, and he was sure those were her finer qualities. The woman would not be easy to spend time with, which he would have to do if she became his fiancée.

Anthony saw the vendor ahead and pulled his horse to a halt beside the cart.

"It's a lovely morning, my lord," the woman said.

"I'll reserve opinion until the sun fully rises, Milly," Anthony said, dismounting. "I'll take a fruit pie please."

"We've apple today, my lord."

Anthony had been eating these pies for many years, as they were the best in London. Not that he'd tell his cook that. The only issue with stopping at Milly's cart was the advice that came with any purchase.

He put her age around sixty. Tall, thin, and usually wrapped in multiple layers of clothing, Milly was never shy to tell him what she thought on any subject. That Anthony was an earl with a dark reputation did not bother her in the slightest.

"It's a troubled mind that has you out here at this early hour, my lord," she said, handing him the pie.

"All is well, Milly." Anthony took it, and a large bite. He sighed at the taste of buttery pastry and spiced apple.

"A lady is my guess."

He didn't show by a flicker of an eyelash she was correct and instead kept eating.

"Well now, if a woman is rousing you from your slumber, my lord, she must be someone important," Milly continued.

She had bright green eyes and a narrow face, with lips that disappeared into her mouth when she smiled, because the top row of her teeth was missing.

"There is no important lady in my life, Milly."

Milly's husband, John, usually manned the stall with her. Where she was tall, he was half a head shorter and a great deal wider. Where she rarely smiled, he always did so.

"He's a woman on his mind, John," she said as her husband moved to her side.

"I never said that, Milly."

"I can tell." She tapped her nose. "It's in the eyes."

"A piece of advice for you, my lord, if I may," John said.

"Can I stop you?" Anthony said putting the last bite of pie in his mouth. He contemplated another but thought it wouldn't sit comfortably as he galloped about the park.

"If she's the one—"

"Not everyone needs love like you two."

"All true, my lord. There's them that are comfortable living with a person who doesn't hold their heart. But if you find someone that makes you want to spend time with her and fills your thoughts, then it's best you keep her."

No woman had ever produced such a reaction in him, and he doubted he could feel that level of emotion. Something was dead inside Anthony, and he'd realized that a long time ago.

"Well, thank you both for the advice, but I'll leave that kind of thing for those foolish enough to fall in love and be off for my ride."

"We'll see if you have to eat those words, my lord," Milly said, bobbing her head.

Anthony mounted and headed to the park.

Getting his aunts off his back would be a relief. There would be no ball, or whatever else they had planned for him. Miss Spencer would also be safe from Cavendish and the gambling. The thought of her under that man's control turned Anthony's stomach.

Reaching the park, he nudged his mount's sides and soon they were galloping. Few people were about, which suited him, as he could be alone with his thoughts.

He wondered what arguments Miss Spencer would present when he called upon her. Because she wouldn't yield easily to what he'd proposed. That wasn't her way.

Clearly the family had fallen on hard times, which is why she'd taken the drastic steps she had. Anthony also had no doubt Miss Spencer was the one to hold the family and its finances together. He knew Heathcliff Spencer was a simple soul.

The thunder of hooves had three horses approaching. He tensed when he saw the riders. Greville, Cavendish, and Calthorpe. The last two Anthony knew were in London for the season. Greville had not been, until now.

Greville raised a hand to halt Anthony, and he thought about riding on briefly but wouldn't give any of these men the satisfaction of doing so.

"Lord Hamilton," he said. "How lovely to see you again, and out so early. Care to join us?"

"Thank you, but no." Anthony didn't elaborate. He owed these men nothing. Cavendish glared at him, still angry over their exchange at Hugh's that night. "In town on business, Greville?"

The man had aged a great deal, and not well. His face was lined, skin a sickly shade of gray. He looked a shadow of the thug he'd once been. Anthony hoped he died a slow and painful death.

Forgiveness, he'd heard, was good for the soul, but as he did not have one, that wasn't of consequence.

"Just so," Greville said. "Visiting friends also," he added.

"He's also in town to cast his eyes over the woman who will be the future Lady Cavendish."

Anthony kept his cynical smile in place, but did not comment on the matter of him marrying Miss Spencer, as that would not be happening. He'd make sure of it.

"How is life in the country, Greville?" Anthony asked, much to the surprise of the three men. He rarely made conversation, and especially not with them. "I believe you live close to the village of Brawley?"

The man nodded, suddenly wary.

"Lovely place. I've spent time there over the years. The food in the tavern there is excellent."

Anthony saw the shock on each of their faces.

"I believe they've had some trouble lately." He appeared to consider his next words. "I can't remember exactly what, but I believe some women have disappeared."

"I-ah—"

"Village gossip is beneath us," Cavendish cut Greville off. "Good day, Lord Hamilton."

He turned to watch them gallop away and thought that he and his friends would need to do some investigations of their own into the missing women, if Greville's reaction to his question was any sign of his guilt.

❯❯❯❯❮❮❮❮

FOUR HOURS LATER, Anthony did something he'd never before done. He approached the front door of a young lady to express his interest in her. Of course, his was not real interest, but still, were anyone to see him, they would be shocked.

The area was not the best London had to offer, but not the

worst either. The red house was two stories and butted up against others like a row of books on a shelf.

He knocked three times on the front door and then stood back to wait. Anticipation over seeing Miss Spencer again grew as he heard footsteps on the other side of that wood. He dismissed it. This was a business arrangement that would suit them both.

"Good morning," Anthony said to the butler. "I am here to see Miss Spencer."

"She's not here, sir."

Why that surprised him, he had no idea, but it did. He'd thought she'd wait for him to call, and yet considering her nature, of course, this would be her response to his order last night.

"Do you know where she has gone?"

The man considered him through a set of piercing brown eyes.

"I'm a friend," Anthony said, forcing a smile onto his lips. "Old friend," he added when no response was forthcoming. "The Earl of Hamilton," he found himself tacking on. Another odd occurrence. He never had to explain to anyone who he was.

"Who is it, Humphrey?" a voice called from behind the man.

"Lord Hamilton, Miss Prue."

"Really?" A hand nudged the butler to one side, and then there stood Miss Prudence Spencer.

She was a softer version of her older sister. Where Miss Spencer scowled or glared, this one smiled. In a simple day dress of cream with sprigged lavender, she looked sweet. Anthony much preferred the sharp edges of Evangeline Spencer.

"I was looking for your sister."

"She's, ah…" She looked around her as if her sister was hiding nearby. "Out."

"So I understand. Do you know when she will return?"

"I'm afraid not. Evie is shopping."

Evie. He'd only ever thought of her as Miss Spencer. It was odd how just a name changed her in his eyes. He could see her as a beloved sister and daughter now, even if she was excessively irritating.

"And you did not care to go?" he said attempting a genuine smile to put her at ease, because she was now wringing her hands, which was often the reaction his presence produced in innocent young woman. Not Evangeline, however. She'd never feared him.

Prudence Spencer shook her head.

"Do you know which direction she took?"

"I don't know. Can I be of any help to you, Lord Hamilton?"

He studied her face. Was she aware of what happened last night? And that her sister masqueraded as a man to ensure her family had what they needed?

"I need to speak to your sister on a matter we discussed at the Bailey ball. She asked me about something, and I have the information she wanted. I would like to give it to her personally," he lied.

And this, Anthony thought, was what happened when you got involved with someone you had no business being involved with. Questions were raised, and you told a lie so no one knew what you were about, and then you had to remember that lie. It was exhausting. He did not know how his aunts did it constantly.

It was simply best everyone feared you as they kept their distance.

"Hello, what's going on here?"

Heathcliff Spencer appeared, a wide smile on his face, as always.

"Lord Hamilton, what has you calling at our humble abode?" Baron Spencer rarely spoke in a moderate tone; he boomed. "Are you visiting my dear Prudence, per chance?"

It annoyed Anthony that Miss Spencer's father naturally thought his youngest daughter was why he had called.

"I have called to see Miss Spencer, my lord."

"Have you really? Now that is a surprise don't you think, Prudence?"

The daughter in question winced, and then her lips pursed in a tight line.

"You'll have to come in and take tea with us, Hamilton. My eldest daughter has gone to Covent Garden. Apparently, she's shopping for—"

"Yes, thank you, Father. I'm quite sure Lord Hamilton doesn't need the details," Prudence Spencer said cutting her father off.

"Thank you for the offer of tea, but I will have to decline, as I have an appointment. I shall call to see Miss Spencer another time." Anthony then bowed and walked back out the gate.

The door shut with a definite snap, and he was quite sure that Prudence was now taking her father to task for nearly telling Anthony that Evie, as he would now think of her, was out shopping for the household supplies.

Climbing back on his horse, he headed toward Covent Garden. He and Evie had things to discuss, and they would do so today.

CHAPTER FIFTEEN

"I FAIL TO see how two bruised potatoes could cost that exorbitant amount, sir."

"Exorbitant!" Mr. Chester glared at her, but his eyes twinkled. "I'm insulted, Miss Spencer. Wounded down to my toes. My heart is bruised!"

"Perhaps if you throw in that misshapen turnip, I may be persuaded to purchase your bruised potatoes. But," Evie held up a hand, "I think it exceedingly shabby you would try to foist them on me."

She'd first come to the markets to purchase food for the household and other necessities with their cook/housekeeper. Evie had then taken her time getting to know several of the vendors. Mr. Chester was her favorite.

"Foist, is it?" He puffed out his broad chest and stroked his moustache.

"Foist," Evie confirmed.

"Oh, very well, but I will not give you both these carrots," he said placing them in the small pile of vegetables before her.

"Excellent. Because I will not accept them."

After the haggling portion of her vegetable purchasing was over, she kissed Mr. Chester's cheek and wandered on.

Mrs. Humphries would be somewhere haggling also.

The markets were loud, the air permeated with so many scents she couldn't identify them. Meats, poultry, fish, and vegetables, there was so much to look at and buy here. The place was alive with noise and color. Evie loved it.

She only purchased what their household needed, and usually one treat for herself and one for Mrs. Humphries to eat on the return journey.

"He's a handsome one," Miss Furner, behind the bread stall said.

Evie, who had been studying the array of loaves on her table, turned to see who she was talking about. She tensed. Lord Hamilton was walking toward her.

Drat. She'd left the house deliberately hoping to avoid him. She wasn't ready for the conversation he wanted to have. It had been a cowardly move, but she was tired from tossing and turning all night and needed to be at her best when they talked again.

Her eyes were itchy and tired, and her body weary from replaying his proposal and the consequences if she said yes, or no, inside her head. She had no wish to battle wits with this man when she was not her usual self.

Turning away, she looked for an escape route, even as she knew it would be futile. The man would catch her if she ran, as he had last night. Evie walked toward him instead of away. *You are no coward,* she reminded herself.

Life was excessively unfair. It was not her fault her father was hopeless with finances, and yet here she was, presented with two men wanting different things from her, neither of which she wanted to accept. Tamping down the frustration, Evie forced herself to smile.

"Lord Hamilton." She sank into a curtsey. "How lovely to see you, and here of all places." Her words rang with insincerity.

"Miss Spencer." He bowed deeply, a mocking smile on his face as if he knew it was not lovely at all.

She found it excessively unfair that he looked his usual vital self. No smudges from worry or lack of sleep under his eyes. His face was not pale or wan as hers likely was, but a healthy glow tinged his cheeks.

In that moment she loathed him for who he was. A man who needed no one for his survival. A man who could wake and dress in that deep blue jacket of the highest quality, and the blue and gray striped waistcoat. Everything about him screamed wealth and confidence.

Horrid beast.

"Is there a reason you are fixing that dark scowl on me, when all I've said is your name?"

"How did you find me?"

"I called at your house, as I'd said I would, but you were not there."

She refused to blush over that. They both knew she'd left the house to avoid him.

"Your father told me you had gone to Covent Garden," he added.

Evie fought the urge to pinch the bridge of her nose.

"Allow me to carry your bag, Miss Spencer." He reached for the handle, but she held fast.

"I can carry my own bag, thank you."

"And yet it would be ungentlemanly of me not to," he said with a hard tug, which pulled it from her grasp.

"You are always ungentlemanly!" she snapped.

"Did you rise on the wrong side of the bed this morning, Miss Spencer? It seems to me you are out of sorts."

"Of course, I'm out of sorts, so stop toying with me," Evie snapped. "Tell me someone who wouldn't be, considering my circumstances."

"Perhaps we could have this conversation in private?" His free hand took her wrist and then he was walking, and Evie had little option but to follow as his long strides led her toward the exit.

"Can I be of assistance, Miss Spencer?"

"I am to, ah, talk with Lord Hamilton briefly, Mrs. Humphrey. If you will take my bag also, please, I shall see you shortly at home."

The Spencer cook/housekeeper studied Lord Hamilton for long seconds, and then nodded. She held out her hand, and he passed her the bag he'd taken from Evie.

"I'll just walk behind you," Mrs. Humphrey then said, clearly not trusting Lord Hamilton. *Clever woman.*

"In that case, I'll carry that bag as yours looks heavy," Lord Hamilton said surprising both women. He took the bag back from Mrs. Humphrey.

Evie couldn't be sure, but thought Humphrey had told his wife exactly what Evie got up to at night when she was impersonating a Frenchman. The woman had said a few cryptic comments in her hearing that told her she was not impressed.

She was sure the Spencers' household staff were not like others. They seemed happy to offer their opinions freely at any given time.

"Well then, shall we?" Lord Hamilton said walking and towing Evie with him. "I feel as if I just passed some kind of test with Mrs. Humphrey, who I guess is your butler's relation?"

"Wife," Evie snapped. "And not a maid, so she should not be walking behind us.

"I am not your enemy, Evie, and the offer came from her not I."

Her name coming from his lips was a shock.

"You can't call me that," she rallied.

"Possibly not, but your family did earlier, and I like it," he said. "Somehow it makes you appear approachable. A facade that I am fully aware is not true."

"We all live behind facades, my lord. You are not the most approachable man either."

"I would never lay claim to such a thing," he replied calmly.

"I don't give you permission to use my name, however," she said. "Unhand me at once."

"You sound like the heroine in one of those ghastly novels my aunts would read."

"Yes, well, one wouldn't expect someone like you to lower

yourself by reading such a book."

Evie couldn't be sure but thought he sighed. "Surely, as your fiancé, I should be allowed to call you Evie?"

"Where are you taking me?" she demanded instead of answering his question. "And you are not my fiancé."

"Somewhere I cannot wrap my hands around your neck and squeeze, which means we need to stay in public."

"I can't believe you just said that!"

"I'm quite sure other people have spoken to you in such a manner before, considering your caustic nature."

"Yes, well, from what I've seen, your nature is hardly sunny, my lord. In fact, I believe some refer to you as ruthless, and other less flattering descriptions."

She shot him another look in time to see his lips tighten.

"Listening to gossip, Miss Spencer. I thought better of you."

"There is always a thread of truth to gossip."

"I found you last night in men's clothes gambling, Miss Spencer. I got you home safely and offered a proposition that would aid us both for the remainder of the season. Perhaps you could think about that instead of my ruthless nature?"

She could almost believe she'd hurt him.

"Forgive me," Evie said. "I did not sleep well, and I am never at my best when things are not within my control."

"I cannot fault you for that, as I am the same," he said in a somber tone.

"Where are we going?"

"To take tea. My stomach is empty, and I am never at my best then either."

"Tea?"

"It's a beverage that is poured from the spout of a teapot. Some drink it with milk, others honey, I believe."

"No, really?" Evie muttered.

He led her across a road after these words and into a lane she'd never entered before. He stopped before a narrow wooden door in need of a fresh coat of paint. Looking up, Evie saw a small sign with the words The Best Tea in London.

"It's the truth," he said, following her eyes. "It's tucked away, but people know of its reputation for excellent scones and tea."

"I don't think I should be seen alone taking tea with you, my lord."

"Possibly not, but your—" He looked behind them to where Mrs. Humphrey stood a few feet back. "What is her position?"

"Cook/housekeeper," Evie said, as there seemed no point lying now.

"Cook/housekeeper is with us."

"A lady's reputation can be easily damaged," Evie said.

"Yes, it can, but then a person who gads about in men's clothes is not someone to question that, surely. Besides, we are to be betrothed. I'm sure it's fine to be seen with me."

"We are not to be betrothed," she said firmly.

He opened the door after placing a kick to the bottom left corner as it was sticking and nudged her inside.

"Come along, Mrs. Humphrey," he added.

Delicious scents hit Evie, and she inhaled deeply. The interior was small, and she had to add, shabby, but most of the tables were full of people.

"Stop pushing me about the place, my lord," she hissed when a large hand, now on her spine, continued to direct her.

"Move your feet and I won't have to."

She muttered something unflattering beneath her breath.

"I have excellent hearing, Evie. Perhaps you might remember that. Now, sit." He pulled out a chair. "I will return shortly."

"My name is Miss Spencer," she said.

He waved Mrs. Humphrey into a seat at the table behind them, then Lord Hamilton took the one across from Evie.

"Relax, Evie," he said as her fingers tapped the table.

"I should not be here with you, my lord, but as I am, then say what needs to be said, and I shall leave." Evie took control of the conversation.

"Tea and cakes for Mrs. Humphries," Lord Hamilton pointed

to the table behind them, "and the same for us," he added to the young girl who took their order. "Four fruit buns also."

"Please," Evie snapped. "And you can't eat all that."

"Please, and I can, because you will help me."

"I am not hungry," she lied. In fact, she was and had planned to eat something on her walk home until he'd appeared.

He studied her again. "You are an exceedingly stubborn woman, aren't you, Evie?"

"Miss Spencer," she snapped. "It is not right for you to call me Evie."

"Very well, let us get down to business," he said looking like a lion with the appearance of being relaxed, but ready to swipe you with a paw if necessary.

What she wanted to do was walk out the door, but she was also no coward. He knew things about her that could ruin her family. She had to stay and listen to what he said.

"I need a fiancée for the remainder of the season, and you need someone to help remove you from the clutches of the perfidious Cavendish. Shall we make a deal?"

"I'm not sure I should," Evie said.

"Because?" He raised a dark brow.

"Because then I am not available to marry anyone, should they ask," Evie said battling the rush of heat she felt filling her cheeks. "I'm sure my sister will attract an offer, but what if she does not? I need to be…" Her words fell away as she grappled to find the right ones.

"The standby, should your sister fail?"

Evie nodded.

"Just so I'm clear," he said. "Your family's financial situation is dire?"

The shame of those words had Evie looking to the left, and away from his piercing gaze.

"Yes or no, Evangeline?"

"Miss Spencer, and damn you, yes," she whispered, still not looking at him. "We have the funds that I have won, but they will not last long. It is extremely expensive to live in London and have a season."

"The shame is not yours." The soft-spoken words had her looking at him again. "As I am sure it is because of you that your family have kept up appearances," he added.

"Is there a point you wish to make, my lord?"

His smile was small.

"That you need money, and I can help you with that if you will help me."

Their tea arrived then, so she said nothing further. Mrs. Humphrey looked more than happy with her situation when Evie glanced at her.

Once they were alone again, she said, "Why do you want to help me, Lord Hamilton?"

"Because, like you, I have no wish to marry until I must. My aunts are determined to change that."

"You are an earl. Surely you can just say no?" Evie asked before giving in and picking up a fruit bun.

"I have no wish to discuss my reasons with you or anyone." The words came out clipped.

"And yet I must tell you everything?" Evie said. "A man I barely know or trust."

CHAPTER SIXTEEN

"**N**OT EVERYTHING," ANTHONY conceded. "The things that matter with regards to our engagement."

Anthony wasn't sure what had possessed him to bring her here to this tea shop. It wasn't a place nobility frequented, and he had stumbled upon it one day and eaten the best wedge of cinnamon cake, so he'd returned often. It had been his secret, until now.

He'd tracked her down at the market, haggling with a vendor over potatoes and turnips. Anthony had wondered when, since he'd left Blackwood Hall, he'd ever been hungry and came up with no memory of that happening.

He may be cold and emotionless, and his life spent indulging in things he should not, but his needs were always met, and well.

Standing at the market, taking in the frayed hem of her skirts, sitting inches above her sturdy boots, the left foot resting on the right, he'd felt an unpleasant burning sensation in his chest, which Anthony told himself was indigestion, but he had a terrible feeling was emotion.

She was haggling over vegetables. The realization had been a humbling one and following on from that had been the need to help her. Anthony rarely felt those kinds of urges.

He'd found himself drawing closer to her, and then she'd turned, and they'd locked eyes. Hers had flashed fear, and then anger.

Anthony knew how to hide like that. How to push the fear away and replace it with anger. It allowed him to distance himself from others.

"Would you like tea, Evangeline?"

"You can't pour my tea," she said, clearly horrified. "And my name is Miss Spencer."

"Why?"

"It is my name."

"No, why can I not pour your tea?"

She actually spluttered.

"And I will ask again, why?" He raised the teapot and poured.

"I-you, it is not done." She was clearly scandalized.

"I did not take you for one who was a stickler for rules, Evangeline, and before you say Miss Spencer, I will call you Evie or Evangeline when we are engaged, so pick one."

She fell silent at that and took another large bite of the fruit bun. Evangeline did not nibble her food like other women he knew, which had him fighting a smile.

"So, you or your sister must make a match, or it will be disaster?" he said returning to the reason she was seated across from him, with her cook/housekeeper a few feet away more than happy eating cake.

"Yes."

"Tell me, Evie or Evangeline, do you have money?"

"If it must be one of those, then Evangeline will do," she said in a prim tone. "And I'm not sure I understand the question, my lord."

He'd thought her eyes a simple brown, but they had flecks of gold in them. Surrounded by dark lashes and brows. She was a beautiful woman, and he wondered why the rest of society had not worked that out yet.

"Quite a simple one. Do you have money that you can give to me to invest for you, to make more money?"

That silenced her. Her lips formed a perfect O. Anthony sat back in his chair, as the urge to close the distance between them and taste her surged through him.

You don't get urges.

He didn't help people either...not quite true, but never a member of society who could use it against him.

"So, to silence you one must shock you. I will keep that information handy for the future," Anthony said picking up his tea for no other reason than he felt a need to do something with his hands, because he wanted to touch her cheek. Test the texture and heat of it.

What was happening to him?

"Before you ask me why, again, let me tell you that if I make enough money for you then you will not need to wed, and your sister could possibly have more than one season, and perhaps a dowry?"

That caught her attention.

"But surely it is not possible to make such a sum when we are halfway through the season?"

"I can try on your behalf."

"You would do that?"

He sighed again. "I am not the complete monster some believe me to be, Evangeline, and I admire and respect you for what you are trying to do for your family. Do I think that charade as Renee was foolish and far too risky? Yes," he said cutting her off as she opened her mouth. "But, if I help you, then you will be helping me."

"I don't know what to say."

"Yes, would be an excellent start." Anthony wasn't sure why he wanted her agreement as much as he did.

"But you are a gentleman. Surely you do not invest?"

"You really do have a poor opinion of us, don't you, Evangeline?"

She nodded, which made him bark out a laugh surprising both of them. Anthony rarely did anything in public but look cynical.

"I have a man of affairs who is exceedingly good with making money. I have been known to excel at it also."

"But you gamble," she said.

"Only what I can afford to lose."

"Unlike Lord Beaton."

"Yes, unlike him and others," Anthony said.

Her head tilted to the side as she studied him, and suddenly he felt exposed, like she could see right down to the scared boy he'd once been.

"However, I doubt you have enough money, Miss Spencer, so I won't make you any promises." The words came out harsh.

"Of course." Like him, her face changed and was suddenly empty of emotion.

Good. It was best this way. They would never be friends. This was business only.

"So do we have a deal for the remainder of the season? If I can make you money I will, but our engagement will deter Cavendish from pursuing you."

"It seems underhanded."

"You go out at night dressed as a Frenchman and fool everyone you see. I doubt it's any more underhanded than that," he said.

"I did what I must."

That bloody chin rose again, challenging him. The problem was, women never did that, and he was finding it... what? Intriguing? Refreshing?

"If you wish for your sister to marry well, your connection with me would help with that," Anthony added.

She was considering his offer; he could see that. Thinking through every angle in that fertile brain of hers.

"She has no dowry?"

"She doesn't, no. We were hoping her nature and beauty would surpass the need for that."

"Which is naïve," Anthony said. "No man would overlook such a thing. Many need the money their future wives will bring with them."

Her eyes shot sparks at him for daring to call her naïve.

"If I may speak plainly, Miss Spencer?"

"You weren't?"

He wanted to laugh again but managed to swallow it down.

"Your sister may be pretty and well-mannered, but she will not secure a match this season without a dowry. But," he raised a hand as she opened her mouth to no doubt fire a volley of insults his way, "if you are betrothed to me it will be believed that a dowry will come with her, and that I will be paying it."

"But that will be a falsehood."

"Do you not have family who can help provide one?"

She shook her head. "My grandparents were not happy that my father married my mother, who," she gave him a pointed look, "brought no money to the marriage, or came from a family with a higher ranking than theirs."

"I see."

"But they loved each other," Evangeline continued. "They were happy together."

"With no money," Anthony added.

"We were happy, and my mother was excellent with money. We did not realize our father's ineptitude until it was too late. I'm not sure why I am telling you this," she added quickly.

"There is no point hiding things now, Miss Spencer. The gloves are off."

"But I am the only one baring my secrets, my lord."

My secrets are far too dark for a sweet woman like you.

"So do we have a deal?" Anthony watched her closely for any sign of what she was thinking. It was long moments later, after a bite of the superb fruit bun, swallowed down with tea, that she spoke.

"We both speak plainly and can readdress this at any time?" she asked.

He nodded.

"I can't believe I'm considering this."

"Think about Cavendish," Anthony said, and saw her shudder. "Plus, I will help you find a suitor for your sister."

"On that note, my lord. May I ask you about men who approach my sister? My father…" She looked down at her teacup, thinking about what to say next.

Anthony thought a few society members could learn a thing or two about thinking before speaking from this woman.

"Is not a reliable source, and I fear although a man may look suitable, he will not be."

That she would trust his word on the men who would court her sister made him feel odd. Few people would come to him with something like this.

"You may ask me, and I will give you my honest opinion," he said.

She stared at him again, like she could read his mind, which Anthony knew was foolish, but he felt exposed.

"Very well. I agree."

He nodded.

"We will be seen together often. Driving in the park and at the theatre," he added.

"Yes, and my sister will have to be with me."

"Not all the time, Evangeline."

"Very well, not all the time."

"You have a maid?"

She nodded. "She is not there always, but I will ensure she is when we go driving. Do you really believe we can convince your aunts, and society?"

"Matches are made all the time between people who feel nothing for each other. No one will question us on the matter."

"You mean no one will question you," she said.

"If anyone is rude to you in any way, then I expect you to talk to me on the matter."

"Very well, and it is likely I will have more questions."

"I would expect nothing less from you," he said solemnly.

She frowned. "Are you laughing at me?"

"I don't laugh, Miss Spencer."

"What, never?"

He didn't answer that.

She huffed out a small breath, looking like a disgruntled child.

"We will go driving in the park tomorrow, and then I will take you to the theatre, along with your father and sister, the following evening."

"I accept your gracious offer, Lord Hamilton." Her face looked like she'd sucked on a lemon.

"You will not like this either, Evangeline, but to make this work, I believe you need to keep what we are doing a secret from your family."

"I don't keep things from my sister."

"People will be watching you and your family, Evangeline. To make this work, we need them to believe us. Your sister's reaction will be important. If she, like the others, believe we have—"

"If you say fallen in love, she will definitely not believe that. We have barely spoken two words to each other, and those were angry ones. My sister is nobody's fool, my lord."

"I am aware of that, but you could tell her that you and I talked at the Bailey ball, and I apologized, as did you, for the way we had spoken to each other."

"I've always disliked apologizing."

"It's not something I enjoy," Anthony said. "For now, we keep this between us."

"And you will not tell your friends?"

"I fear they will know something is off, as I have vowed often I am not ready for marriage."

"My sister knows me better than anyone."

"Then we shall cross those bridges if they arise," Anthony said. "But for now we will not disclose our engagement and simply appear as if we are getting to know each other."

She nodded, seeming happy with that.

"Do you need money to buy dresses?" Had he slapped her, the effect would have been the same. Angry color filled her cheeks, and her mouth opened and closed several times before she spoke.

"We are not a charity case, my lord." She then rose to her feet. "Good day to you."

Anthony watched as she snatched the last fruit bun off the plate before him and walked from the teashop. He did not start laughing until the door was closed.

CHAPTER SEVENTEEN

E VIE SLAPPED PRUE'S hands aside as she attempted to pinch some color into her cheeks.

"Is there a need to pinch so hard?"

"You are pale, Evie, and while I know that is a combination of nerves and fear, Lord Hamilton will not."

They were in their bedchamber and Prue was fussing with her appearance.

"I'm still shocked by what you told me, Evie. To think he apologized to you, and now is taking you driving in the park today. It's very romantic."

Prue thought many things were romantic.

Evie had broached the subject of Lord Hamilton taking her driving last night, as casually as she could, to her father and sister. Heathcliff Spencer was delighted, and Prue shocked.

"I thought you disliked each other?" had been the first words out of her mouth. To which Evie had replied "not anymore" with as much conviction as she could.

"It is only a drive in the park, Prue. Don't make more of it than need be. But I find that I do like him more after we talked." The words felt like they were choking her. Looking down at her gloves, she avoided her sister's eyes. "As I explained last night, you know I thought it would be you that had suitors falling all over themselves for your attention, which they are...will be," she added quickly.

"But now you have one, and he is the powerful and wealthy Lord Hamilton. His reputation worries me, Evie. It is terrible. The rumors around that man make me worry for you."

"Prue—"

"Miss Haddock said that he has five mistresses and a gambling den in his town house."

"Don't be ridiculous," Evie said. While she knew his reputation, she believed a lot had been embellished. There had to be some good in that man, because his three aunts adored him, and Lords Corbyn and Jamieson were loyal to him.

"While you will not openly acknowledge it, Evie, I know you are only doing this for father and me."

"As you would, and likely will. This season was for one of us to find a match, Prue."

"Evie—"

"But I like Lord Hamilton. He does not flatter me, and we have spoken on many interesting topics. He is no fool, and as you know, I can't abide those."

"Really?" Prue looked relieved. Evie had said the right things to ease her worry.

"Yes."

"Well then, let me look at you." Prue held out Evie's arms. "If you are to drive around the park with the devil, you must at least look good."

"He is not the devil." Evie sighed.

"He is not far from it according to many who walk in society." Prue studied her. "The lemon is a perfect color for you. Perhaps I should just—"

"If you touch my cheeks again, I will slap you. Now back away, as I heard someone knock on our door."

"Oh, very well. I only want your happiness, Evie," Prue then said solemnly.

The sisters hugged. "I know, as I want that for you."

"Will you take Sarah with you, Evie?"

"I will, yes." Their maid would accompany her. Which was

silly as far as Evie was concerned. She'd been walking about London alone since arriving here, but she also knew what sticklers society was for rules.

She followed Prue out the hall and down the stairs. Evie could hear the deep voice of Lord Hamilton as she drew closer. He was talking with their father in the small front parlor.

She wouldn't feel shame having him here. Yes, it was not grand like the places he was used to, but it mattered not. He would not be in her life for long. This was a deal between them that would last the rest of the season.

Entering the room, Evie found the immaculately dressed Lord Hamilton seated across from her father. They appeared to be discussing horses, which her father loved but could no longer afford to purchase.

"Ah, here they are, my lovely daughters," Heathcliff Spencer said regaining his feet along with Lord Hamilton.

"Miss Spencer, Miss Prudence Spencer." He bowed deeply.

"Lord Hamilton, how lovely to see you," Prue said. Evie bobbed a curtsey and managed a tight smile.

They must spend time together to convince people they were engaged...or soon would be. Would anyone believe he could be interested in her? After all, he could have his pick of any woman, even if half of them were terrified of him, and she was hardly a catch. Older than the average debutante and not as pretty, there would surely be questions.

"Allow me to tell you how lovely you look today, Miss Spencer," Lord Hamilton said.

"Thank you." The words felt like they were choking her. Prue and her father were watching closely, and she hated lying to them.

"Shall we go?" she asked.

"Of course." He smiled, seeming completely at ease, while her insides were churning like butter.

Prue squeezed Evie's hand and told her to have fun. Her father kissed her cheek, and then they were outside and climbing into his carriage. She took the seat beside Sarah, while Lord Hamilton sat across from her.

"It's a lovely day for a drive," he said as they started moving.

"Yes, lovely," she agreed.

She felt his eyes on her as Evie's went to the window to watch the scenery until they entered the park. They circled slowly behind other carriages and horses, and then Lord Hamilton tapped on the roof, and they halted.

"A walk, I think." He opened the door and stepped down.

Evie couldn't very well argue and demand to continue in the carriage, so she took his large, gloved hand and climbed out. He assisted Sarah to do the same.

"Put your hand into the crook of my elbow, Evangeline." The words were spoken softly, but she heard the order behind them.

She managed a jerky nod, and then her eyes were scanning the people before them. Who had seen them together? She saw two groups looking their way.

"I look exactly as you do when I am forced to eat boiled salmon, Evangeline. Smile for pity's sake. If we are to convince anyone you have fallen madly in love with me, you need to work on your acting skills."

"I like boiled salmon." Evie smiled after she'd said the words. "The problem is, I don't like to be fake and loathe that about some in society. Plus, I don't remember us ever discussing falling madly in love." The very thought made her stomach clench.

"I doubt either of us are the falling madly in love kind. However, this is something we both decided upon, so put your back into it, Evangeline."

"Very well. I shall try." She smiled up at him, fluttering her eyelashes. "I cannot tell you how lovely it is to be here today, walking in the park with you, Lord Hamilton."

He frowned. "I will need to be on my guard with you. That was very convincing for all you said you couldn't act. Will you try to use my name now, Evangeline?"

"Anthony." It sounded off and misshapen on her lips.

They walked a few more steps before he spoke. "Excellent. What is your favorite color?" he asked.

"Yellowy orange."

"Not just yellow, or orange?"

"It is the color that strikes the meadow at the edge of my father's land when the sun begins to rise."

He sighed.

"You don't like my color choice, Anthony?"

"There now. You're getting the hang of it, Evangeline."

She only just resisted the urge to poke out her tongue.

"As to your question," he continued. "It makes my choice of green seem bland," he said. "Are you one of those people who describe things in flowery prose?"

Evie wondered how many people, besides those closest to him, knew this man had a sense of humor. Not many, she guessed, as he was usually leaning on ballroom walls with a mocking look on his face.

"Well, there are many greens. Perhaps the color of the leaves on a walnut tree, or a silver birch? When the sun hits—"

"Dark green," he drawled, interrupting her. "Let's move on as I am woeful at descriptions, and clearly you are not. Favorite food."

"That's easy. Boiled salmon and potatoes."

"You're a mean person, Evangeline."

"Surely not?" Now the nerves had eased slightly, she realized she was enjoying herself, much to her surprise. "My favorite sweet foods are plum cake and barley sugar candy."

"I am partial to eclairs and sugar plums," he said.

"Both excellent choices," she agreed.

They were walking down a path behind others out for a stroll. Some shot them curious looks. Lord Hamilton nodded, or doffed his hat, and Evie smiled. It was getting easier, she thought. As soon as that thought entered her head, she saw him.

"It will be all right, Evangeline. Trust me." He placed a hand over the one she had on his arm. "Breathe easy and continue to smile."

She concentrated on inhaling and exhaling as Lord Cavendish stalked toward them with another man she knew as Mr. Calthorpe. As they drew closer, she saw the anger mottling Lord Cavendish's face.

"Miss Spencer. What is the meaning of this?" He spat the words out as he reached them. "Unhand the woman I plan to marry at once, Hamilton."

"Cavendish, Calthorpe," Anthony said, in his slow drawl. "Lovely day for a walk with a beautiful woman."

"I demand to know why you are walking with Miss Spencer, Hamilton, when you know my intentions toward her."

"I know nothing about you, Cavendish, and have no wish to," Lord Hamilton said.

Evie tensed as Lord Cavendish leaned in, his eyes narrowed and mean as he glared at Anthony, and then her.

"Come here, Miss Spencer, and away from him!"

"Back away, Cavendish, before I make you." Lord Hamilton's voice, though not growling like Lord Cavendish's, still conveyed a menacing threat.

Evie now saw the man most of society feared.

"Miss Spencer never once indicated to me she found your interest in her favorable," he added. "Do as I say, Cavendish, and move back, because you are making a scene, and while I care little for that, I know appearances are everything to a man like you."

"I don't take orders from you," Cavendish snapped, but his eyes shot left and right.

People had stopped to watch, and in that moment, Evie wanted to return home and close the door and never leave the Spencer house again.

"When it comes to Miss Spencer you do, Cavendish."

"What? You have no claim on her," Lord Cavendish spluttered. He fell back a step, clearly shocked.

"Exactly. What are you about, Hamilton?" the man with him, Calthorpe, said. "Some kind of petty revenge you're still seeking for the harmless games at Blackwood Hall?"

Evie felt the arm beneath her fingers tense. Lord Hamilton's expression was once again wearing that mocking smile, but when he looked down at her briefly, she saw the rage. She wondered what lay between these men. *What had happened at Blackwood Hall?*

"You were a coward then, and you're—"

"Lord Hamilton has asked me to marry him, and I have accepted," Evie said quickly, cutting off Lord Cavendish. "We are blissfully happy at the prospect, and I would ask you to respect my decision, my lord." She dug her fingers into the hard muscled arm.

"Extremely happy," Anthony said, in a voice cold enough to freeze water.

Lord Cavendish looked about to have an apoplexy. His face was flushed red, and his hands clenched into fists.

"I knew nothing of your partiality toward each other," he gritted out. "Miss Spencer and I spoke just the other night—"

"You spoke, Lord Cavendish. I did not. Nor did I agree to what you proposed."

"You knew my intentions, woman. Knew what I wanted."

Anthony's hand once again settled on hers. The gentle squeeze was reassuring.

"Her name is Miss Spencer, and if you speak to her like that again, Cavendish, you will be walking away with a bloodied nose... at the very least."

Had he really just said that in a public setting? She felt a small surge of heat that he was protecting her, even if this, what was between them, was not real.

"You threatened me, Lord Cavendish," Evie continued, keeping her voice soft so those craning to overhear, could not.

"Did he? Care to tell me how, Evangeline?"

"No." She shook her head to ensure Lord Hamilton understood. "It no longer matters."

"It matters to me," he said darkly.

"Misunderstanding," Cavendish said glaring at her. "Woman's not the most intelligent, if you grasp my meaning, Hamilton. You may want to revise your intentions toward her."

Before Evie could tell Cavendish exactly what she thought of him, Lord Hamilton released Evie and started to remove his jacket.

"Wh-what are you doing!" Mr. Calthorpe yelped.

"Cavendish insulted the woman I am to marry."

"It was not his intention," Calthorpe added. "Tell him it wasn't."

"It was not my intention," Cavendish said reluctantly.

Anthony stopped his movements, and picked up Evie's hand, placing it back on his arm. "Miss Spencer is to be my wife. Therefore, under my protection. I suggest you think long and hard before insulting her again, Cavendish."

"You will both regret this," Lord Cavendish hissed.

"Be careful. That sounded like a threat to me, and I believe I have already told you I do not take well to those," Lord Hamilton said.

Both men turned and stalked away, leaving Evie wanting to do the same. However, noting the curious looks around them, she forced her lips into a smile, and wondered what she had now found herself in the middle of.

CHAPTER EIGHTEEN

"L ET US WALK," Anthony said attempting to cool the inferno raging inside him. "Evangeline, move your feet now."

His words shocked her into taking a step, and soon they were walking down the path. Anthony usually kept his composure around those men, but today he'd felt the urge to plant his fist in their faces. The anger from his youth was there, but there was something more now. Cavendish had insulted Evangeline, and that had him seeing red.

"I'm sorry you were exposed to that." He looked at her, taking in her tight expression. Was she about to weep? "He has gone, and I will not allow him to harm you again."

She exhaled loudly. "I did not give him any reason to believe I wished to be the future Lady Cavendish, Anthony."

It was the first time she'd willingly called him by his first name, and he liked the sound of it on her lips.

"I know that, just as I know it would have been he who bullied and intimidated you, Evangeline. Now tell me what threat he held over you."

"He knew of our situation."

Cavendish would use every means he could find to get what he wanted, and that had been Evangeline.

"I loathe that man. He calls himself a gentleman and yet he is far from that. He—he makes me so angry. How dare he speak as if he owned me?"

"So, your maidenly sensibilities are not upset then? This is pure rage?" Anthony asked, feeling his own mood lighten.

"We have had only a handful of conversations, and suddenly, because he has decided I would be a suitable wife and mother to his children, he is angry I did not fall in with his wishes. Beastly man."

"Extremely." The thought of Cavendish in a bed with Evangeline made his stomach curdle. "It seems our engagement has been expedited, however."

She stopped, turning to face him. "I'm so sorry. That just came out of my mouth before I could stop it."

He wasn't sure what it was about this woman that he liked, but her forthright nature was definitely part of it.

"We had already decided we would become betrothed, Evangeline, but I think we should return shortly and tell your family, and then I must inform my aunts."

"Oh dear, yes they should have known first."

He let his eyes run down her neck to the soft swell of her breasts above the bodice, and felt his body respond to that...her. Her lovely eyes were filled with worry, and she trapped her full, curved lower lip between her teeth. He wanted to lean in and pull it free with his.

His mistress supplied his needs, and he'd never experienced the want to have more with another woman. Anthony had always believed that was because he couldn't. That something had died inside him at Blackwood Hall. But right then, he wanted this woman, and that would never do.

"We shall walk for a while longer," Anthony rasped before clearing his throat. "Then return to your family to tell them our news."

He could not get out of it now, so he would see it through. But Anthony was a master at keeping himself distant from people. Evangeline would be no different.

"They will be shocked," she said, once again taking his arm. "As will yours."

"But mine will be ecstatic also, as they will no longer need to compile lists."

"Lists?"

"Of suitable women for me to court."

"No!" She gasped. "Really?"

"Really."

"Who is on the list?"

"You were."

"Me? That does surprise me, as I have little to offer. I'm too old, poor, and speak my mind."

"You are," he said, which had her shoulders stiffening. "In my defense I was agreeing with you."

She harrumphed.

Looking around them, he saw they were receiving plenty of glances, and no doubt some had overheard the altercation with Cavendish and his slimy friend. They would be gossip fodder for days.

He would have to watch his old enemy closely. Anthony had a feeling this was not over with yet. The man had a mean, vengeful streak. He knew this firsthand. He would not have that turned on the woman at his side.

"Lord Hamilton." Lord Medway approached with his wife.

"Miss Spencer," Lady Medway said. "It is a lovely day for a walk." The look in their eyes told Anthony they wanted the details of what had just happened with Cavendish. Normally, these two would never approach him, but clearly their thirst for gossip overrode their fear of him.

"It is lovely," Evangeline said.

"We just saw Lord Cavendish, and he did not appear happy. Do you perchance know why, Miss Spencer?" Lady Medway asked, shooting Anthony a nervous look.

"We don't know," he said in a hard voice, which had them bobbing their heads and scurrying away.

"Was that necessary?" Evangeline said.

"I loathe gossip, and the only reason those two approached

was for that. They usually avoid me, and I prefer it that way," Anthony said.

"Do you like people fearing you, then?" She looked up at him. "Because if you do, your reputation has succeeded in ensuring that."

He grunted.

"People will be shocked to hear that society's biggest rogue, Lord Hamilton, is engaged. Surely you can allow them that."

He'd not given enough thought to this. It had simply been a matter of getting her away from Cavendish and his aunts to stop hounding him. Anthony had believed they would both win from the arrangement. He wasn't so sure now. The man he'd always been was not someone who bent to society's standards. He had no wish to change that because of his fake engagement.

"Let them be shocked. I'm not changing who I am."

"As no one would expect you to. After all, you are a man with a title and long list of ancestors at your back." The words came out with a bite to them.

"I can't help who I am, Evangeline."

"Neither can I," she snapped back. "Or I would not now be fake engaged to you. I am tempted to flee back to the country and stay there until the season is over," she muttered.

"I didn't think you a coward, Evangeline," he mocked her, and was rewarded, as Anthony had known he would be, with her shoulders stiffening.

"If you said that to another man, he would take exception and challenge you, Lord Hamilton. Because I am a woman, I cannot."

He didn't give in to the smile. "Of course you are right. Forgive me."

"I would if I knew you meant it."

This woman, he thought. Cavendish would have loathed her resolve and wit. *He'd have broken her.*

"Evangeline, if Lord Cavendish comes anywhere near you again, or says something to upset you, you must come to me immediately."

"I can look after myself."

"Don't be naïve. He is a dangerous man. Trust me on this matter; you cannot be alone with him. I must have your word. That man is dangerous and not someone you will win against."

"I am not naïve, and I'll thank you for not speaking to me like that again."

No one who wasn't in his inner circle took him to task like that. It shocked him she had.

She looked up at him under the brim of her bonnet then. "What is between you and Lord Cavendish?"

"History, and nothing that concerns you." The words came out coated in ice, and thankfully she heeded the warning in them.

"Very well, I will keep my distance from Lord Cavendish."

A further three groups of people plucked up the courage to approach them. One held Lady Beasley and her daughter. Anthony remembered his aunts telling him she had hoped to be his future countess. He was suddenly quite happy to have Evie at his side and masquerading as his fiancée.

Evangeline handled the barbs thrown her way with ease, and Anthony barely spoke a word.

"That Miss Beasley would like to see me burned at the stake," Evie said when the women left.

"Some say I am a catch."

"Really?" She looked him up and down. "I thought everyone was terrified of you?"

"Oh, they are, but they're not terrified of my fortune, and most fathers can overcome that if they can get their hands on it by foisting their daughters on me."

"Charming."

"Who is your favorite poet, Evangeline?" Anthony thought he should find something to discuss with her in a public setting.

"I don't like poetry."

"To not love poetry is surely a crime when you walk in society. What will people think, Miss Spencer?"

"That I'm a philistine with a forthright nature and am too old to change."

He'd been in a rage not long ago and now he was barking out another laugh.

"And you." She looked up at him, the sun picking up the gold flecks in her eyes. "Who is your favorite poet?"

"I like many," he said.

"Favorite poem then?"

"Cyriack, this three years' day these eyes, though clear,

To outward view of blemish or of spot,

Bereft of light, their seeing have forgot;" Anthony said.

"Nor to their idle orbs doth sight appear.

Of sun, or moon, or star, throughout the year,

Or man, or woman. Yet I argue not," she added.

"I thought you said you didn't like poetry?" Anthony managed to get the words out of his dry mouth. She knew his favorite poem.

"I don't, but my sister loves it and is constantly quoting it."

"I believe John Milton is one of the greatest English poets of all time," Anthony said as he turned them back toward the carriage. He rarely talked about his love of poetry to anyone, and yet he was doing exactly that.

"I think you and my sister will get along well," she said. "She is constantly thrusting books in my direction and demanding I read them."

"And yet?"

"And yet I would rather continue reading the tales of Captain Broadbent and Lady Nauticus."

"You cannot be serious? That is utter drivel," Anthony said.

"It is not drivel. It is entertaining, and escapism, unlike the long winded, boring poetry you and my sister enjoy." Her eyes were sparkling now as she met his gaze.

Evangeline Spencer enjoyed a good argument. He tucked that away with the other things he already knew about her.

"You will get on exceedingly well with Toby," he said as they reached the carriage.

"Oh?" She raised a brow as he held out a hand to help her inside. "Is he an intelligent and articulate man then?"

"You are a mouthy woman, Evangeline Spencer."

"Thank you. I do believe that was a compliment."

"It wasn't."

"Well, I will take it as such."

She released his hand and settled inside the carriage. He helped her maid, then joined her.

HEATHCLIFF SPENCER COULD not have been happier when Anthony had asked to speak to him in private, upon their return to the Spencer house.

If he thought it was all a bit rushed and odd, the baron never said so. He had instantly given Anthony his permission to wed his eldest daughter. They then joined Evangeline and her sister in the small parlor to celebrate.

"It's all very quick," Prudence said, handing him a cup of tea and a hard stare. "I mean, Evie never told me you two had even had a meaningful conversation, and we are close and share everything. Today you go driving in the park and now you're engaged. You'll forgive me if I struggle with what has happened."

This Spencer was not quite as happy as her father, if the frown on her face was any indication.

"I have given my permission, Prudence," her father said. "And what a wedding it shall be."

The man reminded him of one of those long necked, bulbous vases his aunt Petunia favored. Large body, but very little substance from the neck up.

"We are happy," Evie said and even to his ears it sounded forced. Anthony shot her a look, and she smiled. A full wide one that did not reach her eyes. "It is wonderful," she added.

"I have never been this happy," Anthony lied.

"It is as if I woke in the dark and now the sun has risen," Evie said clearly to best him.

"Evangeline is what I have been waiting for my entire life," he said solemnly. To ensure he got in the last word, he rose as she opened her mouth to spout another lie. "And now I must be off but will see you this evening at the Rothersham ball."

Anthony bowed and headed for the door before she could stop him. However, he knew she would be on his heels.

"Prue is not convinced," she said the minute they had stepped outside the door.

Anthony turned to look at her and noted that Prue's face was pressed to the parlor window to their right.

"Perhaps this will do it." He leaned in and kissed her before she could protest. Soft, he thought, and sweet. Anthony pulled back and looked into her dazed eyes.

"Behave yourself, and I will see you tonight." He then walked to his carriage before she could speak, still clearly shocked over what he'd done.

He looked at her, raising a hand as the carriage rolled away, but she was still simply staring at him, stunned. Anthony knew exactly how she felt, because that simple kiss had left him reeling.

CHAPTER NINETEEN

H<small>E'D SENT WORD</small> to his friends that he would collect them for this evening's ball, as they deserved to hear the engagement news from him. Toby was first. He climbed in and took the seat across from Anthony.

"Lord, I'm fatigued. I fenced with Jamie today, and the youngest Scuttlethorpe, who is far too energetic, but I could not let him win. Where did you go? We expected you to arrive."

"I had business to attend to," Anthony said. His friend went on to explain details of his fencing matches, and he was happy to let him, as his mind was on other things.

When they pulled up at Jamie's house it did not take long for him to join them.

"Is there a particular reason you felt the need to have us both arrive at the Rothersham ball with you?" Jamie asked when the carriage started rolling again.

"I am engaged to be married to Miss Evangeline Spencer," Anthony said. "I spoke to her father today and he has accepted." He sat back and waited for the questions.

"What? Since when have you wanted to wed, and for that matter to her? Who, and correct me if I am wrong, you told me you found excessively irritating," Toby said. He was frowning now.

"And that she would be the last woman you would marry," Jamie added.

"We have talked lately and have common interests. This benefits us both." Anthony kept his expression blank.

"No," Toby said slowly. "There is more to this, and we want the reasons now, or no one is leaving this carriage."

"What he said," Jamie added, hard-faced. "All of it now, Anthony."

It had been a faint hope at best that they'd believe him. They were his brothers in every way but blood. He could not get much by them.

"Can you not just say, congratulations, Anthony, I am extremely happy for you both?"

"No," they both said together.

"I always believed you would be the last to wed among us, so you will allow us some surprise, that you, the man who conforms to no one and has taken a vow of licentious behavior, is now engaged," Toby said.

"You make me sound degenerate," Anthony snapped, even if the words his friends spoke were true.

"We know you are more than what you have led society to believe, Anthony," Jamie said. "But you don't trust easily after what happened to us, and it was my belief you would never allow a woman close enough to hurt you."

"My wife does not need to be someone I will share my every thought and life with. Plenty don't," Anthony protested. "Many barely see each other."

"All true, but I too believed you wouldn't wed until you were nearing your last legs and had to produce an heir," Toby added.

"In fact, you once told us you will wait until you are at least sixty but can still perform your marital duties to take a wife," Jamie said.

His friends had excellent memories. Now was one of those times he wished they didn't.

"It is done," Anthony said with a finality many would heed and not question further.

"Things can be undone," Jamie said, not one of those people.

"And while I like Miss Spencer and find her an intelligent conversationalist, I also know that neither of you like each other."

Anthony sighed. "I told her I wouldn't tell anyone, just as she promised she would not."

"But there is something smokey about this betrothal?" Toby added.

"Is she blackmailing you?" Jamie demanded.

That made Anthony bark out a laugh. "You think I would allow anyone to blackmail me?"

"No, but I can think of no other reason," Jamie said.

"I found Miss Spencer in an awkward situation—"

"What awkward situation?" Toby asked.

"Do you need all the details?"

"Every last one," Toby said.

"Not a word of this can leave this carriage." They both nodded solemnly.

"She was dressed as a man gambling in Hugh's. A Frenchman. I'd seen her...him before. Mr. Renee, she called herself."

"I don't know whether to be impressed or outraged," Jamie said looking dazed.

"Did she really?" Toby whistled. "Why?"

"Money, of course. She was hardly gambling in disguise for the fun of it," Anthony said.

"How did you know that Mr. Renee was Miss Spencer?" Jamie asked.

"I saw a birthmark on the back of her neck, and then there is the way she stands—"

"What way does she stand?" Jamie interrupted him.

"All her weight on her right leg, with the left foot sometimes resting on it."

"I didn't even know you were aware of Miss Spencer, and yet clearly you've been watching her," Toby said.

"No. As you already know, I saved her in the street one day when a horse would have knocked her to the ground. I turned back after I walked away to check all was well and she was standing like that," Anthony said.

"Still—"

"There is no still about it," Anthony said. "This is convenience for both of us. The Spencers have no money, and one of the daughters needs to marry. Cavendish has decided that Evangeline will be his future wife, and she has no wish to be so, but will find it hard to refuse if he persists."

"No woman should have to wed that man," Toby said, now angry.

"Exactly."

"Evangeline?" Jamie asked.

"If we are to carry this off, we must at least look like we are familiar with each other," Anthony said.

"I understand why she needs a fake fiancé, but not you," Toby said.

"Your aunts," Jamie said before Anthony could speak. "This will put them off hounding you to marry."

"Exactly.

"But why the rush? Surely just showing interest in Miss Spencer for now was enough?" Toby asked.

He explained about the walk in the park and Cavendish's outrage seeing them together.

"I loathe that man, and Calthorpe," Jamie said.

"Amen," both Toby and Anthony added.

"But what about when it ends? You will be all right, but not Miss Spencer," Toby said.

"We are hoping that with her engagement to me, then more gentlemen will approach her sister. If she contracts a good match, Evangeline will retire to the country with her father."

Why the thought of never seeing her again made his chest hurt, he wasn't sure, but Anthony knew one thing, he didn't like it.

"What if no match is contracted and you have taken Miss Spencer off the market when she could have married well?" Toby asked.

"It is done," Anthony said. "We cannot go back. When the season ends, she will leave London and declare she no longer wishes to marry me."

Toby made a scoffing sound. "Do you seriously believe anyone will think that the truth?"

"You are an earl, Anthony, for all you are one who cares little for convention," Jamie said. "She is a nobody and is not popular. She's too old, and her looks—"

"She is intelligent and beautiful," Anthony snapped. He realized his mistake when both men looked at him in silence. "What?"

"You are defending her."

"We have talked, she is not as irritating as I once believed."

Toby smiled.

"Why are you looking like that?" Anthony demanded.

"No reason at all, and Miss Spencer is a very nice woman. She will be good for you."

"It is not a real engagement." Anthony felt he needed to reiterate that point.

"Have you told your aunts? They will be ecstatic."

"They are visiting friends for a few nights. I will speak with them upon their return tomorrow, if the news has not already reached them."

Toby clapped his hands together. "Well then, I foresee far more excitement in the remainder of the season than we've had in years."

"We, of course, will help you in any way we can," Jamie said. "I've always enjoyed anything that sits society back on their heels, and I think tonight will be exactly that."

"It is not real," Anthony said again.

"So you've said," Toby added. "She'd be good for you, though. Miss Spencer would not let you continue on with your licentious ways."

"No, please, tell me exactly what you think of me," Anthony drawled.

"She's intelligent enough to keep you on your toes, too," Toby said.

"I think she could outwit him in all honesty," Jamie said.

"If you are both quite finished," Anthony snapped.

"For the first time in a long while I find I am excited," Toby said.

"As you can imagine, I am happy to have given you a reason."

"I can't believe she dressed as a man to gamble," Jamie said.

"She was quite good at it too," Anthony had to concede.

The carriage slowed then, and minutes later drew to a halt. All conversation ceased and soon they had joined the other guests lined up to enter.

"I believe congratulations are in order, Hamilton?" These words came from Mr. Reginald, who stood with his wife and two daughters in front of them.

"Thank you," Anthony said.

"Prepare yourself, my friend. Those that have always been terrified of you will now see you as someone they can talk to," Toby said.

"Why?"

"Because they will want an invitation to the wedding of the year," Jamie whispered, laughter in his voice.

"Miss Spencer though?" Mrs. Reginald added. "Imagine our surprise." Mrs. Reginald's pursed lips and narrowed eyes told Anthony she was not happy about his choice of future wife.

"I am a very happy man," Anthony said forcing his mouth into a smile.

"And so it begins," Jamie said grinning.

"For the entertainment value alone, I thank you," Toby said.

"Earl, allow me to congratulate you."

And so, it went. Every person in the waiting line seemed to want to speak to Anthony.

"Surely not all these people want to come to the wedding, if there were to be one?" Anthony said. "I'm the man no one speaks to for fear I will debauch their daughters." He felt extremely uncomfortable with this sudden popularity.

"It will stop soon. You're just not used to people actually wanting to speak to you," Jamie said.

"We will, of course, tell everyone how happy we are about your engagement to Miss Spencer," Toby said as they reached the ballroom. "And we are never far away, should all this sudden popularity overcome you."

"Dance with both Spencer sisters," Anthony snapped. "Also, watch Cavendish. If he approaches them, I want to know."

"Consider it done," Jamie said.

They were announced as they entered the ballroom, and suddenly all eyes were on him. Anthony kept his face expressionless. He cared little what anyone thought of him.

"Right, three o'clock." Toby said when they moved into the crowds.

Anthony looked to his right and found her. People surrounded Evangeline. Her sister was also there, but not Heathcliff Spencer. Evangeline's expression was polite, lips curved in a small smile.

"I wonder if her well-wishers were as polite as yours were," Jamie said.

"My guess is not. She looks ready to commit murder."

"How can you tell?" Toby asked.

He didn't answer, just made his way toward her.

She was beautiful in a pale blue dress. The neckline exposed the swell of her breasts, and beneath was a bow of emerald satin. Her hair was styled with ringlets around her face, and an emerald ribbon circled her head.

Nudging his way into the circle, he overheard Miss Lambeth say, "But the shock, Miss Spencer, that you could become engaged to such a man, when to my knowledge you barely know each other!"

"Good evening." Anthony moved to her side. He then took Evangeline's hand and tucked it into the crook of his elbow. "You were saying, Miss Lambeth?"

"Oh… ah, well, I was offering my heartfelt congratulations, my lord."

He stood as the discussion dwindled, and suddenly everyone had somewhere else to be and left.

"Well," Prudence Spencer said. "Your arrival was timely, my lord. You scared them all away."

"Prue!" Evangeline was clearly scandalized by her sister's words.

"I've had years of practice," Anthony said as he heard the first strains of a waltz. "Will you honor me with this dance, Miss Spencer?"

She nodded but didn't speak, and Anthony thought that was because she wanted to breathe fire. He placed her hand on his arm.

"Good evening, my sweet," Anthony said when he had her in his arms.

Her eyes shot up to his from his necktie. "Why did you call me that?"

"We are in public." He bent to whisper in her ear.

"I don't think couples call each other that, and I don't think I want to do this anymore," she whispered back in a furious tone.

"Too late," Anthony said.

"People are rude."

"It's taken you this long to work that out?" he said looking around them. Prudence Spencer was dancing with Mr. Landon, and Toby the widow Lady Blake, who Anthony knew he'd spent several nights sharing a bed with recently.

"No, I knew that before, but no one usually bothers with me. Now, apparently, I am worthy of their attention and probing questions about why someone like you would want to marry someone like me."

"I too have noticed people want to speak with me, when normally they run the other way," he said. "I'd hate to think I was becoming respectable," he drawled.

"I doubt even I could make you respectable, my lord."

He snorted, then looked down into her face, and there it was again, that fiery feeling in his chest. Why did this woman chase away the cold? But Anthony knew it wouldn't last; nothing ever did.

CHAPTER TWENTY

E VIE HAD ARRIVED at the ball and instantly been bombarded with questions and snide comments under the guise of congratulating her on her engagement. Women who had never spoken or acknowledged her suddenly appeared to be her best friend…if her best friend wanted to subtly attack her, that was.

One thing was now abundantly clear, however. People thought the Earl of Hamilton could have done better.

"It's all very well for you to find the situation funny, yet I cannot. So far, someone has hinted that I may carry your child. Or I have compromised you."

"Someone actually said those things to you?" He raised a brow.

"They did not say the words outright, but I understood the meaning. Society may look polished and cultured. It may titter and take tea from dainty cups while eating sandwiches no bigger than my finger—"

"I believe they are called finger sandwiches."

Evie looked at him and while his face held no expression, which she'd seen many times, those eyes were another matter entirely. He was laughing at her.

"And what did you reply to the person who alluded to you carrying my child, Evangeline?"

"Isn't it considered vulgar to speak to a woman of such things?"

"Possibly, but I doubt your sensibilities are hurt as you are not the average society miss."

She huffed out a breath. "They weren't."

"And I will remind you at this juncture that it was not I who told Lord Cavendish about our engagement. That was you, Evangeline."

"I know," she snapped, "and if I could go back and change that I would."

"You can't, so make the best of it," Anthony said. "Remember Cavendish."

She shuddered.

"Has he approached you?"

"No. I think he will keep his distance now," Evie said looking around her for the man. She could not see him, thankfully.

She watched Prue dance by with Mr. Landon. "May I ask you something, my lord?"

He nodded.

"Do you know Mr. Landon?"

His eyes went to Prue, who was laughing at something her dance partner said.

"Not well, but enough that I can say I have heard nothing that would put your sister off marrying him, were it to come to that."

"It's vexing being a woman," Evie said. "I cannot ask questions as a man can, but it is just as important to me that Prue be happy as it is she marry someone with money."

"The Landons are comfortable," he said. "Now, the music is about to end, and I will caution you to hold your counsel and think of the end result before telling someone exactly what you think of them for their impertinent questions, Evangeline."

"I am not a fool, my lord. I know what is at stake."

"And yet, I'm quite sure you can be pushed into losing what little control you have." The side of his mouth tilted up, which Evie knew constituted a smile.

"I'll have you know that my control is excellent," she added.

He'd kissed her outside her house the day he'd spoken to her father. Just a simple brush of his lips over hers, and she'd not been able to stop thinking of that moment since. She wanted him to kiss her again, which was the perfect reason to keep her distance from her infamous fiancé.

"I assure you, Lord Hamilton, I am quite capable of playing the pretty when required. I was just shocked at the onslaught of questions and comments when I arrived. I have recovered now."

"Dance with my friends; they know about us."

"You told them, when I was not allowed to tell Prue?" Outraged, she glared at him.

"So you haven't told her?"

Evie refused to look away, even as she wanted to.

"You told her didn't you, Evangeline?"

Her name seemed to roll off his lips in a way it had on no one else's lips before.

"She followed me about the house, constantly firing questions at me until I broke down and told her. People think she is the amiable Spencer, which let me assure you is not true. She's as tenacious as a fox on a hunt when required."

"She is just able to hide it better than you. I have a sister with a temperament like yours."

"She must be wonderful then."

"She is."

"Is she not in society?" Evie had a feeling he did not like to talk about the people closest to him.

"No, she lives in the country with her husband."

His words were cooler now, and were she anyone else, she would heed the warning that this was not a subject he wanted to pursue.

"Are you close?"

"I have no wish to discuss anything personal with you. This is a business arrangement. Please respect that."

The man who had teased her just moments before was gone again. The ruthless earl was back.

"Of course. Thank you for the dance," Evie said as the music finished. He led her back to where Prue now stood and then left with a curt bow. Before she could speak to her sister, Lord Pyne had whisked her away to dance.

"Hello, has your fiancé wandered off already?"

Evie smiled at Lord Corbyn, whom she knew was Anthony's friend.

"So it would seem, my lord."

"Would you like to dance or walk about the room pretending to be interested in the exquisite decor and well-dressed guests?"

"I would like to walk, thank you."

He held out his arm, and she placed her fingers on it.

"I believe there is a gallery through that door. We could view the somber ancestors if you like?" Evie nodded.

The room had plenty of people wandering about but was not as crowded as the ballroom. True to Lord Corbyn's word, there were indeed many somber-looking ancestors staring down at them.

"Why do you believe no one is allowed to smile in a portrait?" Evie asked.

"I believe a smile is harder to hold for long periods," he said.

"Which makes sense had I given it more thought."

He laughed. "Sometimes we need others to point out what we don't know."

"I'm afraid one of my weaknesses is my need to know everything," Evie said.

"If that is the case, then I can only imagine the arguments you have already had with Anthony."

This time Evie laughed. "I know that you know, my lord."

"I thought you might."

"The original idea was Lord Hamilton's, and I foolishly expedited matters in the park," she said.

"I know the details and lay no blame at either of your doors. Circumstances forced you into the betrothal. Plus, my friend does nothing he hasn't thoroughly thought through first. So, his betrothal to you was something he wanted."

Evie felt a small jolt of pleasure at that and squashed it. Lord Hamilton felt nothing for her, as she did for him. This was merely a business arrangement.

"I doubt either of us wanted it."

He did not reply to that for a long while.

"Anthony is my oldest and closest friend besides Lord Stafford. He is also one of the best men I know. Don't believe what you see or hear about him in society, Miss Spencer. Not all of it is true."

Why had he just told her that?

"His aunts seem lovely," Evie said, unsure what else to say.

"They are wonderful ladies, and we have a lot to thank them for," Lord Corbyn said.

"Were you all childhood friends, my lord?"

"We have been friends from a young age, yes. We became so at school."

"I would like to have had an education, other than what I learned from my mother and books," she said.

"I'm sure your education was a great deal more fun than ours, Miss Spencer." His eyes were on the painting above them, but she knew he wasn't seeing the austere-looking gentleman.

"Lord Corbyn." She patted his hand, needing to ease the sudden tension in him. "I'm sorry if your school life was not what it should have been."

He looked down at her and she saw a flash of pain, and then it was gone.

"It was hell," he said quietly. "But that is in the past, and now I am to dance with the lovely Lady Barlow. Come, I will take you back to your sister."

"I will stay, my lord, and wander. I rather enjoy studying all the austere-looking ancestors."

"Thank you for walking with me, Miss Spencer. I enjoyed our talk."

"As did I, Lord Corbyn."

She watched him walk away from her, thinking the entire conversation unusual. Why had he said that Anthony was one of the best men he knew? It was not like she had a future with the man.

Evie wandered, nodded to people, but did not stop. If she kept moving, no one would question her about her sudden engagement and the reasons behind it.

"Do take a look at the stars, Miss Spencer, they are really something this evening."

"Thank you, I will, Lady Beasley," Evie said, surprised the woman was talking to her, considering she wanted her daughter to be the next Countess of Hamilton.

"And do accept my congratulations on your engagement," Lady Beasley added with a smile.

"Thank you." Stunned at the woman's change of heart, Evie felt the least she could do was look at the stars. Stepping through the open doors, she walked to the edge of the balcony. The air was cool and held the scents of London.

"Oh, Miss Spencer. Do help me!"

Looking around for who was calling her Evie glanced over the railing, and found Miss Beasley below, wringing her hands.

"What is wrong, Miss Beasley?" Evie started down the stairs to her right.

"A man, he has fallen, and I fear broken his leg. You must help."

"I will get help," Evie said reaching her.

"Oh please, just come, he is groaning in agony. It is that way. I can't stand the sight of blood, and his head is bleeding. I shall get help."

"Very well." Evie picked up her skirts and ran down the path. Torches lit the way, but it grew darker the farther she ventured. Looking around her, she saw no sign of an injured man.

Stopping when she reached a small opening with seats, she heard someone moaning to her right. Stepping from the path she hurried in that direction. The man was bent at the waist, with his back to her.

"Are you all right, sir?"

He straightened, and then turned. Evie began to back away as Lord Cavendish smiled at her.

"I don't think so, Miss Spencer." He grabbed her arm.

CHAPTER TWENTY-ONE

ANTHONY WAS TALKING with Toby and Jamie when someone tapped him on the shoulder. Turning he found Prudence Spencer with a worried look on her face.

"Lord Hamilton." She curtseyed. "Have you seen my sister?"

His eyes immediately looked for Evangeline, like they had since he'd left her.

"No. How long has it been since you saw her?"

"Not long, but I fear something is not right, and I have looked everywhere, and it is not like her to leave me." She looked close to tears now. "I fear something has happened to her.

"Your father—"

"Has not seen her."

"I took her walking in the gallery a while ago," Toby said. "She wanted to stay there and study the paintings."

"I have just come from there," Prudence said.

"Can either of you see Cavendish?" He said the words softly, so only Toby and Jamie could hear.

His friends rose to their toes, and then both shook their heads.

Where are you, Evangeline?

"Lord Hamilton, if I may have a word."

"Lady Raine," he said, bowing to her. "If you will excuse me, I am looking for my fiancée."

The woman was one of society's beauties. Married to the

powerful Earl of Raine, she was not someone he knew well, or usually talked to.

"That is what I wish to speak to you about," she said softly. "I overheard Miss Beasley telling a group of people that she heard Miss Spencer say to her sister she was going out to meet with another man in the gardens."

"I beg your pardon?"

"Exactly. Make haste, Hamilton. That girl is perfect for you. It's about time you changed your ways."

"Ah—"

"Move." She shooed him away.

Anthony left, moving through the guests with his friends and Prudence on his heels. Stepping outside, he didn't see Evangeline on the balcony, so he made his way down the stairs.

"Go right," he directed his friends. "Prudence, return to the ballroom."

"I cannot—"

"Your sister has no wish for you to ruin your reputation. Allow me to find her on your behalf." She wanted to protest, but knew his words were true. She nodded and retreated to the stairs.

Anthony ran down the shell path to the left, searching everywhere as he did so.

Where are you, Evangeline?

Anthony may not have known her long, but he knew she would never have simply walked out of that ballroom without telling her sister where she was going.

"I say, is that Miss Spencer?"

Anthony stepped off the path into the trees at the words. It was there he found Evangeline in Cavendish's arms. She was struggling to pull free. He took all this in, in seconds. Just as he took in Calthorpe and his sister. Both looking smug, watching everything unfold.

"Unhand her now, Cavendish, and I may just let you live," Anthony said moving closer.

"Well now, I'm sorry to say that your fiancée is free with her favors, Hamilton. I should imagine you'll be happy to discover this before your marriage to Miss Spencer."

Before he could plant his fist in the man's face, Evangeline had wrenched free and swung hers. It connected with Cavendish's jaw, snapping his head sideways. She then raised her knee into his groin. He bent groaning.

Anthony would have laughed if he had it in him. Instead, he said, "Come to me, Evangeline."

She spun, eyes wide, face leeched of color to look at him.

"I didn't... he's ly-lying," she stammered.

Anthony could have killed Cavendish with his bare hands in that moment, for the utter devastation he saw on her face.

He'd had many such urges since Blackwood Hall, but he'd thought making Cavendish suffer slowly was a far better punishment for the hell he'd subjected Anthony, Toby, and Jamie to. But not now, looking at Evangeline's pale face he contemplated cold blooded murder.

"Come here now," he said holding out his hand. When she moved it was to stumble toward him. He pulled her into his arms and held her tight. Her entire body was shaking, and his rage climbed. He needed an outlet, and his eyes were on Cavendish, who was now on his knees.

"Anthony, what has happened?" Toby and Jamie arrived.

"Miss Spencer just assaulted Lord Cavendish, and that was after she threw herself at him in a wanton manner!" Calthorpe said.

"Look after her." Anthony pushed Evangeline gently toward his friends. He then advanced on Calthorpe and his sister.

"I say, Lord Hamilton—"

They were the last words he spoke. Anthony punched him hard in the jaw, sending Calthorpe stumbling backward. His sister shrieked. Anthony pulled Calthorpe back to his feet, blood now streaming from his nose. He then dragged him to where Cavendish now stood, bent at the waist clutching his groin.

"Before today, I simply hated you for what you did to us."

"Others are coming," Toby said softly.

"I will not bruise and bloody you both as I wish to, but I will seek retribution for what you have done to my fiancée in other ways you will not see coming," Anthony said.

"Your fiancée is—"

Anthony stopped his words with a fist, and the satisfying sound of a crack had Cavendish's head snapping back again. Calthorpe's sister shrieked once more.

"Heed me," Anthony said, making both men look at him. "If the foul deed you did this night reaches anyone's ears. If anyone hears a lie about my fiancée making advances to you, or if anyone speaks slanderously about her, then I will find you, no matter where you hide."

"Y-you can't threaten us," Calthorpe said, now blotting his nose with his handkerchief. "I will tell everyone that you hit me without provocation."

Anthony's smile held no humor. "I have a reputation for a reason, Calthorpe. It would pay you to remember that, and the fact I care little what people think of me."

Calthorpe looked scared, Cavendish furious.

"I suggest you watch your backs, gentlemen, because I will be aware of your every move from this moment on."

He turned and looked at Calthorpe's sister. "I will ruin you, if one word of this reaches anyone. Do you understand?" Her nod had him dismissing her.

"You two go first, and we will follow," he said to Jamie and Toby when he reached them and Evangeline. "It is best we return, as if we have just taken a stroll in the gardens for some privacy," Anthony said.

His friends agreed with a nod and left without another word.

"Take my arm, Evangeline."

She did. Her fingers shook as they gripped the sleeve of his jacket.

"We shall walk now, slowly, and you will collect yourself, because we must return to the ballroom. Do you understand?"

"Do you believe me?" The words were a whispered plea. The woman who had brought Cavendish to his knees was broken in that moment.

"I do, Evie. I know that none of what just happened was of your making."

She exhaled slowly. "Th-thank you."

He fought the need to hold her until she stopped shaking, but he couldn't, because the rage inside him would scare her.

"No thanks are needed. I'm only sorry you were subjected to whatever Cavendish did to you." He almost didn't want to know, because he feared he would release her and storm back to that scum.

"It was Lady Beasley who lured me to look at the stars. I-I thought she was being nice, and then her daughter was out here and told me someone was in danger. She begged me to help. I ran, and he was there—"

"It's all right," Anthony said lowering his hand over hers as the panic rose in her voice. "No one will harm you again."

The sob was small, but he heard it. He released her arm and slid his hand around her back, pulling her close. Her fingers gripped his lapel as Evie pressed her face into his chest.

"It will be all right," he said to the top of her head, as much for himself as her. He needed this contact to calm the rage inside him. And she needed it to reassure her she was safe now.

Anthony knew he had to release her before anyone saw them, but it was one of the hardest things he'd ever done. He never sought physical contact with anyone, but he wanted it with her, which was why he let her go.

"He didn't hurt me; it was just the shock. No man has... has behaved like that around me before. Lord Cavendish grabbed me. He then told me I was his woman, not yours."

"I'm sorry you suffered because of me," Anthony said attempting to tamp down the need to finish what he started back there in the trees. He put her hand once again on his arm, and they walked to the house.

"I don't know what lies between you, but I think it was not just you he wished to punish, Anthony. I think he wanted to hurt me for daring to refuse what he'd offered."

He worked through what he should say to her about his past dealings with Cavendish, because she deserved something after what she'd suffered.

"Cavendish, Calthorpe, and another were the older boys in Blackwood Hall where we lodged during our school years."

"Was he as horrible as he is today?"

He looked down at her, studying the delicate side profile. The ridge of her cheekbone, and a long curl over a small ear. Anthony had never thought of her as small because her personality was so large, but he realized she was.

"Yes, and even more so. He was a thug and a bully," Anthony said. It was odd, but in that moment, he could not find the anger he usually felt when he remembered those days. His rage was solely on Evie's behalf.

"I'm sorry if you suffered because of those men, Anthony."

"Thank you." It was humbling that she could think of him in that moment.

"Evie, when we return, there may be murmurs. I'm sure that if Miss Beasley was part of that entire business, she will have been spreading untruths about the place," Anthony said, remembering what Lady Raine had told him.

"Prue—"

"Was the one who said she could not find you, "Anthony said.

"Then I must get back to my sister."

"You're sure?"

She nodded.

"We went for a walk in the gardens, Evie. Remember to say that and only that if you are asked anything about where you have been."

"Of course, and thank you again."

She'd become Evie to him and he Anthony to her in the last

few minutes, and he could think of her no other way now.

He led her to the stairs, nodding to the few guests who looked their way as they climbed. She took a deep breath before they entered the ballroom. Soon they were moving through the guests until they found Prudence Spencer.

"Evie."

"I am well, Prue. Lord Hamilton and I went for a walk in the gardens. I am sorry I did not tell you, but you were dancing."

Prudence's eyes shot from her sister to Anthony's.

"And now, I am to dance with my lovely fiancée again," Anthony said.

"And I will dance with her equally lovely sister," Jamie said, appearing.

They moved to the floor, and he placed Evie in a line across from him. Two dancers to her left was Miss Beasley, who was frowning as she noted who Anthony's partner was. He gave her a hard look that had color filling her cheeks. She quickly turned away.

As the music began, he met Evie in the middle, and she managed a smile.

"Good girl," Anthony said as he retreated.

Through the dance she smiled, as did he, and he watched Miss Beasley's frown darken. Toby stood to the side of the dance floor, watching them. When their eyes met, he shook his head, which told Anthony that Cavendish and Calthorpe had not returned.

But he had a feeling this wasn't over, even after he'd threatened both men. Cavendish was vindictive and held grudges. It worried him he'd come after Evie and her family.

When the music finished, Anthony knew he should dance with others, as should Evie if they were to mislead the gossips. He led her back to where Toby stood.

"Come, Miss Spencer, I believe this is our dance," his friend said.

He danced with others, as did she, and by the end of the

evening, they had squashed any rumors, which was helped by the fact Cavendish and Calthorpe had not reappeared.

"Splendid night," Heathcliff Spencer said, totally unaware of what his eldest daughter had suffered earlier. One look at Evie's face told Anthony not to mention it.

"I will call on you tomorrow," he said helping her into the carriage. She didn't answer, simply nodded, and he closed the door.

He stood watching it roll away and wondered what the hell he was to do now.

"I think I need a drink," Toby said, joining him. "And then we need to discuss how to keep your fiancée and her family safe."

"Because while you may have terrified Calthorpe into silence, we both know Cavendish is a tougher nut to crack," Jamie added. "Your fiancée is in danger, Anthony. You have to know that."

He did, and suddenly the engagement he'd thought was an excellent scheme for both him and Evie wasn't, and he was now faced with the fact she was in danger, and it was up to him to keep her safe.

CHAPTER TWENTY-TWO

E VIE HAD SLEPT fitfully and risen with smudges under her eyes and in a vile humor, which boded well for no one in the Spencer household.

"If you snap at me one more time, Evangeline, I will not be responsible for my actions," Prue hissed at her from across the small table where they ate their morning meal.

Their father was humming at the end while drinking his tea and reading the paper, as usual oblivious to undercurrents... or anything, if she were honest.

Oh, to be that way, Evie thought with a healthy dose of annoyance. *It must be lovely to be oblivious to everything going on around you.*

"Would you not be a little out of sorts, were you in my position, Prudence?"

"Yes, but I am not the enemy. I am your sister, for better or worse," she muttered.

Evie poked out her tongue.

"Get your bonnet; we shall take a walk. This house is too small for your vile humors. We shall exercise them from you."

"I am not a horse, Prue."

"More of a nag I would say."

Evie lobbed her toast crust at her sister. Prue caught it with ease and smirked, then popped it into her mouth and made a humming sound. "Father, we are going walking," she then said rising.

"Lovely day for it," he said not even glancing out the window. "Have fun."

The Spencer sisters donned their bonnets, and both took a light shawl, as the weather was not exactly cold, but there was a hint of a breeze, and headed outside.

Arm in arm, they began to wander.

"Are you all right, Evie? We both fell asleep so fast, I did not have a chance to thoroughly discuss exactly what happened with Lord Cavendish?"

"I am well. The man is a nasty individual who tried to scare me, but didn't succeed," she lied. In fact, he had succeeded. She'd been terrified, and then Anthony had arrived, and she'd known relief so fierce it had nearly dropped her to her knees right alongside the moaning Lord Cavendish.

"Do you remember when we had that maid, Daphne?" Evie asked Prue.

"Tall, and had a tale for every situation?"

"That's the one. She taught us that move with our knees if we wanted to ward off a man's unwanted attentions," Evie said.

"You didn't?" Prue slapped her hand to her mouth.

"I did on Lord Cavendish, and it works," Evie said feeling a great deal better than she had moments ago. Going for a walk was an excellent idea.

"I'm glad you are not to wed him."

"Me being fake engaged to Lord Hamilton does not solve a great deal, and yet I did not want to wed Cavendish, so at least in that I am relieved."

"And last night I was suddenly a great deal more popular than I was the night before," Prue said. "And Mr. Landon is to call on me later today. We are going driving and stopping to see the exhibition in the park. Several aspiring artists will have set up their easels and will have works on display. Christian is quite taken with art, Evie."

"Christian, is it?"

"That is his name."

"Very well, I shall come with you," Evie added.

"I thought to take—"

"I shall come," she said firmly. "I want to get to know him, if as I suspect you like him very much?"

"I do," Prue said, and Evie could hear the excitement in her voice. "Very much."

"Well then. I'm coming with you."

"You won't question him thoroughly over everything will you?"

"Of course not."

"You've got your fingers crossed, haven't you?" Prue said.

"No, and I promise I will sit in the carriage's corner gazing out the window, saying nothing."

Prue snorted her disbelief.

They walked, and Evie's thoughts went to Anthony. She and society believed him a reckless man with dangerous habits, but she now knew there was so much more to him. He could tease and laugh but also be gentle. Then there was the man who had found her last night and saved her. He'd looked savage, and then he'd chased her fears away when his big arms had closed around her.

She also knew that Lord Cavendish and others had attended the same school as Anthony and his friends, and after what happened there they loathed each other.

"Will you talk to me about what took place in that garden, Evie?" Prue asked suddenly.

"No, it is done with. I wasn't harmed, and the less said about it, the better."

"You cannot shut everything you have no wish to discuss away in that large brain of yours, Evie. Sometimes it helps to speak on matters that upset you, or they fester like that sore I once had on my knee."

"Charming."

Prue turned and started walking backward so they faced each other.

"You think things will hurt or upset me, so you don't discuss them."

"You will trip if you keep that up," Evie said.

"Then I shall trip, and it is not up to you to save me."

"Prue—"

"I mean it. I am not the only Spencer daughter. There is another."

"I know, me," Evie said in a tone that should warn her sister to shut up. It didn't work.

"Exactly, and since mother's passing you have taken on the responsibility for Father and me, but you don't need to. I can look after myself and help with him."

"Of course I need to," Evie scoffed, feeling just a little offended that her actions were being hurled back in her face with a lack of appreciation that stung.

"Do you think I am incapable, then? That my only strength is to smile sweetly and catch a husband?" Prue asked.

They had both stopped now and were glaring at each other in the street where anyone could see them. Neither Spencer sister cared.

"Someone had to take charge and ensure there was enough money to feed and house us," Evie snapped. "I was the oldest, and on the shelf as far as society is concerned, therefore—"

"Says you," Prue said in that annoying tone only a younger sibling could have, that got right under an older sibling's skin with far more ease than it should have.

"Don't be childish," Evie snapped. "I was the one to do it. I am good with figures—"

"I am equally as good," Prue snapped back. "But you assumed the mantle of—"

"Prue," Evie gritted out. "I did not sleep well, and it has been a trying few days. If you wish to have an argument that lasts longer than five minutes, can we postpone it until tomorrow? If not, then prepare for me to lose my temper."

"Even when we argue, you are taking control."

"Do you think I wanted this?" The words exploded out of Evie. "Wanted Mother to die, and Father to be hopeless with money and send us destitute?" She turned and walked away from Prue, then back again. "And another thing—"

"Oh goodie, there is another thing," her sister said, brows drawn together in an angry line like a set of drapes keeping out the cold on a winter's night.

"I want a better life for you!"

"I want a better life for you!" Prue yelled right back in her face. "Don't be a bloody saint and sacrifice your hopes and dreams for me, Evie!"

Evie actually staggered back a step at those words and pressed a hand to her chest as if she could stop the pain.

"I want you and Father to be happy, warm, and safe. If that is being a saint, then I am guilty." Her voice was cold. "Now it is time to return, as Mr. Landon will arrive shortly."

"Don't take that pious tone with me, Evangeline Elizabeth," Prue seethed. "It is always your way to end an argument on your terms. Well, not in this case. I am correct, and I will have my say."

Evie turned and walked away.

"I think you and Lord Hamilton could have a proper marriage," Prue said, shocking Evie again, as she'd not expected those words to come out of her sister's mouth. "He has a fierce reputation that, in truth, terrifies me, but I have seen the way he looks at you."

Prue hurried past Evie, and turned again to walk backward, which was now extremely vexing and no longer worrying. In fact, she hoped she tripped. Then this discussion? Argument? Was over.

"You cannot be serious," Evie said, stomping on the seed of hope those words planted inside her. "We have a deal. I am helping him avoid his aunts' pressure to wed, and he is helping me avoid marriage to Lord Cavendish and make you popular so you can marry well. We have a bargain, which will end with the season."

"Things change, and I saw how gentle he was with you last night—"

"Must you romanticize everything?" Evie snapped.

"I am not romanticizing; I am being truthful, and if you were not so mule-headed and opened your eyes, perhaps you could see what I do."

Evie scoffed. "You have known him only a handful of days, and barely held a conversation and suddenly you know he is a good man with a bad reputation, who would be good for me?"

"Yes."

"No!" Evie shrieked. "Lord Hamilton and I have nothing in common, nor do we wish to. He will wed someone with blood as blue as his when the time is right and carry on with his licentious lifestyle. Now this discussion is over."

"No, it is far from over," Prue said. She then turned and the Spencer sisters stormed back to the house in a silence so loud she was sure they heard it an hour's drive by carriage away.

They rarely fought, and if they did, it was over quickly. This felt different. A deeper conflict that could have consequences, and yet Evie was hurting too much to bridge the gap. She'd done everything she could to give Prue this season, and her sister was behaving like she was a pious saint for putting her family's welfare before herself.

Was she?

CHAPTER TWENTY-THREE

ANTHONY HADN'T SLEPT more than a few hours after returning home last night. He'd thought about gambling or calling on his mistress. Neither had created so much as a flicker of interest in him. So, he'd gone to the room downstairs where he'd hung a punching bag and beat it until he could think no more.

Cavendish wanted to ruin Evangeline Spencer because of him. She may believe she played some part in that, but he knew differently.

He should never had entered this foolish arrangement between them, because now she would need to be protected... by him.

Sipping his coffee, he wondered at this feeling inside him. The fierce need he'd felt last night to maim Cavendish and Calthorpe for hurting her. Anthony had worked hard not to show anger or pain. He fought his demons by doing the things that made him feel, and they'd grown more daring and aggressive. But now he wasn't sure anything would draw his attention away from her.

Where before he'd actively sought anything that would rid him of the cold and make him feel, even for a few minutes, now he wanted to feel nothing when she was near.

Anthony knew something was changing inside him, and he didn't like it, because he couldn't control it. He reminded himself again to keep his distance from Evangeline Spencer.

His aunts arrived in a flurry of excitement as Anthony was

eating his breakfast. They burst into his parlor all talking at once.

"Anthony!" Aunt Petunia ran to him with her short black dog, Monty, on her heels. It yapped and turned circles as he regained his feet, bracing for the inevitable. "You're engaged to Miss Spencer! We could not be happier."

"So happy," his other two aunts parroted.

"Monty, enough!" he bellowed as the dog kept barking excitedly.

"He is just happy, aren't you, darling?" Aunt Aggie said. "We traveled straight here once we heard the news."

"How is it you got the news of my engagement miles from London?" Anthony said as he waved them into seats, resigned his morning meal would be shared with his aunts. Monty then leapt at him. He caught the dog and returned to his chair.

"A note arrived from Bessie. You remember her dear, Lady Riddle. Well, her daughter told her, and she sent word immediately, which is what you should have done."

"I wanted to tell you in person and had planned to do so today."

All three of them harrumphed.

"Tea, Dibley, and lashings of it, as we have much to discuss," Aunt Petunia said. "Before we go to the exhibition."

"Much to discuss," Aunt Lavinia added. "Also, Dibley, if Cook has baked some of those lemon biscuits, we would not be displeased."

Stroking Monty's soft ear, he watched his aunts order his butler around. It was like being buffeted by a gentle breeze when they arrived. But Anthony would allow these three women to do whatever they wanted within the safety of his home.

He remembered the day they'd saved him as if it was yesterday. Two years after he arrived at Blackwood Hall, his aunts had called to see him. Anthony had been told to dress well and say nothing by the Housemaster. He'd done the first, but not the second.

They'd taken him for a drive while forcing the food they'd

brought with them into his hand. He'd broken down. Lost control and wept. They'd demanded to know why, and Anthony had shown them exactly what he was regularly subjected to. He'd exposed the welts, bruises, and marks on his body.

It was rare he saw anger on his aunts' faces, but he saw it that day. The carriage had turned around and returned to Blackwood Hall. Aunts Petunia and Lavinia had then left him with Aunt Aggie and stormed the walls of Blackwood Hall. They had never told him exactly what was said, but from that day onward, the lives of Anthony, Toby, and Jamie had changed for the better. It had not all been easy, but they no longer woke each day terrified for what they'd have to endure.

If they'd done nothing else for him, they'd have his eternal gratitude for that alone, but they'd been a constant source of love and affection in both his and Harriet's lives.

"Now, when is the wedding to be?" Aunt Aggie asked.

"We have not discussed that as yet," Anthony said, feeding the dog some ham.

"Not at the table please, Anthony," Aunt Petunia said as she did every time he fed Monty.

He would need to tread carefully with these three. They could sniff out a lie at ten paces.

"We want to meet her," Aunt Aggie said.

"I thought you already had, which is why she was on the list?" Anthony said.

"Yes, but just in a social situation," Aunt Petunia replied.

"You put a name on the list, and you did not even know the character of the woman? Shame on you," he said, teasing her. "All of you," he said.

"Oh, pooh to that. Now hurry it along. We are going to the exhibition and for a jaunt around the park, as we have the open carriage, and you are coming with us. I want all the details of your betrothal."

"Am I?"

"Yes, I want to hear everything," Aunt Aggie said.

"And if I say no, you will all harangue me until I agree?" Anthony asked.

"Exactly. Finally, you are learning," Aunt Aggie said smiling. "But the art will be lovely to see."

"You do know most people fear me, don't you?" he drawled.

"Yes, but not us."

They left forty minutes later, Anthony next to Aunt Lavinia and the other two seated across from him with Monty.

"You will be married in St. George's, of course," Aunt Aggie said.

"Of course," Anthony agreed, because there would be no wedding, so he would simply agree with what they wanted.

He wondered how Evie was this morning. Cavendish had scared her, and then she punched and kneed him in the groin. He'd been proud of her for that. At least he knew she could disarm a man if need be.

But not one who grabbed her from behind.

"Do you care for her, Anthony?" Aunt Lavinia asked.

"That will come, Lavinia. There is no need for any of that yet. As long as there is respect the rest will happen," Aunt Petunia said.

"But he is our boy, and I want him to be happy," Aunt Lavinia added with an uncharacteristic snap to her words.

"I will be happy," he said squeezing her hand. "Have no fear."

She smiled and nodded, pleased with his response. "Because you deserve that, my boy, considering you have not been for so long."

"I'm happy," he protested, uncomfortable that she knew this about him.

"No, you are not. No one lives the life you do, pursuing the things you have, and is happy, Anthony," Aunt Aggie said. "But I have hopes that Miss Spencer can change that for you."

He shouldn't have done it. His engagement to Evangeline had stirred up so much emotion, and when it was over, his aunts would be heartbroken. But it would be for the best.

Anthony was not a man someone like Evangeline Spencer should be married to. His demons would destroy her.

They drove through London with his aunts waving at and greeting anyone they came across.

He had spent many hours both night and day wandering these streets. It was as familiar to him as his estates, and likely more so. Sampson's Confectioners caught his eye.

"Stop if you please, Huntley," he said to his aunts' driver.

"What's wrong?" Aunt Aggie looked around her.

"Nothing. I want to purchase some sweets. I will return shortly."

"I tell you that boy has changed since he's become engaged," he heard Aunt Lavinia say as he walked to the shop. Rolling his eyes, he then purchased what he needed and returned minutes later with two bags. One he handed to his aunts, the other he kept in his pocket, after popping one sweet into his mouth.

"Do you know I don't believe I've had a lemon drop for years," Aunt Aggie said. She then sucked loudly. "Delicious."

While they discussed the need to eat more lemon drops, he thought about his next move with Evie. He needed to ensure Cavendish and his lot were no threat to her. But how?

Entering the park, he enjoyed the cool, crisp breeze on his face. People knew he was related to these three, but he rarely spent time with them in public, so those they passed were surprised to see him rolling around the park in an open-topped carriage.

Anthony had many responsibilities, and now it seemed he had more. The Spencers. They had no money, which he needed to address. He'd said he'd help Evie with investments, but their immediate need was more pressing. Prudence Spencer needed to wed and wed well.

The carriage stopped as the art exhibition appeared. He saw plenty of easels, some set up with completed artwork, others with artists painting. Studying the scene while his aunts chatted with Ladies Barber and Harper, whose carriage had pulled up alongside, his eyes landed on the back of a woman who was walking behind a couple. *Evie*. She stopped to study a painting. Standing slightly to the right while her sister and Landon strolled on. To her left was another group, and Miss Beasley was among them.

"Excuse me," he said to his aunts. "I see someone I wish to speak with. I shall return shortly."

They waved him away, and he climbed from the carriage, making for Evie. She was moving again. Head down, shoulders hunched and to him, she looked dejected. Had something else happened? He increased his pace but was too late to intercept her before the other women.

"Well, if it isn't Miss Spencer. I wonder you dare to show your face after last night," Miss Beasley said loudly, unaware that he was behind her.

Evie turned and saw him, her eyes widening.

"I know what you did with Lord Cavendish," Miss Beasley hissed. "We all do."

"Oh? And how is it you know that, if it was not you and your mother who lured me outside on the pretext of helping someone?" Evangeline said.

"Hello, my sweet." Anthony moved to her side. He then placed a hand on her back. "How are you today?"

"Lord Hamilton!" Miss Beasley looked shocked. Her friends, however, were shooting her questioning glances.

He bowed to the women, still smiling, which he was sure did not reach his eyes. This woman and her mother had lured Evie into Cavendish's clutches. The outcome could have been a great deal worse had he not found her.

"What were you discussing when I arrived?" Anthony asked feigning ignorance.

"I-ah, was just discussing a rumor I overheard," Miss Beasley said quickly.

"Rumor?" Evie said, her tone ice cold.

Looking down at her, Anthony noted she was pale and had

smudges beneath her eyes. Clearly, she hadn't slept well.

"You lured me to Lord Cavendish, Miss Beasley—"

"I cannot believe you would speak such slanderous lies to me!" She clutched her chest.

"Lies are they?" Evie snapped.

"Allow me to finish this for you," he said running a hand down her rigid spine.

"I—"

"I am to be married to Miss Spencer, Miss Beasley," he said before Evie could continue. "She is to be my wife," he added, just to make sure the woman understood. "If anyone threatens or harms her again, there will be consequences for those involved."

"My lord—"

"Consequences that neither you nor your mother will enjoy."

Miss Beasley gulped so loudly they all heard it.

"Do you understand that from this day forth, everyone will show my fiancée and her family the utmost respect?" Anthony had kept his voice calm, as if they were simply chatting, but his meaning was clear to everyone in this small gathering.

"Evie?"

"Carry on with your walk, Prue, all is well," Evie said, keeping her eyes on Miss Beasley. "I've done nothing to you. Why would you want to harm me?" she added.

"You are engaged to me," Anthony said. "And that is enough. Isn't that right, Miss Beasley?"

The woman was puce with embarrassment now. She'd not expected Anthony to come to Evie's aid. She'd thought to drive a wedge between them. Little did she know their engagement was not real.

"A word of advice before you leave us, Miss Beasley. Stay well clear of Lord Cavendish and his friends. If you think I am dangerous, they are doubly so."

Her mouth fell open at Anthony's words. She then turned and fled with her friends on her heels.

"Well," Evie said, exhaling the word in a loud breath.

"Exactly. Let's walk behind your sister and Landon."

"A distance behind," she muttered.

"Pardon?" He picked up her hand and lowered it to his arm, seeing as she hadn't put it there already.

"Nothing."

That single word had conveyed her need for him to ask no further questions and to put distance between them. As someone who had lived his adult life doing just that, he allowed her the quiet she wished for as he looked at the paintings.

"I like that one." He pointed to a landscape minutes later. It was of the scene before them, a small glimmer of water in the distance. Carriages and horses on the road, and people promenading.

"I like that one better." She pointed to the right where a man was painting a night sky with very little color.

"Because it mirrors your current mood?"

"My mood is fine, thank you," she snapped.

"Perhaps one of these will help sweeten your sour countenance." He held out a barley sugar. She took it with a muttered thank you and popped it in her mouth.

He let her have her silence as he listened to her sucking on the sweet. Visions of them in bed together with that mouth on him had his barley sugar wedging in the back of his throat. Anthony coughed several times to dislodge it.

"Are you all right?"

"Yes," he rasped.

"Suck it slowly and it will not shoot to the back of your mouth."

"Thank you. As you can imagine, that had not occurred to me in the years since I've been eating them."

"Sarcasm is a sign of a small mind," she said haughtily.

"Yours must be minute then." Her only response to that was a hiss of breath.

A loud yapping had them both turning to see Monty approaching at a sprint.

"Bloody dog," he muttered.

"Whose bloody dog is he?" Evie dropped to her haunches right there in front of everyone looking, of which there were many after his chat with Miss Beasley and what happened last night. In fact, they seemed to be the center of attention in the park today.

Monty ran at her, dancing on his hind legs, licking her face until Evie started giggling.

"Who does he belong to?" she asked.

"He is my aunts' dog, Monty." Anthony lifted her to her feet, ignoring the heat in his chest as he studied her. Her smile did not reach her eyes. They still looked sad.

"He's lovely."

"He's a spoiled dog, but yes, he is a good boy. I brought him for them three years ago, and they dote on him."

Anthony bent to stroke Monty, who immediately flopped on his back to have his belly rubbed.

"He is of course mannerless as you can see. It is not done to expose your belly in public like that, Monty."

When he rose, she was giving him one of those unsettling looks that told Anthony she could read every thought in his head, but all she said was, "He's lovely."

"What's wrong, Evie?" he said, because right then he would have done just about anything to make her happy again.

CHAPTER TWENTY-FOUR

"**N**OTHING IS WRONG, my lord."

"You are an exhausting woman. One minute I am Anthony and the next Lord Hamilton, or my lord."

"This is exhausting," she said. "I had thought it would be a simple matter of getting through the season, but it has turned out to be so much harder, and none of it was of my making."

"As it is not of mine."

"I know." Her shoulders slumped. "If you must know, my sister and I are arguing."

"What about?" He wandered to another artist and studied his work, and as she had her hand on his arm, she had to follow.

"I'm not sure why I should tell you."

He handed her another barley sugar, which she took.

"Are you inundated with people you could speak with then, Evangeline? From what I have seen, you are friendless here in London." He had to be honest with her, because it was the only way to get a reaction.

"I am hardly that."

Anthony made a show of looking around him.

"They would not all be following me about like ducklings, now, would they?" She frowned in displeasure, and he wondered what it was about this woman that intrigued him. Perhaps it was that she did not flirt with him or drop silly inane comments into a conversation.

"Very well, perhaps you are correct, even if it was rude of you to point out my friendless state," she said, and then crunched loudly on her barley sugar.

"I'm a rude person. I thought you already knew that."

"There is that," she said. "I don't have friends here, but that is because this is my first season and I am too old to make any, and not worthy of anyone's attempts to try. However, I have encountered several chaperones that appear nice."

It angered him she had no friends because she was a far more interesting woman than most in society.

"What are you and your sister arguing over?" he asked.

"I refuse to tell you that, as it will simply give you more ammunition to fire at me." Her words did not have their usual strength behind them, which told Anthony the argument had upset her.

"Let me guess," he said. "You have been telling her what to do, and she doesn't want you to treat her like a child anymore? Or you don't like Landon, and have exceedingly high standards for Prudence's future husband, and let her know that?"

He was merely guessing, but Anthony had a sister, and she loathed him attempting to control her.

"You cannot know that." She shot him a look and their eyes met. It was Evie who pulled away first.

"I'm astute. Ask anyone."

"Oh, please, everyone thinks you a rogue with no conscience or scruples," she scoffed.

"But not you?" He wasn't sure why he'd asked that question, but right then he needed to know the answer.

"I think a man who loves his aunts and did what he did for me last night, and has the respect of his two friends, is not a bad one. But I believe you have no wish for anyone to know that about you."

"My reputation is justified, Evangeline," Anthony got out around the lump in his throat. *She had seen what others hadn't.*

"I know you want people to believe that, Lord Hamilton."

His chest felt warm again, as if the cold inside him was thawing.

"There you are!"

Grateful for the distraction, Anthony watched his aunts hurrying toward them while he reminded himself that this was temporary. Evangeline would never be his wife.

"Oh, now look at you both. What a picture you make!" Aunt Petunia said taking Evie's hands.

"Good day to you, Lord Hamilton."

"And you, Prudence," he said to her sister when she arrived with Landon. "A lovely day for a walk."

Her face looked like Evie's, sad and worried.

"Some of this artwork is quite stunning," Landon said.

He was a good man. Fair and had money. But of course, there was the matter of no dowry that he possibly did not know about.

"All is well, my lord?" Prudence asked, as Landon moved on to inspect the paintings again. "Regarding the business with Miss Beasley, I mean?"

"All is well."

Her eyes went to her sister, who was chatting with his aunts, but she did not speak again, just went to greet his relatives.

"We could not be happier," Aunt Petunia said, her eyes teary, which made Anthony's guilt climb. Calling off the engagement would devastate his aunts.

"You must take Evangeline to meet Harriet at once, Anthony," Aunt Lavinia said suddenly. "It is only right you do so."

"She lives four hours from London, Aunt. Perhaps another time?" Anthony said.

"The Hampton house party!" Aunt Aggie said suddenly. "Harriet lives nearby. You could introduce your fiancée to her then. It is only a few weeks away, from memory."

"Oh, we are not attending," Evie said quickly.

"Of course you are, and we shall see to it," Aunt Petunia said. "You leave that to us. We will stay with Harriet, but of course will visit you there."

"I don't—"

"Don't fight it," Anthony whispered in her ear. "Besides, it will have Prudence and Mr. Landon spending time together daily; I will ensure he is invited. There will also be other eligible men there. Plus, it gets you out of London and away from Cavendish."

She looked like she wanted to argue.

"Wouldn't you enjoy that, dear?" Aunt Petunia said to Prudence.

"Oh yes, very much so," she said, which sealed Evie's fate.

"Excellent," Aunt Aggie said. "We shall be off then, as we have much to do."

They always had "much to do."

"I shall find my way home," Anthony said.

They left as they had arrived, chattering like a nest of chicks, and Anthony started walking with Evie's hand on his arm again. He liked the feel of her close, which should worry him a lot more than it did right then.

"My mother was like your Aunt Petunia," she said as the silence stretched between them.

"What was she like?"

"Strong, determined, and beautiful. We always knew she loved us even when she was cross."

"You take after her, then?"

She looked at him, brow raised. "Perhaps in the strong and determined part."

"I'm sure your family know you still love them when you are cross with them, like now," he added, looking at Prudence, who stood a few feet away with Landon, shooting her sister looks. Neither of them mentioned he thought her beautiful, which she was. Not a classic beauty, but all her own.

"Go and talk to your sister. You are blood. It is important that you always make up after an argument. One never knows what will occur to ensure you don't."

"What does that mean?"

"Aunt Aggie lost her husband the day he left the house in a rage. They were arguing over something that she doesn't even remember, and he fell off his horse and broke his neck."

"Oh no, that must have been devastating."

"I don't think she's ever recovered," Anthony said and wondered why he was sharing something so personal with this woman. It was odd how she didn't ask him questions, and yet he wanted to tell her things. Especially him, a man who never shared anything about himself.

"Then I'm glad she has her sisters and you in her life," Evie said.

"For better or worse," he added. Anthony wasn't sure why he was suddenly doubting the way he'd chosen to live, but it had to stop, and likely would at the end of the season.

"I'm not sure we should attend that house party, Anthony."

"Why? You will enjoy it, and I'm sure some people attending will be nice. Not all of society are sharks, like me."

She didn't laugh at his poor attempt at humor. Instead, she was frowning.

He felt like there was more to her words, but he couldn't work out what.

"Why don't you want to go?"

"I don't like society," she said, and it sounded lame to both their ears as she was currently entering it most evenings.

Silence was a powerful tool, so he used it then to his benefit as they strolled on.

"As you know, we are here for only a single season, my lord," she said.

"And we've circled back to my lord."

"As I was saying, a single season," she said with a bite now to her words. She then paused, clearly unsure how to proceed.

"Just say the words, Evangeline. I already know you are living with two identities and an inch from social ruin."

As he was looking at her, Anthony saw her head turn to the left and then the right before she spoke.

"How did you realize Mr. Renee was me? No one else did."

He weighed his answer carefully, not wishing her to think he'd been watching her.

"That day I found you wandering around looking at Lord Bailey's exotic plants. Your head was bent, exposing the back of your neck. I saw the marks you have there. I then saw them on Mr. Renee the night I realized who you were."

Her eyes were on her sister's back, but he knew her thoughts were on what she would say next. Conversing with Evangeline Spencer was entertaining because he never knew what would come out of that lovely mouth.

"Surely others have such marks."

"You have the foot standing thing also," Anthony said as he nodded to Mr. Jacobs. The man was so startled he tripped and stumbled several steps but managed to stay upright.

"Foot thing?"

"You put all your weight on the right leg and the left foot rests on top of it, Evangeline. I have seen no one but you do that."

Anthony was suddenly uncomfortable with how much he knew about this woman.

"I like to observe people, and because I dislike meaningless conversation just for the sake of hearing my own voice, I spend a lot of time doing that."

"Are you suggesting I like meaningless conversation?" She looked indignant now.

"Where in my statement did you gather that?"

"Nowhere," she muttered. "Sorry."

"You must spend a lot of your life apologizing if you are quick to assume everyone is judging you," Anthony said.

"You have no idea," she added. "But I am not important or wealthy, so judgment is always a conversation away."

"How cynical you are, Miss Spencer, but back to why you have no wish to attend the house party."

Her sigh was loud. "We don't have enough dresses," she

hissed. "There, are you happy I am completely humiliated?"

"Ecstatic. I woke up this morning thinking how happy I—"

"And you say I am annoying," she interrupted him.

A loud scream reached them, coming from somewhere up ahead. Evangeline started running, so he followed. Anthony was faster and rounded the row of trees which led to the water first. He found a rowboat overturned, and the occupants in the water.

"Mr. Benjamin has gone under several times, and Miss Little is hampered by her dress, and I can no longer see her!" A frantic Miss Beasley uttered these words. "W-we are friends, and I know she cannot swim."

Shrugging out of his jacket, Anthony attempted to pull off his boots, which wasn't easy, but he managed it with a lot of hopping. When he was done, he looked at the boat's occupants and found Evangeline wading into the water.

"Get out of there at once!" he roared, following her.

"There are two of them. You can't save them both!" she called back.

"You're fully clothed!" he bellowed.

"I will stand here, and you can bring them to me!" The water was up to her chest now. "Hurry!"

He looked behind him and saw no one else disrobing, so he plunged into the water and started swimming. Passing her, he did not take long to reach the man who was floundering about in the water like a child taking his first swim.

"Where is Miss Little?"

The man lunged at him and took them both under.

"Stop thrashing your arms, Benjamin!" Anthony bellowed when they resurfaced. He still couldn't see Miss Little. *Was she under the boat?*

"There!" Evie shrieked.

Following her hand he saw the woman surface, frantically slapping at the water, before sinking again.

Wrestling Benjamin under his arm, Anthony propelled him toward Evie, who was now paddling toward him.

"You'll drown, you fool. Go back!"

Of course, she ignored him, then took hold of Benjamin, who instantly clung to her.

"Desist!" she yelled at him, "or I will let you drown, Mr. Benjamin."

Deciding Evie had the man under control and that her sister and Landon were now wading in to assist her, Anthony swam in the direction he had last seen Miss Little. Diving under the surface, he tried to find her. It took him two more attempts before he saw a flash of white. Swimming toward it, he reached out and grabbed an arm.

Surfacing, he saw she wasn't conscious or, he thought, breathing. He started back to the bank, where a crowd had now formed. Evie was out now and being wrapped in Landon's jacket.

When he could stand, Landon helped him bring Miss Little in. Miss Beasley was sobbing loudly as they laid the limp form of her friend down on the grass.

"Let me in," Evie said, as people crowded around. "Move back, I said!" she snapped, and then she was there, crouched on the opposite side of the still form.

"Raise her legs!" someone cried. "The water will run from her mouth."

"Do not raise her legs!" Evie roared. "I read a card that the Royal Humane Society created on how to save a person from drowning," she added.

"What shall we do?" Anthony asked.

"I need to breathe into her mouth," she said.

"Everyone, move back!" Prudence yelled. "My sister needs room."

He watched Evie take a deep breath and then release it like she did before firing an arrow from her bow.

"P-put your hand under her neck please, and lift it slightly, my lord."

He did as she asked. Evie then opened Miss Little's mouth and appeared to give her breath.

"I say, what is she doing to poor Miss Little?" he heard some-one ask, shocked.

"No, I've heard about this. A man was saved after he fell into the Thames and stopped breathing by someone doing what Miss Spencer is."

While the debate raged above them, Evie continued to breathe life back into Miss Little. Anthony wasn't sure if the woman was too far gone or if Evie's efforts would work, but in that moment he had never in his life been so awed by another human as he was by Evangeline Spencer.

Evie lifted her head, and he watched Miss Little's chest rise and fall.

"I can't tell if she's breathing, Anthony." Her words were desperate.

"She is breathing, Evie. Now we must roll her to her side," Anthony said, and between them they maneuvered Miss Little, who instantly started coughing and spluttering up water.

"Dear Lord, Jessica!" Mrs. Little appeared with two other ladies. Anthony watched Evie rise, and the women dropped to take her place.

"She is breathing, Mrs. Little, but spent some time in the water," Anthony said.

"You saved her, my lord," someone said.

"I brought her in, but it was Miss Spencer who saved her," Anthony said looking around for Evie, but he couldn't see her in the crowd that had formed.

Regaining his feet, he searched but still couldn't find her.

"If you are looking for Miss Spencer, Lord Hamilton, she asked Miss Prudence Spencer and Mr. Landon to take her home," Lady Howe said.

She'd left before he could speak to her. Before he could assure himself she was all right.

"What you both did was extremely brave, my lord. Allow me to thank you."

The acknowledgments came then, and Anthony felt as uncomfortable as the people delivering them. He was nobody's hero, and these people knew that, but were willing to overlook the man he was for what he'd just done.

But it was not he who was the true hero this day. It was Evie, and she'd left before he could tell her that.

CHAPTER TWENTY-FIVE

E VIE HAD RETURNED home after saving Miss Little, exhausted. She'd brought a woman back to life, and that was both a terrifying and exhilarating thought. All she'd wanted to do in that moment was get far away from that crowd of people. Her hands had been shaking, and she'd been close to tears, so she'd urged Prue to get her away from there.

Prue had then helped Evie shed her wet clothes and change, then Evie had fallen onto her bed and slept the entire rest of the day, not waking until morning. When she did, her head was stuffy, and her chest burned.

What followed was an illness that laid her low for nearly two weeks, which considering the visitors who had called at the Spencer house, was both a blessing and a curse. The curse was her throat was raw, and her entire body felt like she'd been stomped on and then rolled over by a herd of cows.

Today was the first day she felt more like herself. She'd risen, bathed, and was now sitting in the small chair beside the bed watching Prue pack for the Hampton house party, which she did not want to attend, but had no choice in the matter. Preparations, it seemed, had been made while she was ill.

"There are a great many flowers in this room and downstairs when I ventured there earlier," Evie said.

"Lord Hamilton brought some, and others also. He has called often for news of you. I'm quite sure he didn't believe me when I said you were recovering, and he wanted to check for himself," Prue said as she pulled a box out from under the bed.

"Tell me you didn't let him in here to see me?" He'd brought her flowers. Why did that make her feel warm, when for days she'd been ice cold?

Prue dropped the box on the bed and looked at Evie. "You looked all pale and interesting, with your lank hair stuck to your head. Of course I did."

Evie grabbed a pillow off the bed and threw it at her.

"Prue?"

"Hmm?" Her sister was lifting the lid off the box.

"I'm sorry that you feel I am controlling, and I promise to ask for your help and opinion in the future."

"Apology accepted. But we both know that's a lie, Evie."

She laughed, because her sister was right. She liked to be in control, but then she wasn't the only one. Control was important to Anthony too.

She'd missed him. It was as simple as that. Missed their debates and the way he challenged her. She'd thought about him endlessly as she lay in her bed for days. He was becoming a problem for Evie because she was beginning to feel a great deal more for the man than she should, and that would never do.

Your arrangement with him is only temporary.

"Lord Hamilton said he was displeased you had left that day without telling him," Prue said.

"What? Why? I was cold and my dress was stuck to me exposing...well, everything," Evie said, waving her hand about.

"You should have told him. He was worried, and you're engaged." Prue pulled a dress out of the box that Evie had never seen.

"Fake engaged, but you're right. I should have at least told him I was going. I'll concede to that." But she'd needed to get out of there because she couldn't completely discount that she may have been ill, and there was no way she would do that in front of at least a dozen members of society.

"It's a miracle," Prue muttered, shaking out the dress.

"What is that?" Evie asked, getting to her feet to inspect the dress.

"Has your illness addled your mind? Clearly, it's a dress." Prue held it up with a smile.

"I can see that, but it's not one of ours."

"Well, when you were sick Lady Petunia and her sisters arrived and took me shopping. I argued, of course," Prue said, "but they were insistent. We have four new dresses each, and several bonnets."

"Dear Lord," Evie whispered. "Tell me that isn't true." He'd done this. Lord Hamilton, after she'd told him they did not have enough dresses for the Hampton house party.

"Very well, it's not true, Evie," Prue said, gently folding the dress and lowering it into the open trunk.

"No. This can't be happening. We can't accept this kind of charity from him. It's humiliating. How will I ever face Lord Hamilton again?"

"They are beautiful dresses," Prue said removing a cream one from the box. "I knew your sizes so was able to have them made."

"Can you not see this makes us beholden to him? After the season is over, we are leaving and will likely never return. How will I...we repay him for this?"

Prue dropped the dress and grabbed her shoulders. She then gave them a little shake. "He is a wealthy man, and you are engaged to him—"

"I'm not!"

"Very well, fake engaged, but the point is, he cannot have you turning up at a house party looking like the poor cousin of your great aunt, who is now living on the charity of her family because her husband stole all her money and—"

"I get the point. There is no need for one of your stories," Evie snapped.

"Excellent. So, you understand why he did this?"

"I don't like it, but I understand it." Society valued appearances above all else, and even the infamous Lord Hamilton could not be seen with a fiancée dressed in ill-fitting, worn clothing.

"It was a very kind thing he did also, Evie. To spend money on you when he did not have to."

She nodded, knowing that he was capable of that too. She'd seen him dive into the water to rescue Miss Little and Mr. Benjamin, who would have drowned had he not. Those were not the actions of the callous man he portrayed himself to be.

"So now you need to get ready as a carriage will be arriving soon," Prue said slamming the lid shut. "Make haste, sister. We are about to go on an adventure neither of us foresaw before the season started."

"Now? Today?"

"Now, today. A bath is coming. You will wash, and we will leave in two hours. The drive will be taxing, but you can sleep the entire way if you wish to."

"How can we afford a carriage to Lord Hampton's estate?" Evie demanded.

Prue ignored her and flung open the door. "Humphrey!" she then bellowed.

"Don't yell at the staff, sister. How are we affording a carriage, and who ordered it?" Evie said.

"You called, Miss Prudence." Humphrey appeared in the doorway.

"Yes, Humphrey, I want to take this downstairs for when the carriage arrives. Grab that end, and we shall do so now."

"You will not bloody do so!" Evie roared. "You'll answer the question."

"Do you think a future countess should curse like a sailor, Humphrey?" Prue asked as she lifted her end. "Because I'm sure I don't."

"It's not seemly," he said, and then they were gone, hefting the luggage out the door. Evie followed.

"Answer the question, Prue, and you know well and fine I am

not going to be a countess."

Her sister made a great show of panting and making noises that suggested she was putting a great deal of effort into what she was doing. Evie knew better; she was avoiding answering her.

The chest was deposited by the front door.

"In the parlor, now, Prue."

"Oh, very well," her sister said stomping past Evie into the room. "Bring tea if you please, Humphrey. We will need our strength for the journey, and then there is the fact my sister has been unwell. Do you remember how quiet it was for those few blissful days when she couldn't speak?"

Humphrey thought better of answering that question and walked away.

"The carriage, Prue. How is it we can afford one, when to the best of my knowledge you never once mentioned it to me, and I did not tell you how to pay for it?" Suddenly exhausted, Evie sat after asking the question.

"Lord Hamilton is providing the carriage."

Evie stared at her sister like she had developed an eye in her forehead.

"He asked if we had a carriage, Evie, and I said no, and that we would hire one, as I know you would have wished me to do," Prue said, now seated beside her on the sofa. "He then said, I have two, you can use one of them."

"Who has two carriages when you are only one person?" Evie asked.

"A wealthy earl is my guess. Who perhaps drives his aunts about the place?"

"I thought they had their own carriage. We saw them in it one day in the park." Evie pinched the bridge of her nose hard to find some clarity in her foggy head. "We cannot allow him to pay for our clothing and a carriage, Prue. It is just not right."

"At the time Father was here, and we were taking tea with Lord Hamilton and his aunts, and one of them said, I can't remember which one, what a capital notion and I'm sure the

Spencers will be a great deal more comfortable in your carriage, Anthony. Especially considering your illness."

"Lord Hamilton and his aunts came here to take tea with you and Father while I was upstairs on my deathbed?"

"We checked on you," Prue rushed to add. "You slept the entire time. Lord Hamilton was very worried and asked if he should call a doctor as you had been ill for so long. So he did and—"

"Tell me you are joking," Evie said feeling faint for perhaps the first time in her life. How would she ever repay that man what her family now owed him?

"No, I would never joke about this. The doctor came and declared you had a chest inflammation and were extremely unwell. Lord Hamilton then made him return daily to check on you, until the doctor finally said you were improving," Prue said. "Do you know that fierce reputation he has in society is completely unjustified? He can be a bit brisk, and occasionally gruff, but he is very kind, Evie."

She had no idea what to say to that. Why had he done all these things? Was he worried about her holding up her end of the bargain?

"What did Father say with all of this going on?" Evie asked, instead of "tell me more about Lord Hamilton."

"Naturally, he was worried about you and relieved when the doctor called. Father then said capital, and we would love to travel in comfort. Thank you, Lord Hamilton. He also loves parties and anything that involves him lolling about the place with people and eating a lot of food. So, the idea of a house party appealed to him."

"Of course it did," Evie said feeling nauseous.

Looking at her sister's face she saw only happiness.

"You're excited about the house party, aren't you?"

"I am." Prue clapped her hands. "Christian is coming."

"Christian?"

"Mr. Landon."

"Ah, right. I remember that was his name now. He seems a nice man."

"He is, and was worried about you also, Evie."

"I should have asked, is Miss Little all right?"

"She has recovered and called to see you along with Miss Beasley, but as you were still unwell, they left again."

"Good Lord, Miss Beasley was here?"

Prue nodded. "We've been quite busy with people knocking on our door to ask after you since you saved Miss Little."

"Well then, let's hope with my return to health my popularity wanes quickly," Evie said.

"I love being popular," Prue said regaining her feet. "Now, you are all caught up, and it is time for you to get up those stairs, wash, and put on the dress I have set aside for you to travel in."

"I feel like while I slept my life has slipped from my control," Evie muttered.

"Excellent. It will do you good to feel that way. Now move."

She did as her sister asked because she was too tired to argue. Besides, a long carriage ride would give Evie time to work out how long it would take to repay their debt to Lord Hamilton. She feared it would be many years.

CHAPTER TWENTY-SIX

"A ND EVANGELINE IS now well?"

"I have not seen her," Anthony said to Toby as they wandered through the grounds of the Hamptons' large estate.

House parties were not something he usually attended, but he'd come to this one because here Evie would be safe, and here she could finish her recovery.

"It's nice to get out of London," Jamie said.

The gardens here were extensive and tended by five gardeners. You could walk them for hours and not see everything. Lakes were stocked with trout for fishing, and parties went out daily to ride over the hundreds of acres of land.

But it was the huge conservatory that Hampton had built to cantilever over the water that intrigued Anthony. It offered a spectacular view of the night sky through the large telescope erected inside. An avid star gazer, Hampton had told Anthony he must view it before he left.

He, Toby, and Jamie had arrived this morning. His aunts had left a few days earlier and were visiting with Harriet, whom he would see tomorrow. But the person he most needed to see was Evie.

It had been two weeks since she'd saved Miss Little, and while her family had told him she was well, he wanted to see that for himself.

"I cannot believe she just plunged into the water?" Jamie said.

"As I told you the last two times we discussed this, yes, she did, and in her dress."

Jamie whistled. "I've been thinking if you are not actually going to wed her, I may ask for her hand, as she seems the perfect wife to me."

The flash of rage Anthony felt at his friend's words was instant. *Mine*, he wanted to roar.

Damn bloody woman! She'd worked her way inside him, and he wasn't sure how to get her out again. Anthony had panicked when he'd heard she was ill, fearing Prudence was lying to him and she was worse than they were leading him to believe.

"Anthony?"

"Sorry, what did you say?" He looked at Toby.

"What's wrong?" Jamie asked.

"Nothing."

"There is definitely something," Toby said. "You're changing, my friend."

"No, I'm not," Anthony said, feeling a stab of panic at the words because he'd felt like that was exactly what was happening to him.

"You are. You've lost some of your hard edges—"

"I have lost nothing," he cut Jamie off. "I went to Hugh's two nights ago and gambled until dawn." And he'd hated it and wanted to go home because Mr. Renee was not there.

"Society no longer speaks of you in fearful whispers," Toby said. "I wouldn't go so far as saying you're a respected member yet, but you're on the way."

"I—"

"Lord Bethany told me he thought you were top-notch last week," Jamie added.

"I am exactly who I have always been," Anthony gritted out.

"Cold, calculating, and unemotional, do you mean? A man who won't reveal himself unless his doors are closed, and only we, or your aunts, are present?" Toby asked.

He had been all those things, but knew Evie had changed

him. He couldn't allow it to continue...could he?

"Both of you, be quiet," Anthony snarled.

"Very well, but for what it is worth, we like the changes," Toby said.

"Now let us discuss our visit to Brawley while we are here," Jamie said. "If Cavendish, Greville, and Calthorpe are involved in those girls going missing, we must bring them to justice."

"Agree," Toby and Anthony said.

"After that business with your fiancée, there is no more hiding in the shadows and seeking revenge unseen anymore," Toby added. "They know you are watching them now, Anthony."

"I want them to pay for all of it, but especially scaring Evangeline."

"Because she's important to you now?" Jamie said.

"He hurt her because of me. I cannot allow that to go unavenged."

"You put your fist in both their faces," Toby drawled.

"It was nowhere near enough," was all Anthony said.

They walked back to the house as yet another carriage rolled into the courtyard. This one, he knew.

"Is that your carriage, Anthony?" Jamie asked.

"It is. The Spencers are arriving in it."

"You are really playing the part of the besotted fiancé well," Toby said.

Ignoring them, he walked to the carriage as it stopped.

"I have it, thank you," he said to the footman hurrying to the door.

Opening it, he found Evie first, sleeping against the side of the carriage. He drank in the sight of her and felt the knot of fear inside him finally unravel.

"She's been asleep for at least two hours," Prudence said loudly. Her sister did not wake.

"Out you come. I shall wake her. You stretch your legs," Anthony said holding out a hand for Evie's sister.

"Well sprung carriage you have, Hamilton," Lord Spencer

said climbing out behind his daughter next. "But I'm pleased to have arrived."

Anthony climbed inside. "Evie." He touched her pale cheek. She didn't wake. "Evie," he said more loudly.

"Our mother said a herd of bulls could rampage through our house mooing and Evie would sleep through them," Prudence said from the doorway. "Pat her cheek, as we have no water to flick at her."

"You flick water at your sister?" Anthony turned to look at her.

"It is a sister thing, my lord."

He snorted, and it was then Evie opened her eyes. She sat upright, blinking furiously.

"Hello, Evangeline."

"Anthony?" Her voice sounded like a rusty door hinge.

"She does not wake well, my lord," Prudence said from the doorway. "It is best to keep your distance for at least an hour."

"Yes, it is I," he said, giving in to the need to touch her. His thumb ran over a soft cheek. "Are you feeling all right after your long journey?"

She nodded, and then blinked again. Lastly, she rubbed her eyes like a child. He found it ridiculously endearing.

"Are you now alert enough to leave the carriage?"

"I think so. That was a long journey." She frowned. "In your carriage. You shouldn't have let us use it. Plus, there are the dresses, Anthony. You have spent too much money on us. I did not need a doctor; that, too, was a cost to you."

Looking about for her bonnet, he found it on the floor. Picking it up, he lowered it onto her head.

"No, really, I don't know how we can repay it all," she said, lifting her chin as he tied the ribbons. "Stop that," she hissed, realizing what she was letting him do. "Someone may see."

"You are my fiancée. I'm sure I can help you with your bonnet ribbons, considering how ill you have been, Evangeline."

"But we're not... not really."

"We are in the eyes of society, and to give that lie credence, then we must do things like this." He bent to kiss her softly. No one could see, as his body was blocking the view, but he needed to taste her lips again. When Anthony raised his head, they formed a perfect O.

"Don't do that again," she whispered.

"I like being told what to do about as much as you, so perhaps you should remember that, Evangeline."

"It's a failing," she whispered, "which clearly we share."

"So it would seem. Now come along."

Her eyes met his then. "I owe you an apology, my lord... Anthony."

"Just Anthony."

"I'm sorry I left quickly that day when you saved Miss Little, but I did not want the fuss that would follow, plus my clothes were sticking to me in an unseemly manner."

"Running away solves nothing, Evie. However, I understand, and you were wet, cold, and very likely in shock. But it would have relieved me to know you were all right," he said. "But now you are well, I can tell you how courageous and foolhardy you were."

"I was not foolhardy," she said, eyes narrowing.

He backed out of the carriage and held out a hand for her to join him.

"Foolhardy," Anthony added, helping her to step down. He then kept her hand and placed it on his arm. "You could have drowned plunging into that water recklessly like that."

"I was helping!"

"Oh goody, she has regained her wits," Prudence said dryly.

"There were others—"

"No one was rushing forth to help," Evangeline snapped, interrupting him.

Anthony felt lighter inside than he had in days and knew that was solely because she had arrived. His fake fiancée.

"Good day to you, Miss Spencer," Jamie said. "Ignore my

friend. You were extremely brave."

"She could have drowned," Anthony snapped.

"I know how to swim," Evie said.

"Exactly." Toby stepped forward. "Lovely to see you again, Miss Spencer, and I am pleased you have recovered."

"Not quite. She's still tired and pale," Mr. Spencer said. "But my eldest daughter is strong. She will bounce back to her old self in no time."

Because she's had to be strong, Anthony wanted to say but kept that thought to himself.

"Well, that is all behind us," Prudence said. "Come, let's find our rooms, and then you can go back to sleep, Evie."

"I don't need to sleep anymore. I want to explore the gardens."

She wore a dress in pale blue, with cream lace around the cuffs and neckline. He wondered if it was one he'd paid for. Anthony knew Evie would have a great deal more to say about the money he'd spent on her and her family. He looked forward to it. He loved arguing with this woman.

"About the dresses," she said out of the side of her mouth as they made their way into the house.

He snorted. "It is done, Evangeline. What are you going to do? Unstitch them and take the cloth back?"

"It's a thought," she muttered, which had him barking out a laugh.

CHAPTER TWENTY-SEVEN

A FTER SHE LEFT Anthony and the heated discussion about money she was in no way finished with, Evie and Prue went to their rooms. They weren't large, but big enough, considering they had shared a room and bed in London. Prue's was across the hall, and their father's next to her.

Everywhere she looked inside the Hampton manor house was grand. From the furniture to the floorings and drapes. Floor after floor of wonderful antiques and paintings. It was by far the largest house she'd ever entered, and she could not wait to explore. But first she'd just rest for a while because that bed looked comfortable.

An hour later she woke disorientated. The illness had made her weak and tired, and it would take time for her strength to return. Rising, she washed and then changed into a new dress. This one was a simple apricot in soft material that fell in elegant folds to the floor. She'd never worn anything like it before.

A dress Anthony had paid for. That soured her pleasure in wearing it slightly.

She knew pride influenced her feelings, but Evie felt humiliated because the Spencers couldn't afford their own clothes.

As there was nothing she could do about this now, she left her room in search of her family and food. She knocked on Prue's door. When she didn't answer, Evie tried her father's, but there was no answer there either.

Hoping she didn't get lost, Evie headed left and thankfully found stairs. She saw glimpses through windows of manicured lawns and bordered gardens. The furniture smelled of lemon polish and was expensive and elegant. Stopping to study the contents of glass-fronted cabinets, Evie wondered if Anthony's estate looked anything like this. Did he have more than one? Not that she'd ever see them. However, he interested her, so it was natural to be curious, or so she told herself.

It was nothing to do with the kiss he'd given her in his carriage. He'd been pleased to see her, she was sure of it, just as she had to see him. It was ridiculous how one man could make her heart beat faster. A man she had no rights to, Evie reminded herself.

The chandelier when she reached the bottom was bigger than any she'd seen, and she was excessively pleased it was not her job to dust it. Evie stood, staring up, awed at the light catching on the glass for long seconds, until the sound of someone clearing their throat drew her eyes to the enormous doorway.

"Miss Spencer."

She watched Miss Beasley approach and with her was Miss Little, who was now looking a great deal better than last time Evie saw her.

"Miss Little, I am pleased to see you have fully recovered," Evie said noting how uncomfortable both young ladies looked.

"Oh, Miss Spencer, I can never say thank you enough for what you did for me," Miss Little rushed to say. "What you did..." Miss Little pressed her hand to her lips. "W-was so incredibly brave."

"I know I have no right to ask this of you, Miss Spencer," Miss Beasley then spoke in a subdued voice. "But I would ask your forgiveness for the way I have behaved toward you this season."

Both ladies looked ready to cry.

"Please, there is no need—"

"I would be dead were it not for you!" Miss Little ran at Evie then and hugged her tightly. She had surprisingly strong arms.

Evie, never comfortable with displays of affection from people she didn't know, awkwardly patted her back. "It's all right, Miss Little. Really," she added as the girl started sobbing.

"What I did that night to you is unforgivable," Miss Beasley said, stepping closer to Evie and the still sobbing Miss Little. "I'm so sorry, but when Lord Cavendish asked me to lure you outside for him, I knew it was my chance, you see. I enlisted my mother's help."

"Chance for what?" Evie asked as she gently eased Miss Little back.

"To ensure you did not marry Lord Hamilton," Miss Beasley said in a wobbly voice. She too was close to tears. "My mother wished me to wed him."

"I see," Evie said, understanding exactly in that moment the pressure Miss Beasley's mother had put on her.

"Helena!"

Looking to the door behind the two women, Evie watched Lady Beasley enter.

"Come here at once."

"I am speaking with Miss Spencer, Mother, and apologizing for our behavior."

"I have nothing to apologize for! You will come here now," Lady Beasley said.

"No, I won't, Mother. I will return shortly. Lucinda and I are thanking Miss Spencer for saving her life also."

Lady Beasley looked ready to commit murder, but instead turned and walked back out the door.

"Please, do not fall into trouble with your mother for me. Your apologies are accepted," Evie said.

"I realized after you saved Lucinda, Miss Spencer, that I was horrid to you, and I found I did not like the woman I had become. Especially when you willingly risked your own life to save someone who had not been nice to you." Miss Little, who was still clutching Evie, sobbed harder.

"We all have our faults, Miss Beasley," Evie said easing out of

Miss Little's grip again. "Mine are many, as my family will tell you, but I think it is important to be honorable and kind each day, if you can be nothing else."

Miss Little pressed her face into the handkerchief Miss Beasley thrust at her.

"Yes, I am going to try and do that," Miss Beasley said.

"And now I am extremely hungry. Would you point me to somewhere there is a table full of food?" Evie said.

"Thank you for your forgiveness. I'm not sure were our roles reversed I would have been as generous," Miss Beasley added.

"Do you know, I think you would have," Evie said. "Shall we move on from this moment?" Both girls nodded.

They informed her where the food was and that there was a croquet competition taking place on the west side of the house.

They escorted her outside, and then Miss Beasley and Miss Little went to where their mothers sat with a group of other women. Evie hoped Lady Beasley was not too hard on her daughter.

She followed a path around the outside of the house, taking in the lovely green hills in the distance and the gardens she was going to explore.

Entering another door, she found a sideboard with several platters full of tempting food. The room was empty bar an elderly gentleman snoring loudly slumped in a chair. Picking up a plate Evie loaded it with small sandwiches and a wedge of plum cake. Wandering back outside she stood studying her surroundings and devoured everything.

"Hello, Miss Spencer."

She tried not to stiffen as Mr. Calthorpe appeared. Evie nodded.

"Are you going to inspect the croquet my cousin has set up for the guests?"

"I am at present eating, sir. Perhaps after." She crammed another mouthful of cake in so she couldn't speak again.

"I will escort you."

She shook her head, then fought to swallow. The cake wedged, and she coughed but got it down without spitting it all over him. Not that he didn't deserve that.

"Are you all right?"

Evie nodded.

He did not have the mean look of his friend Cavendish. However, he had been present when Evie was lured outside and stood by with his sister to watch as she struggled to get free. His jaw only showed a faded tinge of yellow now from the punch Anthony had given it.

"I'm sorry, Miss Spencer, for my behavior. It was unforgivable."

Evie wondered what it was about this place that people suddenly felt the need to apologize to her?

"I'm afraid I should have known better, but Lord Cavendish has been my friend for some time you see."

"I wonder he is still your friend, sir, if he has questionable behavior."

"We have been friends since childhood," Mr. Calthorpe added. "It is not easy to walk away from that."

She nodded, unsure what to say, because unlike Miss Beasley she didn't want to forgive this man, because he'd played a hand in mistreating Anthony and his friends. That, as far as she was concerned, was something she would never forgive or forget.

"Excuse me," Evie said taking her plate back inside. She then selected two large sugar biscuits and hoped Mr. Calthorpe would be gone when she returned. He'd said "my cousin" so that meant Lord Hampton and he were related. Her mother always used to say you can't pick your family members, but your friends you could be fussier with.

Walking outside she saw no sign of him and started down the path in the direction she hoped to find the croquet, or at least her family. Her feet crunched on the path as she nibbled on the first biscuit. On either side, trees rose and then met in the middle above her, creating a canopy that allowed shafts of sunlight to peek through. She couldn't see around the trees to where the trail led but heard someone approaching.

"Hello, you're awake." Anthony appeared, his face softening as he smiled at her.

The man was just too much of everything. Too large, too handsome, too appealing. She could go on but stopped herself and swallowed the mouthful of biscuit she'd just taken.

"Hello, is the croquet that way?" Evie pointed her biscuit in the direction he'd come from.

"It is. Is that for me?" He stopped before her. Not an acceptable distance away, and far too close.

"Pardon?"

"Is that biscuit for me?" He pointed to her right hand.

"I have a father and sister. You don't think it could be for them? Or that I wish to eat it after I have finished this one?" She raised her left hand to show the half-eaten biscuit.

"Well, to save you the dilemma of to whom to give it, I shall eat it." He then lifted her hand and took a bite while she was still holding it.

It was something a couple who were in love may do. Or a couple who had been married for many years and actually liked each other. It was not something two fake engaged people should do. It made her feel weak at the knees, watching his dark head lower and those white teeth taking a bite of her biscuit. Evie took a step back, but because he was holding her wrist she did not get far.

"Are you scared of me, Evangeline?"

In that moment, she understood all those rumors about him. He looked dangerous and wicked standing in the shadow of the trees with small pockets of light dancing around him.

"Why would I be scared of you?"

"Because your pulse is fluttering right here." He tugged her closer and used his other finger to trace the skin over her pulse.

"Why are you touching me?" Evie was never one to talk around a subject.

"Because I can't seem to stop myself." His eyes were serious now.

"You should try."

The finger moved down, and she swallowed, making a gulping sound. He then cupped her cheek.

"Anthony." The name came out breathy and not at all like the way she usually sounded.

"Evie," he whispered and then he was kissing her. Her wrist was released and Anthony's arms wrapped around her, pulling her into his hard body.

For the first time in her life, Evie felt fragile. His arms crushed her to him, and his mouth took hers in a slow, sensual exploration that had her reeling. Her hands clutched the lapels of his jacket to both steady herself and hold him close.

"Open your mouth."

She obeyed the command, and he deepened the kiss, and Evie lost the ability to think at all. Lost every thought but one. *Anthony*.

Chapter Twenty-Eight

H E HAD TO stop kissing this woman. Had to let her go, but Anthony didn't seem able to do either of those things. Evie felt right in his arms, and he wanted to keep her there. Wanted to lay her down and take her where they stood. His body was hard with need for her.

"Anthony."

It was she who eased back, not he.

"We can't do this. Anyone could—"

"I don't care about anyone right now, Evangeline. I care about you," he rasped.

Her brown eyes were so close to his, and he could read every conflicted emotion in them.

"I don't understand."

"That makes two of us. There are things we need to discuss, Evie, but not now where anyone could chance upon us. Right now, you're correct. We need to stop kissing and walk."

He took her fingers and kissed the backs of them before lowering them to his arm.

Out of the corner of his eye he noted her exhale. As he'd just done the same, he understood why. They both needed time to recover from what had happened.

"I dropped my biscuits, and just when I had decided who should receive one." Her voice wasn't its usual forceful tone. There was a huskiness to it now that he'd put there.

"To whom were you giving it?" Anthony asked, happy to change the subject.

He'd just kissed Evie on the path where anyone could have seen them. Yes, they were engaged. Nevertheless, it had not been a wise move on his part. Especially because now he really knew what she tasted like and that she responded to him as she did everything, with enthusiasm.

"Why, Prudence of course."

"You're a mean woman, Miss Spencer."

"I try."

"Are you really recovered from your illness, Evangeline?"

"I am, yes. I haven't been ill in a long time, and I don't want to be again anytime soon. It was horrid."

"I'm sure it was." He'd hated thinking of her lying in that bed in pain.

"Why did you kiss me?"

He'd known of course she'd want answers but had hoped she'd wait, but then this was Evangeline. She never simply accepted things.

"Because I wanted to," he said slowly.

"Do you do everything you want to?"

"Usually. You?"

"Where I can," she said, her tone prim.

He smiled, as he often did in her company. He'd thought to strike a bargain with this woman to benefit them both, but it had turned out so much more than that. For so long, he'd vowed he was better alone. Better not putting his trust in anyone else. *But he trusted her.*

"Mr. Calthorpe is here, Anthony."

"He is Hampton's cousin so that stands to reason."

"I just wanted you to know, seeing as there is a past between you."

"Has he approached you?"

"Yes. I was eating outside, and he did so. There was an apology that I didn't believe was genuine. I told him in a roundabout way that he needed better friends and walked back inside. When I returned, he'd left."

"Good girl. Keep your distance from him, and if he approaches or says anything that upsets you, then come and find me, Toby, or Jamie."

"I will. I'm so sorry you suffered because of those men, Anthony."

For once, he didn't get that jolt of anger and anxiety at the thought of Blackwood Hall. It was Evie, of course. She made him feel calmer.

What did he feel for this woman?

"Evie!" Prudence waved to her sister as they arrived where the croquet was being held. She was standing with Landon, who Anthony had recently taken the time to get to know better.

"There is more food over there should you require it," he said.

"You've already been eating those biscuits I had, haven't you?" She looked up at him with an accusatory look on her face.

"Of course, but one can never have enough biscuits."

"There is that."

They talked with her family and Landon, and then he excused himself to speak with Jamie and Toby, who were flirting with several women.

"Miss Spencer certainly has better color in her cheeks than when she arrived. Care to tell me why, Anthony?" Jamie asked, moving away from the women so no one could overhear their conversation.

"She has been asleep as you very well know."

"You looked quite happy with yourself also when you arrived," Toby added.

"If there is a point to these veiled comments, please reach it before I get a gray hair," Anthony said. He made himself look at his friends and not her. Because when Evie was close, she drew him to her side.

"There is, actually," Jamie said checking to make sure no one was listening to their conversation. "We've decided you like Miss Spencer very much."

"In fact, we think you like her so much you should make the engagement real," Toby added.

It should have given him a shock to hear the words. It didn't.

"No denial?" Toby asked.

Anthony refused to answer that. "Are we to visit Brawley tomorrow afternoon?"

"We are," Jamie said grinning.

"Excellent. Now I'm going to play croquet and beat you both," Anthony added.

They played and Evangeline was, of course, as competitive as he. She argued every point and heckled her sister constantly.

"Do not crow, Evie," Prudence said as their father roared with laughter over his daughter's antics.

"I'm not crowing. This is my victory look," she said, fluttering her eyelashes.

God, he wanted that woman, but could he take a chance and go after what he wanted? Anthony had always believed himself broken, but lately he'd wondered if Evie was the one to put him back together.

"Hello!"

Anthony found his aunts approaching, and behind them his sister, Harriet. He was moving in seconds. Reaching her, he hugged her close.

"Hello, Harry."

"Hello, big brother." She kissed his cheek.

"I thought I was coming to see you?" He gripped her shoulders.

"You think I would wait another day to meet your fiancée?"

She was shorter than he, and slender, but he stared into his eyes when he looked at her. Her hair was a shade darker, but there was little doubting she was his sister.

"Hello, Harry."

"Toby, Jamie!"

He released her, and she hugged his friends.

"Now, I want to meet your fiancée," Harriet demanded.

Anthony met Jamie's eyes, and he shook his head to indicate Harriet did not know, like his aunts, about his engagement being fake. He then took his sister to where Evangeline stood with her family. She was nervous, he could see it in her face, but smiling as they approached.

After the introductions, Harriet took Evie's hands in hers.

"Hello. I'm so very pleased to meet the woman my brother is finally marrying," Harriet said. "I don't envy you the task, and I will add, good luck?"

"Thank you, and I love you too, sister dear," Anthony drawled.

"Be quiet. I wish to talk to my future sister-in-law," Harriet said dismissing him.

The look on Evangeline's face told him Harriet's words surprised her.

"My sister does not fear me, Evangeline, like others."

"Ah, I did wonder," she said with a small smile.

"She really is the perfect woman for you," Jamie said minutes later as they made their way back to the house and afternoon tea.

"And why is that?"

"She will not allow you to have your way and is not intimidated by your reputation."

"There is that."

Jamie was quiet for a few seconds and then said, "Which means what?"

"Which means mind your business, or I shall start my aunts on a hunt for your future bride."

He heard Jamie's teeth snap together and laughed, something he'd done a great deal of since Evie had arrived at the house party.

They spent the day eating and drinking in the sun, while his sister and aunts talked with Evangeline and Prudence. Anthony stole Harriet away for a walk before she and their aunts were to leave.

"I hear I am to be an uncle," he said wandering beside her, away from the other guests. "Congratulations, Harry, I could not be happier for you and Simon. Is he excited?"

"Ridiculously so," she said pink-cheeked. "He would have come but had estate business to attend to today."

"I will call in and see him when I leave," Anthony said.

"She has changed you," Harry said, slipping her arm through his. "You have lost that cynical air you brought home from Blackwood Hall all those years ago."

Anthony wasn't sure what to say to that.

"I never knew what happened to you there, as no one would tell me, but I saw the change in you, Anthony—"

"Harry—"

"I should have spoken years ago," she continued. "I tried, but you shut me out of your life. You'd changed. The gambling and everything else. It was like you were trying to outrun something, but never quite managed it."

That was exactly what he'd been doing, but Anthony hadn't known his sister had seen that.

"I'm sorry, Harry. You're right, it was hell at Blackwood Hall, and doing what I did was the only way for me to cope," he said. "I told myself it was better you didn't know."

"I'm sorry you suffered, brother, but glad that now you have found Evangeline you can find the happiness you deserve."

"I've been happy, Harry. Don't be dramatic." He tried to make her smile.

"I'm not being dramatic. I'm being honest. I like her. She's funny and intelligent. Plus, I doubt she will simply acquiesce to your every wish."

"She's unlike any woman I've ever known," Anthony said, and it was the truth. There would only ever be one Evangeline Spencer.

"Well then," Harry said. "Be happy, Anthony."

He walked her to the carriage where his aunts waited and

then helped them all inside.

"Look after my niece or nephew, sister."

"I will, and you be nice to Evangeline, brother." She kissed his cheek again. "I love you," she said, like she always did when they parted. Anthony had never said it back...until now.

"As I love you... all of you," he said looking around her to the three women shamelessly listening to every word of his conversation with his sister.

He closed the door on their surprise and watched the carriage roll away.

Smiling, he walked back inside to find Evangeline.

CHAPTER TWENTY-NINE

E VIE WASN'T READY to sleep, even though the hour was late. It was the third day of the house party, and she'd spent it walking around the gardens with a small party, including Anthony and Prue. It had been magical, and she felt herself falling more and more under his spell. Each day, she drew closer to him and believed he felt the same.

There was a tentative hope that what they had would become real, and she would one day be Lady Hamilton, Anthony's wife. The thought was both terrifying and exciting.

When she'd returned to her room after a night of music and dancing, she'd told the maid she would not need her and taken down her hair but stayed in her dress. Evie now sat in the small window seat, looking out at the stars.

Lady Hampton had told her she must inspect her husband's conservatory before she left. Looking through the telescope would be a dream come true, because she loved stars. Dared she do so now?

Grabbing her shawl, Evie slipped her feet into her shoes and made for the door. There was no point in rousing Prue, as she would just say no.

Opening it, she peeked out. Evie was no fool, and she'd heard that people at house parties got up to any number of things they shouldn't, like entering bedrooms that weren't theirs for illicit rendezvous. Stepping out, she saw no one lurking nearby.

Although why they would be when the three Spencers were the only ones in this wing, she wasn't sure. Reaching the stairs, she made her way quietly down.

The house took on an entirely different personality in the dark. Shadows lurked everywhere, but as her eyes adjusted, she was able to see slivers of light filtering in through windows.

Reaching the entrance way without detection, she headed right along another hall.

Back in Chipping Nodbury, Evie walked about at night a lot because everyone in her village was sleeping. As a person should be at such an hour. But it had been her time to enjoy the stars alone.

She slipped into Lord Hampton's library, which he'd told her to use as often as she wished. It was full of so many wonderful books. There was also a door that led directly to the gardens. Heading for that, she stepped outside and closed it behind her.

Looking up, she saw the sky was clear and a perfect night to study the stars. Decision made, Evie hurried to the path that forked left toward the lake. It wasn't a long walk, but at night, alone, doubts crept in. Just when she thought about turning back, she saw moonlight shimmering on the water.

Walking over the narrow bridge, Evie opened the door quietly and waited. She did not want to come across anyone in here. Silence greeted her, so she closed the door and moved to the nearest seat. She'd look through the telescope soon, but for now she just wanted to lie on her back and stare at the stars.

The sound of footsteps, and then the door opening had her rising.

"I knew you were reckless, and this confirms it."

The large shadow standing in the doorway was that of her fiancé…fake fiancé.

"Anthony, you made my heart stop. What are you doing here?" Evie gasped.

"Following my reckless fiancée," he snapped.

"Why am I reckless? I was careful and encountered no one.

How did you see me if you were not being reckless also?"

"I was seated in the library when you walked in. I watched you open the door and step outside, and you damn well know it is not the same for me to be wandering about at night alone as it is for you."

He moved closer to where she sat. Now she could read his expression, she saw he was indeed angry.

"It is not reckless here in the country to walk about alone for anyone surely?" she protested.

"And what of Calthorpe or Cavendish? Are they not a risk to you? Or someone who has drunk too much and thinks to take advantage of you."

"Stop snarling at me. You are not my fiancé, this is fake, and I do not take instruction from you." Evie felt her own anger rise.

"I will snarl at you if you are behaving like a fool," he thundered. "I have history with those men that until now has merely simmered below the surface. But Cavendish wanted you as his wife, and I beat him to it—"

"I am not a bone to gnaw over," Evie snapped, regaining her feet.

"To him you are. Use that large brain of yours, Evangeline." His hands grabbed her shoulders. "I don't want you hurt."

Before she could speak, he had pulled her closer.

"You're important to me," he whispered against her lips. "Do you understand what I'm saying?"

"No," she said.

"Me either." He kissed her. It was hard, his lips crushing hers, and it took two seconds for her to respond.

Evie threw her arms around his neck and held on as his mouth devoured hers.

"You are causing me a lot of trouble, Evangeline." His mouth moved to her jaw where he kissed along it. "I can think of nothing but you."

"I am the same," Evie said lifting her chin as he reached her neck.

His hands were moving over her body, leaving heat wherever they touched.

"This engagement," he gritted out, easing back from her. "I think we need to make it real."

The shock had her mouth opening.

"Well?" he demanded, wrapping her hair around his fist and giving it a gentle tug, which had their eyes meeting.

"I-ah. Yes," she said, and then nodded in case he didn't understand what she'd said.

"Good, because I want to make love to you, Evangeline, and I want to do that now."

"Do you?" Her limbs had gone weak, and she had an urge to press her thighs together because heat was pooling there.

"But if you don't want that, then we will wait until after our marriage," he gritted out.

He looked in pain, Evie thought as his hands stopped their movement and he stepped back to put space between them.

"You need to say no now, and then we will go back to the house, because if I keep touching you, I will be unable to stop," he rasped.

This man whom she thought had so much control wanted to make love to her. Evangeline Spencer. He wanted her to be his real fiancée. The thoughts were heady ones.

"Yes." She moved closer. "I want that... all of it."

"Thank God." He cupped her face and kissed her, softly this time. "I shouldn't ask this of you...shouldn't even be contemplating—"

"Anthony, I want this. I know what happens, and I want that now with you—"

"It will only ever be with me, Evangeline."

"Only you," she whispered.

He moved away from her toward the door, and then she heard the key turn in the lock.

"Lord Hampton does not like to be disturbed when he is in here, for which I will be forever grateful."

She didn't speak, just watched him prowl back to her. He shrugged out of his jacket and dropped it on the floor. Then he had his hands on her again.

She rose to her toes to take his kisses, eager to feel more with this man she would spend her life with. Anthony would be her husband. She'd think about that more later, but not now.

"Evie, what are you doing to me?"

She loved the sound of her name on his lips.

"No woman has ever made me want her like you have."

"I've never known the touch of a man, so I can't—"

"Don't finish that sentence. There will be no other man as I believe I've already explained."

His hands went to the buttons at her back, and she felt them pushing each through its hole. The rush of cool air told her he'd parted her gown. One warm hand slid inside, his fingers touching the skin above her chemise. She could do nothing to stop the moan.

"You are so beautiful." Anthony stepped back and looked at her. "Take off your dress now, Evie."

She did, pushing it from her shoulders so she stood only in her chemise. His eyes ran over her, from the top of her head to her toes, and she felt everywhere his gaze landed.

"And you. Will you remove your... ah, boots," she said suddenly nervous for no other reason than she'd never seen a naked man.

"I will remove my, ah, boots," he teased her.

She watched as he tugged them off and then he closed the inches between them. His fingers trailed down her neck, to her chest, and then he was touching her breast.

"Oh my," she whispered as he stroked her nipple, and delicious heat shot through her body.

"Oh my, indeed," he whispered against her lips before kissing her. As his mouth tormented hers, one hand eased under the hem of her chemise. Seconds later, he pulled it up and off her body.

"Beautiful," he whispered, "but then I knew you would be."

"Anthony!" She gasped as he licked one of her breasts, and the tension building inside her rose higher.

"I want to see you." Evie shuddered as his tongue swept across her taut nipple.

He released her to tear off his necktie and pull the shirt over his head. Needing to touch him, as he had her, Evie placed a hand on his chest and felt him shudder. She stroked the slopes and plains of skin over hard muscle. His was a beautiful body, and she was awed that he would be hers to touch from this day forth.

"More," he said, his voice strained. "I want you to keep touching me, Evie. Only you can make the cold go away."

She ran her hands over every inch of him that was exposed to her. Then she pressed her lips to the place above his heart.

"Evie." The whisper of her name sounded broken.

CHAPTER THIRTY

"L ET ME TOUCH you, now," he said as his hand moved up her thigh to that secret place only she had touched before. The breath caught in her throat as he ran a finger down the soft folds between her legs. His thumb brushed the hard bud and this time it was Evie who shuddered.

"Just feel, my sweet." He kissed her again. Hard and deep, while his fingers stroked her. One pushed inside her tight, wet sheath, and the tension rose, then another finger and she let out a shuddering moan and came apart. His lips silenced her cries as his hands continued to torment her until he had teased every tremor from her body.

"Oh my," Evie said easing back. "That was wonderful."

"It was," he said walking her back in his arms until her legs hit the sofa.

"Be sure, Evie." His hands cupped her face. "There is no going back once we do this."

"I'm sure." She leaned in to kiss him. "Make love to me, Anthony."

He removed his breeches, and Evie looked at the hard length of his arousal. She felt fear, but so much more. This man wanted her, as she wanted him. *Her fiancé.* Evie had thought never to experience this, what could lie between a man and a woman, but now she was…always would with him.

"Can I touch you?"

His laugh sounded strangled. "I'm not sure I can take you touching me right now, my sweet."

Evie stroked a finger over the crown of his erection, and Anthony moaned. He let her explore him for a few more seconds before stopping her. He then changed their positions and sat on the sofa.

"Straddle my thighs, Evie. I can't wait any longer to have you."

He pulled her down so her legs were on either side of his, exposing her to his touch.

"Christ, I want you so much." He cupped her face and kissed her softly. "This will hurt you, Evie, but only this one time, I promise."

She nodded.

Anthony kissed his way to her breasts again and slowly licked each, taking the time to suck on her nipples until she was panting once more. Only then did he tell her to rise on her knees.

She did as he directed and felt the smooth, hard edge of his erection pressing at her entrance.

"Slowly, sweetheart." He guided her down onto his shaft. The tip penetrated, and then she was lowering herself onto him. Muscles stretched, and Evie felt pain, but so much more. She wanted this as much as her next breath. To feel the man she loved deep inside her brought tears to her eyes. With a final thrust he took her innocence.

Anthony was hers, as she was now his.

"Evie?" He whispered the words into her hair as he held her still against him.

"I-I'm all right, Anthony. Please don't stop."

His laugh was hoarse, and then he was moving inside her. Easing her up and back down as he took her slowly until that wonderful tension climbed inside her again.

"Anthony!"

"Let go, Evie." He thrust into her again and again until they both found their release.

Breathless, he lay back, taking her with him. Evie rested on his chest as a wave of exhaustion swept over her. One of his hands cupped her head, the other slipped around her waist. She knew it would now always be her favorite place to lie.

Evie felt her eyes close. As she lay there listening to his breathing, the delicious pull of slumber lured her under.

"No!"

The roar had her eyes opening. She was still lying on Anthony. Sitting upright she eased off him. His head was rolling from side to side, in the grip of some kind of nightmare.

"Stop, please stop!" The words were hoarse and desperate, almost as if he was in pain.

"Anthony, it's all right now. Wake up."

He struck out, connecting with her shoulder, sending her to the floor with a shriek of surprise.

"Evie?" He rose on his elbows, looking for her.

"Yes, it's me." She climbed to her feet. "You were dreaming."

She watched him blink several times.

"Why were you on the floor?"

"You were having a nightmare and—"

"I hit you?"

"It was an accident, Anthony."

"No!" He got up, backing away from her as she reached for him. "No," he said, this time softly, and to Evie it sounded like a vow. He then grabbed his clothes and began to dress.

"Anthony, what's going on? Talk to me." She touched his arm, but he pulled away as if she'd struck him.

"Please talk to me." Evie could hear the desperation in her voice.

He turned to face her only after he was finished, his expression empty, face pale.

"I don't want to marry you."

"P-pardon?" Evie whispered, stunned. "You said our engagement was now real, and what we just did—"

"No, I've changed my mind. I have no wish to marry."

His words were cold and hard. If he'd struck her, the shock would have been no less.

"You don't mean that, Anthony. What we shared, just did—"

"Dress now and go back to the house." He cut off her words.

This couldn't be happening. She had reached the gentle man who had just made love to her. This wasn't him, and she refused to believe what he'd said. He did want to marry her.

"Anthony, what is going on?" Evie pulled on her chemise, and then her dress, as he remained silent. "Please. You owe me that much."

"I owe you nothing more than what was in our agreement. After the season is over, we will never see each other again, and both continue with our lives. I will pay your sister's dowry, if that is what it takes to end this."

She didn't flinch at the cruelty of those words like she wanted to, nor wrap her arms around her waist to stop the pain. Because Evie was strong and, in that moment, she would use her pride as a shield for as long as she could.

Something had happened while he slept. A memory of past pain that had him pushing her away. Evie also knew, looking at his tight closed expression, he would not listen to any words she spoke right now. She tamped down the rush of panic that he never would and that what demons haunted him would keep him from her forever.

She needed to say what she must and leave before the promise of tears became a torrent down her cheeks. No way did she want him to sneer at her for weeping, which in his current mood he would.

"I don't know what happened, Anthony, or what that nightmare was about, but I am no fool and know that you were serious when you said you wanted our marriage to be real."

"I—"

"Just as I know the man who kissed and touched me. The man who was so gentle when he took my innocence is not the cold one standing before me now."

"Don't profess to know me, Miss Spencer, I—"

"But if you are too much of a coward," she cut him off, "to face whatever that was, or let me help you fight your demons by your side, then so be it. I will not beg."

"I don't need anyone's help. What I need is for you to leave." His words cut through her with the accuracy of a blade.

But Evie made herself look him in the eye. "You are a liar and a coward, Anthony, but if you wish to live your life in lonely isolation, then do so. But if you change your mind—"

"I won't," he snapped turning his back on her.

"And wish to speak to me again," she continued as if he hadn't uttered a word, "it will be only when you tell me the truth, because I deserve a man who is brave enough to do that. I deserve for the man I love to love me back."

She had the satisfaction of watching his head spin to look at her and walked out the door with hers held high.

Once she was sure Anthony could no longer see her, Evie picked up her skirts and ran back to the house. Reaching her room, breathless, she stepped inside and allowed the first tear to fall. Seconds later, she realized she was not alone as the tip of something sharp pressed into her neck.

"Don't move or make a sound, Miss Spencer, or I will slit your throat and then go across the hall and do the same to your sister. Do you understand?"

Evie nodded, heart thudding so hard in her chest it was painful.

"Light your candle, and then walk to the dressing table, where you will find a note. Write those words on the blank paper next to it." He spoke in a hoarse whisper in her right ear.

She had no idea who the man was, as he was behind her. But what she knew was that the blade in her neck was sharp.

"Hurry."

The knife pressed into her spine now, as she lit the candle, and then moved to the dressing table. Sitting, Evie picked up the pen and wrote. Her fingers shook as she read the words on the note beside her.

Think, Evie. She had to alert Prue somehow that she'd written this note under duress.

"Hurry." The knife dug into her spine, the small sting of pain telling her it had gone through her clothes to pierce her skin.

Dear Prudance,

I could not wed a man like Lord Hamilton when I love another. We have run away together. Please understand and forgive me. I love you and papa always.

Your loving sister Evanngalline.

Evie knew he was watching every word she put on the paper. Leaning over her shoulder to ensure she followed his orders.

"That's not how you spell your name," he said.

"When I correspond with my sister, it is."

The sound of a door banging had him dragging her back to her feet.

"Fold it and place it on the pillow. Make haste."

Evie pretended to trip. One hand tugged her necklace free as he grabbed her and then pushed her to the bed. After placing the note and the necklace on the pillow, she prayed he didn't look.

"Hurry. Open the door and tell me if it is clear. Remember, if you try and alert anyone, I will kill you and then your sister."

"It is clear," Evie whispered.

"Walk to the servants' entrance and take the stairs down. Hurry."

She did as he asked. The man knew exactly where he was going, which told her he was a guest or one of the staff. When they reached the kitchens, she looked around, hoping to see anyone. A movement caught her eye, but before she could search further, the man pushed her forward, clearly not seeing what she had.

She had to escape, because if she didn't, Evie knew she'd never see her family again. *Anthony.* She wouldn't think about him now. There was too much pain there.

When they were outside, he pushed her around the house. They took a path through the gardens before reaching the stables.

"Do not even contemplate making a noise," he said. "I am not alone, and I will have your sister killed while she slumbers."

The thought of anyone touching Prue had Evie biting her bottom lip to stay silent.

She saw the carriage waiting for them on the dark drive. The door was open, and the man urged her toward it.

Panic gripped her. If she got in that carriage, she would die. She had to escape now and run back to the house before him. Evie stopped suddenly, then lashed out backward with her foot. The grunt told her she had reached her intended target. She fled, but someone grabbed her before she'd taken two steps. Then they dragged her back and into the carriage.

Forced down onto a seat, she fought to get free, but there were two men holding her now. Looking up she saw both wore masks so she could not identify them.

"Two gutless masked men," she spat at them. "You will not get away with this!"

"Oh, but we will, Miss Spencer. And I will enjoy breaking you of this nasty habit you have. I believe it's called spirit."

A cloth closed over her mouth and nose. A vile stench filled her nostrils and suddenly her head felt light, and then she knew only darkness.

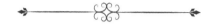

CHAPTER THIRTY-ONE

ANTHONY ENTERED THE breakfast parlor early because he could no longer stand his own company.

Because you are an unfeeling, coldhearted bastard.

Evie would not be in his life. She would not be his wife. Anthony had assured that last night. For one brief moment, he'd thought he could have it all with her, but that was before he'd hurt her.

She'd called him a coward, and she was right. He was. He'd hit her in his sleep while having a nightmare, which was something that rarely happened anymore, but he'd panicked. He'd then done what he did best and pushed her away with cruel words and turned back into the cold, emotionless man he'd taught himself to be.

The look on her face had nearly broken him, but Evie had also learned to hide. She'd pushed her pain down inside and stood before him, expressionless and so beautiful.

He could still see her as he'd made love to her. Hair a tangled mass of curls around her pale shoulders. Lush body naked in the moonlight. He'd never felt anything like he had with her last night. Never felt that close to another person. A connection.

He'd then turned on her, but she'd not wept. Instead, she'd said what she had to in a cold, clear voice. Then, after telling him she loved him, she'd walked away from him, and he'd let her.

Anthony had followed later when he had himself under control and returned to his room to lie on his bed and stare at the ceiling, reliving every moment of making love to the woman he now knew he cared for deeply.

The feel of her soft skin under his hands. Her cry when he was inside her. It would all torment him forever. He was destined to live that night over and over, because no one could ever make him feel as Evie had, again.

"Shall we leave in an hour?" Toby said, walking up behind Anthony, jarring him from his thoughts. "I rose early because I know Jamie wanted to be on the road before the sun rose too high.

"I will be ready," Anthony said, filling his plate with food he had no wish to eat.

He'd wanted Evie as his wife more than he'd ever wanted anything before, and for a few brief moments, had believed he could have her. He'd been a fool.

Now she was hurting and angry, and he doubted would ever speak to him again, which was exactly what he should want. It was for the best. *For her best.*

I deserve for the man I love to love me back.

Evangeline Spencer loved him. Anthony had never thought a woman would say those words to him, especially not someone as wonderful as she.

Ignoring the burning in his chest, *he* walked outside to sit and eat his food. His friends joined him, and he cursed himself for not staying in his room and coming down just before it was time to leave. These two knew him better than anyone. He would need to be careful what he said.

"And where is your delightful betrothed today?" Jamie asked. "I must say I am extremely happy that Evangeline will be your wife."

"I believe we have covered that ours is not a real engagement," Anthony said calmly.

"Yesterday you confirmed to us both that she means a great

deal more to you than a fake fiancée would," Toby said watching him closely.

"The engagement will not go beyond the end of the season. Now," Anthony said, "do we have names you wish to speak to in Brawley?"

"I'm sorry, what did you just say?" Jamie asked.

"Do we have names—"

"Not that part, the other bit," Jamie said.

"If you're ready, we shall leave," Anthony said. "We're to ride, so let us walk to the stables." He never felt panic, but it was there now, clawing at his throat.

He wanted Evangeline Spencer with a need that he doubted would ever wane, and that terrified him. She had given him hope, and that was a dangerous thing for a man who had never allowed himself to believe in it before. Damn this searing pain inside him. For the first time in many years, he longed for the numbing cold that usually existed in his heart.

"Tell us what is going on with you, Anthony. Your face is leached of color, and you look ready to cast up your accounts," Jamie said.

"Don't be ridiculous. I merely drank too much brandy last night."

"You never drink to excess when keeping company with your fellow peers," Toby said flatly.

Damn, he should have said he'd eaten something that disagreed with him. Anthony was usually far more alert than that.

"Get up," Toby said. "Now. We are walking."

"I don't want to walk," Anthony protested. "I want to eat my meal."

"Which you are pushing around your plate," Toby said. "Move your feet, Hamilton."

"Go to hell," he snarled with more venom than he should have used if he wanted to stop further questioning.

"I have no wish to join you there," Toby said, leaning toward him. "What have you done?"

"I have no idea what either of you is talking about."

"My money is on Evangeline being the problem here, but what I don't know is why, or what you've done to ruin things with her," Jamie said.

He reacted to hearing her name before he could stop himself. Anthony's hand clenched into a white-knuckled fist around the knife.

"What did you do?" Toby said slowly.

"Lord Hamilton."

"Yes," he said far too loudly.

"Miss Prudence Spencer has asked that you attend her at once please."

The only reason Evie's sister could want to speak to him was because she had told her what happened last night. Was Prudence Spencer about to take him to task for his behavior? *You deserve it if she is.*

"Of course, I shall go at once," Anthony said rising. "Where is she?"

"In the orchard, my lord."

"Thank you." He faced his friends who had also risen. "I will meet you shortly in the stables."

"Not bloody likely. We're coming. Something is afoot, and we want to know what. If Miss Prudence Spencer can shed light on that, excellent."

"There is nothing afoot, and I don't need your company, so go away," Anthony snapped.

"Why are you hurrying if nothing is afoot?" Jamie said, pulling alongside him. "And you can insult us all you like, but we're still coming with you."

"Evangeline is the perfect wife for you," Toby said. "We think you care deeply for her. In fact, we believe you love her."

Anthony's foot caught on the other one and he stumbled for several steps, only just managing not to land on his face.

"What?"

"She's fiery, strong willed, and won't let you have everything your own way. Plus, she will finally heal your pain," Toby added. "Don't mess things up with her. Make her your real fiancée, Anthony."

She was all of those things and more, and it was because he cared so much for her he knew she was safer without him.

"No, she's not going to be my wife." Anthony then increased his pace and reached the orchard. He found Prudence with her father, but not Evie. Her back was to him, and she was yelling.

"She would never do this, Father! Never leave us like this."

"Prudence?"

She spun, and he saw the tears and devastation on her face. Anthony knew instantly that look had nothing to do with what he'd done last night.

Evie!

"Where is she? Where is Evangeline, Prudence?" His words sounded desperate.

"When she d-didn't answer my knock on her door this morning, I opened it and entered."

Anthony watched Prudence inhale a deep breath like her sister did when she wanted to steady herself. He wanted to roar at her to tell him where Evie was.

"I found this." She thrust a paper at him. "It is her handwriting, but she was forced to write those words, Lord Hamilton. She would never leave us."

He read them twice before looking at her again. Toby and Jamie also read the note over his shoulder.

"Well. I think it's clear what her intentions are," Anthony said feeling like he had something sharp stuck in his throat. *Had she done this to get away from him? Was there another man?*

"No!" Prudence said stomping closer. "Nothing is clear, and if you truly knew my sister you would know she would never do this to her family."

"Prudence," her father cautioned.

"See the way she's written my name and hers." Prudence wrenched it from Anthony's grasp. "Evie is telling me something is not right, and she wrote that note under duress."

"I agree," Heathcliff Spencer said, stepping closer. "My eldest daughter is the most honest and loyal person I know. She would never leave us, or you, without a word."

"Why would someone force her to write that note?" Toby asked. "Surely she's under your protection, Anthony?"

"She wrote that note," he said, turning away from them. "There is no other reason for her disappearance." *If this is what feelings gave you, he didn't want it. The pain inside him was crippling.*

Anthony couldn't seem to think clearly. Evie had left to be with another man. *Correction, you sent her into the arms of another because of your behavior.*

"No!" A small hand shoved him hard in the spine. "My sister would never do this, and shame on you for believing she would."

He spun to face her. "I don't know your sister, and we both know this is not real," he snapped.

"Not real?" Heathcliff Spencer gasped.

"Not now, Father," his daughter said with her eyes on Anthony, looking every inch as strong as her older sister in that moment.

"And what about the other night?" Jamie said moving to Prudence's side to look at him. "Cavendish and Calthorpe," he added. "You don't think they could harm her after the humiliation they suffered at your hands?"

"No…" His words fell away, but suddenly he wasn't so sure. Cavendish would never stop seeking revenge on Anthony for his humiliation.

"My Lord, my sister loves us," Prudence said. "I had thought, watching you and Evie, that something had changed between you since arriving here. Please, if you feel anything for her, then help us find her."

"I may not see much, but I have watched you both together, Lord Hamilton. My eldest daughter cares for you deeply," Heathcliff Spencer added.

He was not the only one surprised by those words. His daughter was looking at her father wide-eyed.

"I know I'm a silly old fool, but I still see things."

Prudence wrapped her arms around him briefly. "You're our silly old fool."

"Take us to where you found the note," Anthony demanded. *Was she in danger?* Had someone taken her to seek revenge on him? The thought filled his veins with ice.

They all hurried back to the house.

"May I be of assistance?" the butler said when they entered.

"Have our horses saddled at once, please," Anthony said. He didn't know where they were going, but if Evie had been taken against her will, he had to find her.

"I'll question the staff," Toby said.

The rest of them ran up the stairs. Far smaller than his, the bed had been made and the room tidied.

"I found it there." Prudence pointed to the pillows.

Anthony wasn't sure what he thought he'd find, but he looked anyway. Dropping to a crouch, he searched beside and under the bed. He saw the chain as he rose. It was beside the nightstand.

"That's Evie's necklace," Prudence said as Anthony held it out. "She never takes it off, even to sleep. It was our mother's. She wouldn't have left it behind."

He would know that if they'd married, just as he would have learned all the sides to Miss Evangeline Spencer.

Anthony studied the necklace; the catch was broken. Someone had torn this off her. The thought of anyone touching her with anything but kindness or love made him burn with rage.

He'd pushed her away from fear of hurting her but ended up hurting her anyway. If he had remained in that conservatory with Evie, then whatever had befallen her would never have happened, he was sure of it.

"Find Calthorpe," he said looking at Toby. His friend left at a run, and Anthony turned to face the Spencers. "Trust me to bring her back to you."

"I want to help. E-Evie is everything to us."

"I know that, Prudence, just as I know now, she would never have willingly left you—"

"You do?"

He nodded at her question. He'd been an idiot to believe otherwise.

"I need you both to stay here and keep up appearances. Tell anyone who asks as to her whereabouts that she has a headache and is resting in her room. Draw the curtains. I shall return as soon as I have her."

"But what if you c-can't find her?"

"I will, because I will not stop looking until I do."

Prudence ran at Anthony, hugging him hard. "Please bring my sister home."

"You have my word." He hugged her back briefly, and then left the room in search of Jamie. He found him in the kitchens with the butler standing beside a young boy.

"What have you learned?" Anthony asked when he reached them.

"Tell him," Jamie said to the boy, who looked terrified. "He won't harm you. Just tell him what you told me."

"I was hungry, and I came to the kitchens as Mrs. Broom always leaves me a slice of bread for if I need it. I saw a man coming in the door. He told me to mind my business and walked into the house. He took the servants' stairs up. I got the bread and stayed here to eat it.

"What did he look like?"

"I didn't see his face clearly because he was in the shadows, and the kitchen fire doesn't throw out much light. He was shorter than you and wore a hat and coat."

"How did he speak?" Anthony asked.

"Odd voice. Like a whisper but not. Hoarse," the lad added. "Like Mr. Davis."

"The stable master," the butler added. "A horse kicked him in the neck, and he never spoke the same again."

"Greville had a friend who talked like that," Jamie said, clicking his fingers.

"Dutton," Anthony whispered.

"I was sitting here, in front of the fire, and I heard footsteps," the boy added. "So I blew out the candle and curled up small."

"Did you see who left?" Anthony asked.

"There were two of them. I'm sure it was the man, but he had another in front of him, and he pushed her toward the door. I saw her hair. It was long. She turned, and looked right at me, but then they were gone."

Evie.

"Your help has been invaluable. Thank you," Jamie said, pressing a coin into the boy's hand.

"Calthorpe left last night, according to Hampton. He had an appointment but said he would be back in a few days," Toby said entering the kitchen.

Anthony handed out more money to the butler, and then they left by the kitchen door.

"It has to be Evie. I saw her last night, and her hair was loose. It had to be after she came back to the house. Someone was waiting in her room," Anthony said.

"When did you see her?" Toby asked.

"Does it matter?" A slither of dread ran through him, but Anthony tamped it down. He would get her back, and someone would pay for what they'd done.

"So you believe now she did not leave with someone else?" Toby said.

"I do."

"I say we ride to Greville's estate. We'll pass through Brawley on the way," Anthony said.

"Yes, Cavendish has the main motive, and we know he and Greville are close, along with Calthorpe," Jamie said.

"What if we're wrong?" Anthony said, as desperation gripped him. "What if there is someone else involved—"

"Everything points to Cavendish," Toby said with a calm he wasn't sure he'd ever feel again. Would he get a chance to tell her she was right? That he had been a coward to push her away instead of telling her the truth about his feelings?

"Let's go," Toby said.

"I think Toby is right, Anthony," Jamie said as they ran to the stables. "Cavendish is the only person with motive."

"He is, but is he foolish enough to take this step? To remove Evangeline from a house party?" Jamie asked.

"He hates Anthony enough to lose what little sense he has," Toby added. "Especially after that night you punched him."

"She is missing because of her association with me," Anthony said. "And when I catch Cavendish, I will kill him this time," Anthony said mounting.

Minutes later they were galloping toward Brawley.

Stay safe, Evie. I will find you.

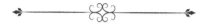

CHAPTER THIRTY-TWO

E VIE WAS JOSTLED awake. Opening her eyes produced a dull pain in her head.

"I'm glad you are back with us, Miss Spencer."

The hideous masked face was swimming into view as Evie blinked several times to clear her vision.

"Who are you? What do you want with me?" she asked slowly, attempting to collect her scattered wits. "What was that vile stuff you pressed to my face?"

"Merely something to help you sleep."

She couldn't place his voice. Gruff. But then he was likely doing that so she didn't recognize him.

"Now, you'll forgive me for this, but needs must I'm afraid."

"What are you—"

"We can't have you taking in your surroundings," he said, pressing a blindfold to her eyes. She couldn't stop him, as her wrists were bound before her. Her wits may be slow, but her feet still worked. Evie lashed out with one and heard a satisfying grunt.

"Bitch!"

"Quiet!" a second voice said.

She was dragged out of the carriage and thrown over a shoulder. Then jostled as he walked. Nausea roiled around in her belly, and she could do nothing to stop the retching.

"Keep walking," a voice said.

"She's emptying her stomach down my back!"

Evie kept retching. She loathed being sick, but right then was rather happy to be doing so all over this horrid man.

She wasn't sure how long they walked, but it felt like at least an hour. Finally, Evie heard a sound, like a bolt being opened, and then the squeak of hinges. More walking and then another bolt, and soon Evie felt herself falling. She landed with a thud on something hard. Someone then wrenched the blindfold from her eyes. Leaping to her feet, Evie struck out with her bound hands. Raising them, she connected with the man's jaw, sending him backward. Unfortunately, he stumbled back out through the open door.

"Close it!"

It slammed, and she heard someone secure the bolt.

Evie slammed her fists on the wood, which only resulted in them hurting and the door remaining shut.

"Damn you!" she roared. No one answered.

Her head felt clearer now, and her belly less queasy, likely due to the fact it had nothing in it, but the desperation clawed at her throat.

She had to get out of here, and back to Prue and their father. *And Anthony.*

Taking in her surroundings, Evie walked around the room. A narrow bed with a thick green coverlet. There was a dressing table with a hairbrush and ewer on top. A narrow wooden chair was pushed up to it.

Moving closer, Evie plunged her face into the water. The cold was a shock, but she needed that. Rising, she grabbed the drying cloth and blotted her face. *Where was she?*

There was a folded pile of clothing on a chair, and several shawls thrown over the back of it.

What was this place, and why did they bring her here?

Light coming through the window told her it was daylight, so she must have been in that carriage for some time. Evie saw nothing but the sea below her. The Hampton estate had been a

three-hour trip by carriage to the sea. For those interested, there
was a trip planned there for tomorrow. Prue had been so excited.

Evie pressed a hand to her mouth as she felt an overwhelm-
ing need to sit on the bed and weep. But there was no time for
that now. She would give in to that later, when she had escaped.

Did anyone know by now that she was missing?

Anthony.

"No. I will not think about that cowardly man," she said. But
the pain of last night nearly dropped her to her knees. He'd
touched her like she meant something to him. Held her as if she
was made from spun glass and then pushed her away.

Damn you for a coward, Lord Hamilton.

The last words they'd spoken to each other were angry and
hurtful. He would have to live with that, as would she… for as
long as these people allowed her to.

No!

Even if Anthony was not brave enough to love her, she needed to survive this for Prue and their father. They relied on her,
and she would not let them down. Her focus had to be on them.

The room wasn't large, and she knew the man who'd carried
her had walked for a while to reach where she was.

Think, Evie.

Pacing away, she walked slowly around the small room.
Picking up the hairbrush she studied it. Silver with an intricate
pattern, it had a long handle. Looking at the window again, Evie
wondered if it would break the glass. But then if she made a
noise, it may bring someone to investigate.

Moving closer she looked through the glass and saw water
below. From her height Evie guessed there were likely cliffs
beneath, and she would plunge to her death if she attempted to
climb down them. But there could also be a ledge somewhere she
could reach.

Grabbing two shawls, she went back to the window and
lowered one onto the floor beneath. The other she wrapped
around the handle of the hairbrush. Not easy work with her

hands bound, but she was nothing if not determined. She was about to strike at it with the handle when she heard footsteps. Grabbing the shawls, she took them and the hairbrush back to the bed. Sitting, Evie draped the shawls over her knees and dropped the hairbrush to the floor, kicking it with her heel under the bed.

The door swung open, and a man appeared in one of those terrifying masks.

"Miss Spencer, we thought you may be hungry after your trip." He took a single step into the room, keeping his eyes on her. *Wise man.*

"Where am I? Why have you abducted me?"

He lowered the tray to the floor, just inside the door, and then backed away. Before he closed it again, he spoke once more.

"This will be your home for quite some time, Miss Spencer. I suggest you eat, as you will need your strength." He then shut the door quietly, and she heard his laughter as he walked away.

She'd known, of course, that something nefarious was afoot. You didn't steal someone away in the dead of night from a house party to make friends with them after all. But those words had a sinister threat behind them, she was sure of it.

"I'd rather die than be held against my will for the rest of my life," Evie declared, getting off the bed.

But why did they want her? Did they think to ransom her and hope Anthony would pay well to get her back?

He would; she knew that. There was a good man under the cold facade. He'd shown that with the care he gave his aunts. Even if he was too much of a coward to come out of hiding and live with her.

Thinking about him hurt, so she pushed him aside again and dropped to her knees to look under the bed. The hairbrush had not gone too far thankfully. Hooking it out with her foot, she regained her feet. Her stomach then let out a loud rumble.

If she was to escape and find her way back to her family, then she must keep her strength up. Picking up the tray, Evie carried it back to the bed. There was something that looked like a beef stew and a slice of bread and jam. She ate the bread.

Evie then planned, which is what she did best. She worked through every option for escape, which, if she was honest, there weren't many. When she was finished with the food and coming up with every scenario that may or may not happen, she took her supplies back to the window.

Wrapping the hairbrush, she then yelled "Let me out!" while smashing the handle into the window so no one heard. A crack formed, but it needed to be bigger if she was to look out and eventually climb through. Yelling again, this time she forced her elbow into the glass, and it shattered.

Taking one of the larger shards, Evie braced it between her knees, using it to saw through the ropes around her wrists. It took time, and she nicked herself twice, but finally, her hands were free. Tucking the glass into her bodice, she was about to clear away the glass from the sash, when she heard footsteps. Dashing for the chair, she carried it back to the door.

Heart pounding, Evie watched it open, and a man stepped inside.

"What the—"

She raised the chair and swung at the back of his head. He crumpled to the floor.

Evie bent and began searching his pockets. Finding a large round ring holding keys, she pulled it out. She then pressed her fingers to his neck and felt his heartbeat. He may be a villain, but she had no wish for this man's death to be on her hands.

Straightening, with her heart in her mouth, Evie walked to the door. Peering out, she saw no one. Stepping outside, she closed it softly. After trying several keys with trembling hands, she finally found the right one to lock it.

Looking to the right she saw a short hall and stairs. The left was a longer one with two more doors leading off it.

Which way should she go? She heard a sound then. Was that someone weeping? Tiptoeing left, she reached the first door. Someone inside that room was definitely crying. Should she open it? Turning the handle slowly, Evie found it locked. *Did that mean whoever was behind this door was also being held against their will?*

Evie couldn't call out and risk someone hearing her, so she tried several keys in the lock until one fit. Pushing the door open, she looked inside.

Three young ladies were sitting, wide eyed and clearly terrified, on a bed, which was the only furniture in this room. Like hers had been, their hands were bound.

"Wh-who are you?" one of them asked.

"My name is Miss Evangeline Spencer. Are you being held here against your will?"

The girls nodded.

"What are your names?" Evie whispered moving closer.

"I'm Molly, and this is Hannah and Rachel."

"Well, Molly, Hannah, and Rachel, I was being held against my will too, in the room next door. Now let's get your hands untied so we can escape."

"How?" one girl asked.

"I don't know, but we have to try. I, for one, refuse to simply sit about awaiting my fate." She went to the one called Molly and worked on the ropes around her wrists. Then between them they got the other two free.

"Come along. We must make haste now." Evie used her no-nonsense voice that rarely worked on Prue but that her father usually took note of.

"Are any of you hurt?" Evie asked as they got to their feet.

Molly shook her head. "They bring us food, but that's it. I don't know how many days I've been here," she said.

"They're planning something soon with us, but we don't know what," Hannah added. "We've heard chanting and other voices nearby. It's right scary."

"It matters not. We are leaving," Evie said.

"You're bleeding, miss," Molly said. "Let me bind it."

It was probably better not to leave a trail of blood, so she allowed Molly to tear strips off the hem of her undergarments and bind the cuts on her wrist. It took precious minutes, and Evie's fear climbed. They had to leave before someone realized what she had done.

"Hurry," she said, heading to the door when Molly had finished. "Follow me and walk as lightly as you can."

"I can't," Rachel whispered. "What if—"

"Do you have family, Rachel?" She nodded tearfully. "And do you wish to see them again?" Evie asked.

"Y-yes."

"Then you must be brave, because if you truly wish that, then we have to escape now."

"She's right," Molly agreed.

Evie opened the door and walked left once more, hoping all three of the girls were following. *Please, let this be the way out.*

At the end of the hallway, there was another door. Evie tried several keys, each one making a noise that seemed loud in the enclosed space, until finally locating the right one.

"Brace yourselves to fight if need be." Evie looked at the girls, and each nodded. "With everything you have," she added. "Nails, feet, teeth, whatever you need, use it." They nodded again, wide-eyed now. "We must escape, and this is our chance."

Opening the door, she entered a large chamber. Holding up a hand, Evie searched and found no one in there, so she waved the girls inside, and locked the door behind them.

At one end of the room there was an altar. Before that was a table with white candles on the floor ringing it. She heard the girls gasp at the same time Evie realized this was some kind of place that people came to worship, and something was likely sacrificed on that table, because leather straps hung on either side.

"D-do you think this is where they would have brought us?" Molly whispered.

Evie did indeed think that, and the thought sent a chill down her spine. They would have suffered in many ways here, she realized.

"It's evil I feel," Hannah whispered.

"Come along." Evie walked across the room to some steps. "We are leaving at once." The staircase veered left and at the top she came to a narrow door. Searching again through the keys, she found the one that fit in the lock.

"Are you ready?" she whispered, and the girls all replied yes. Turning the key, she pushed the door open.

"I hear someone coming," one of the girls whispered.

"Hurry!" Evie stepped through and ushered them behind her. She then shut and relocked the door.

"Run now, and don't look back!"

CHAPTER THIRTY-THREE

B RAWLEY WAS A small village near to the coast that took them three hours to reach. Three of the longest hours of his life.

They'd ridden hard, and conversed rarely, and the entire time thoughts of Evie had plagued Anthony. Was she all right? Had someone hurt her?

He'd spent his last moments with Evangeline Spencer inflicting pain on her, and he would never forgive himself for that.

She was right; he'd been a coward. For many years, Anthony had kept himself distant from anyone but his family and two friends because he'd never allow anyone to hurt him again.

But she'd been different from the start. Evie had infiltrated his soul, and this deep aching pain inside told Anthony it was love he felt for the woman he'd pushed away. Where he'd endured hell before and survived, to lose her now, he knew he wouldn't.

It was terrifying to think she was suffering because of him. That she was going through pain like he and his friends had as boys. *Was Cavendish responsible?* They were staking everything on that being the case, and Anthony prayed they were right.

The Fox and Crown tavern was in the middle of the village. After stabling their horses, they headed there.

"Do not go in there lording about the place. We need to find out what these people know, and to do that, we have to be civil," Toby said.

"I'll be civil," Anthony said, his tone dark.

"And that's you being civil, is it?" Jamie said.

He grunted something unintelligible.

"Do you love her?" Toby asked.

"What?"

"Do you love Evangeline, Anthony?" Jamie demanded. "Don't be a coward and answer the question."

"Yes." He stopped fighting what he knew. "It has to be that, because it hurts, in here." He rubbed above his heart.

"Well then, let's find her," Jamie said after clearing his throat.

The interior was like most he'd entered. Dark, with the tang of alcohol and body odor in the air, and a steady hum of voices.

They approached the man behind the bar.

"Good day," he said with a pleasant smile.

"Good day to you. We are after some information if you could help us," Jamie said.

"Of course."

"A woman has gone missing, and we are trying to locate her," Toby said.

The man's smile fell.

"She is my fiancée," Anthony added.

The man studied him for several seconds, and Anthony withstood it, instead of grabbing him and shaking the answers he needed from him.

"We've had two girls go missing from Brawley, and a further one from the next village."

"Yes, we heard that. One of those girls, Molly Allsopp, is my housekeeper's niece," Jamie said.

"We believe there could be a connection with the boy wandering nearby that a farmer found with markings on his chest. If it's possible, we'd like to speak with him," Toby said.

"My nephew, Frank, was found with the markings on him. Not sure what he can tell you, but I'll get him."

"We'd be grateful," Toby added.

"If you'll sit in that booth, I'll find him for you." The man waved them to the right.

Toby put a hand on Anthony's shoulder and maneuvered him toward the booth.

A young man approached with his uncle just when Anthony was about to storm into the kitchens and find him. He looked nervous, which was understandable, considering three gentlemen wanted to speak to him.

"My name is Frank, and my uncle said you wish to speak with me."

"Sit," Toby said waving him to the empty seat beside Jamie. His uncle stood, watching in case he was needed at the bar.

"Can you tell us what happened the night leading up to you being found with the mark on your chest, Frank?" Anthony asked.

Frank shot his uncle a look, and Anthony had a feeling he didn't want to speak about the matter with him there.

"We've had a long journey, sir. Could we prevail upon you to get us three ales?" Toby said, clearly seeing what Anthony had.

The man nodded, shot his nephew a look, and then walked away.

"Perhaps if you have no wish for your uncle to hear what it is you want to say, tell us everything you know quickly," Jamie said.

"What I did was wrong, and I can't tell my uncle," Frank said. "It would kill him and my aunt. They took me in, you see, when no one else would."

"Your secret will be safe with us, Frank," Anthony said.

"I took the cart with some supplies out for delivery, and on the return journey, I stopped up a track in the forest to eat what my aunt had packed for me. Three men approached me on horseback. They said they needed something picked up and delivered, and I'd be paid handsomely for it. They handed me more money than I could earn in a year, so I said yes."

The boy looked for his uncle, but he was still behind the bar as another customer had arrived.

"One man, he handed me a flask, and I didn't want to insult him, so I took a drink. They then told me they needed supplies collected from the next town over. I tried to say it was too far, and my uncle needed me back, but the words seemed stuck in my throat. After that, I don't remember much. I thought I heard a woman's scream, but I couldn't open my eyes, and my limbs felt heavy."

"Can you take us to where you last remember being?" Anthony asked.

The boy nodded. "When I woke up from whatever they'd put in my drink, I was still in the forest with my horse and cart. But a full day and night had passed.

"Were you hurt, Frank?"

He shook his head. "Just the red symbol on my chest."

Anthony, with a flicker of an eyelash, acknowledged that the boy's words had shaken him. He remembered the feeling of waking with no memory and finding that symbol on his chest.

They drank the ale and left with Frank and a warning from his uncle to look out for him, which they assured him they would.

"Our horses are fast, and if you're happy with it, Frank, I'd like you to climb up behind me," Anthony said when they reached the stables. Wide-eyed, the boy nodded.

They rode back out of town until Frank stopped them. "There." He pointed to a narrow track between the trees.

Anthony turned and soon they were riding deeper into the forest. They stopped when the track opened to a clearing surrounded by trees.

"This is where I was."

Dismounting, Anthony looked around him. There appeared to be no tracks leading anywhere.

"Frank, I need you to stay here and watch our horses. Can you do that?" Jamie asked.

"Aye."

They each took a direction and searched for any clue that suggested someone had been this way.

What if this was not where Evie was? What if someone else took her and is even now—

"Here," Toby said suddenly. "Someone has been this way and covered their tracks. I'm sure of it."

Toby disappeared into the trees. Anthony and Jamie followed at a run. Beyond the tree line, there was a well-worn path.

"Why would someone go to the trouble of disguising this?" Jamie asked.

"It's close to the sea. You can smell it in the air. Perhaps they're smuggling goods in here?" Toby said.

"Or perhaps someone is hiding it for more nefarious purposes," Jamie added.

"This is the right place," Anthony said, suddenly sure of it.

"How do you know that?" Toby asked.

"I just do."

"Because you love her," Jamie added.

He said nothing more, just ran along the narrow track. They checked everywhere. Each time there appeared a gap in the trees, they investigated. So far, they'd found nothing. But they would. Anthony felt Evie was close.

"The sea is closer now," Jamie said.

"Wait!" Toby held up a hand, and they stopped. "What's that noise?"

"Someone is coming," Anthony whispered.

They moved into the trees and hid, waiting. The woman that appeared was not Evie, but scared and running from something, if his guess was correct. He stepped out from his hiding place and in front of her.

"No!"

"I mean you no harm," he said as she backed away from him. "Please, I am trying to find someone. A woman."

"Pl-please don't take me back there," she begged.

"What is your name?" Jamie asked, reaching them.

"M-Molly Allsopp."

"Molly, your aunt is my housekeeper. She sent me to find you. I am Lord Stafford."

The girl stopped moving and pressed a hand to her mouth.

"You are safe now, Molly," Toby said. "But you must tell us all you know at once, as we are very worried for our friend, Miss Evangeline Spencer."

"Sh-she was the one who saved us!" Molly gasped. "She unlocked the doors and let us out. Then someone heard us, and she told us to run."

"Where is she?" Anthony demanded.

"We were all separated—"

"All?" Toby asked.

"There were th-three of us in that room when Miss Spencer saved us," Molly said.

Of course, she would not have just sat there and waited for him to find her. His Evie would have taken charge of her destiny.

"We need to find the others now, Molly," Jamie said. "You must listen to me carefully."

The girl nodded.

"If you keep following this track, it will take you a while, but you will come to Frank from the Fox and Crown. He is holding our horses. He will look after you until we return," Jamie said.

She nodded. "Please help the others."

"We will," Toby said. "Now go."

She did and had soon disappeared.

"Let's go," Anthony said.

They had not run far before they heard more sounds. Once again, they moved deeper into the trees and waited. Heart pounding, Anthony kept his eyes on the trail. *Please let it be Evie.*

Three women appeared, and then he heard her voice.

"Do not look back. Run!"

"Molly—"

"Will be safe, but we are not!"

"Evie!" he roared.

"Anthony!" She spun to search for him.

He reached her in seconds, catching her as she hurled herself into his arms.

"Christ, Evie, I've been so scared," he whispered into her hair.

She was shaking, her entire body shuddering as her hands clung to his neck.

"I have you." He crushed her to him. "You are safe now. No one will hurt you again," he vowed.

"They're coming!" one of the women cried.

He tugged Evie's hands from his neck and pushed her toward the other two.

"Hide now, Evie."

"Anthony—"

"Keep them safe," he said, knowing that would be the only thing that would make her do as he wanted.

She took both girls' hands and tugged them into the trees. He, Jamie, and Toby followed.

They heard the thud of booted feet and watched four men wearing masks appear running.

Pistols raised, he, Toby and Jamie were soon in pursuit.

"I heard voices. They're here somewhere!" one man roared. It's only two nights till Black Mass. We need them."

Anthony knew that voice. He cocked his pistol and yelled, "Halt!"

The men spun and found Anthony, Jamie, and Toby.

"Take the mask off, Cavendish. Now, or I'll shoot you where you stand."

He reluctantly did as Anthony asked, and he got a good look at the man who he was going to kill.

"No shooting, Anthony. We will make him suffer in other ways," Toby said.

"I want him dead."

"But you are better than he."

"That nose looks sore," Jamie said. Cavendish's nose was swollen, and his eyes were black and bruised. "Miss Spencer did an excellent job."

"Get on your knees," Toby ordered.

"What's the meaning of this, Hamilton? Can't we walk about

wearing masks in private?" Cavendish said, but Anthony saw the fear.

"Knees, now!" Toby said.

The men did as he asked.

"Hands on your head," Jamie added.

They moved closer, checking the men for weapons.

"Explain yourself," Cavendish said, still thinking he could talk his way out of this.

"You abducted three women, and then Miss Spencer from the Hampton house party, Cavendish. That's what this is about," Anthony said.

"What women?" he scoffed. "I see no women anywhere."

"How about now?"

"Evie, go back," Anthony growled. She, of course, ignored him and moved to stand at his side.

"Miss Spencer? What are you doing here?" Cavendish said.

Before he could stop her, she'd stepped closer to the man and punched him hard in the face yet again. Cavendish howled with pain and fell sideways clutching his already throbbing nose.

Unmasking the other men revealed themselves to be Calthorpe, Greville, and another.

"Well now, imagine our surprise at seeing all three of you low-life scum together again," Toby said. "Considering what you were capable of at Blackwood Hall, my guess is that has merely increased."

"Move back now, Evie," Anthony said grabbing her around the waist. "Let us deal with them."

"You'll not stop us," Greville hissed. "There will always be more."

Pulling out his handkerchief, Jamie forced it into the man's mouth. "Does anyone else have anything to say?" No one spoke again.

They used their cravats to bind the men's hands and then pulled them back to their feet.

"Now walk." He prodded Cavendish with his pistol.

THE MAGISTRATE WAS summoned when they were back in Brawley. Greville, Calthorpe, the other man, and Cavendish were taken away. Anthony and his friends were also assured the forest would be searched to find the location where the women had been held.

Anthony had left Evie to clean and bind her cuts along with the women she'd saved at the Fox and Crown while he dealt with everything alongside Jamie and Toby.

After her initial pleasure at seeing him, she'd barely spoken a word to Anthony. He'd wrapped her in his coat and held her rigid body before him on his horse. He'd not tried to talk to her, as people surrounded them, but he would soon. The journey back to the Hampton house party was the perfect opportunity.

"Where is Miss Spencer?" he said, entering the Fox and Crown. Looking around, he saw no sign of her or the other women.

"She was worried for her family, so Mr. Greggor said he'd take her to them, seeing as she'd brought his daughter back," Frank said.

"Well," Toby said. "At least we can be sure you'll not have everything your own way."

CHAPTER THIRTY-FOUR

E VIE WAS TIRED and hungry, but for all that, she was now safe and could return to her family.

Anthony had saved her, and she would always be grateful to him and his friends for that. But Evie was in no fit state to stay and face the man who had said what he had to her last night. The man who had taken her innocence and then sent her away.

She was tired and felt weepy, and there was no way she wanted to do that all over him. When it was possible, he would apologize to her for his behavior but still tell her he had no wish to marry her. If he actually wanted to talk to her, that was. No, it was better she returned to the house party and saw him when she felt stronger.

"That's a mighty sigh," Mr. Greggor said from beside her.

He'd offered to take her back to the Hampton house party. She'd refused as surely it was too far. He'd said nothing was too far for the woman who brought his daughter back to him. So here she was, seated beside him on his cart, while he sang softly.

"It has been a long day."

"I'm sure, but you're safe now and will soon be with your family."

He started to sing a ballad that Evie knew so she joined in. Unlike Mr. Greggor who could hold a tune, she sounded like a cat whose tail someone had stood on. But he was polite enough not to mention that fact.

"You have a lovely voice, Mr. Greggor," Evie said when the song was finished.

"Mrs. Greggor likes me to sing to her of an evening." His craggy face split into a smile.

"You love your wife very much?" She wasn't sure why that came out of her mouth, but it had.

"Oh, aye. She's my reason for smiling."

Evie sniffed loudly as tears clogged her throat.

"And you, Miss Spencer. Do you love that man who carried you before him on his horse into the village?"

"What? No," she lied. "Why would you say such a thing?"

"I know the look of a man in love, and he had it." He started singing again then. This time she did not join in.

Anthony didn't know how to love her, but she wasn't telling Mr. Greggor that. She found herself lulled into sleeping on his shoulder as he sang softly. It was the thud of an approaching horse's hooves that roused her.

"Well now, it seems I was right about him," Mr. Greggor said, pulling his cart to a stop as Anthony halted beside them. His face looked like it had been carved in granite.

Evie watched him dismount and stalk to where she sat beside the driver.

"What the hell are you about, Evangeline?" he demanded.

"I'm going back to my family," she said in a cool voice.

"You were just abducted, put through hell, and now you're traveling alone," he snapped.

"I am not alone, as you can see. I have Mr. Greggor with me. He has been kind enough to sing to me." She wasn't sure why she'd said that.

"Good day to you, my lord," Mr. Greggor said raising his cap.

Anthony nodded but kept his eyes on Evie. He then reached up and grabbed her, lifting her off the seat.

"What are you doing? Let me go at once!"

"Thank you, you can leave now. I will see Miss Spencer to her family safely, Mr. Greggor."

"You will not—" He put his hand over her mouth, stopping Evie from speaking.

"Very well," Mr. Greggor said. "I know you're Lord Hamilton and have helped today in getting our girls back, so I know you'll see Miss Spencer home safe."

Evie tried to push the hand aside, but it didn't budge. She then watched Mr. Greggor turn his cart and roll away. Opening her mouth, she bit him.

"Ouch!" Anthony shook his hand, releasing her.

Evie started walking.

"Evie, wait!"

"I don't want to wait. I want to go back to my family, but you sent my ride a-away." She could hear the hysteria in her voice. Evie needed sleep to be at her best; she was not that now.

She'd had a night of utter bliss with this man, and then he'd sent her away with harsh words to be kidnapped. There was only so much she could take before she broke down, and Evie was fast reaching her limit.

"I'm sorry." His hand touched her shoulder lightly. "Please, Evie, stay and listen to me."

The words had her stopping, but she didn't look at him.

"I have no right to ask you to do this considering what you've been through and that some of the blame for that lies at my feet."

"If they had not taken me last night, then they would have tried again, my lord. You are not to blame for what happened to me. What you said before I was kidnapped, however, I lay entirely at your feet." She addressed her words to the road before her.

"You were taken because Cavendish and I have a past."

She said nothing to that. He was so close now, she could feel him behind her, just inches separating them. All it would take was for her to lean back, and she could rest on that solid chest, and she knew he would hold her… but no, she would not weaken now.

"You were right. I was a coward, Evie. It terrified me when I realized I'd hurt you. What I could have done to you."

"But you did not."

"Evie, please look at me."

She took a deep steadying breath and released it before turning.

"My life was hell at Blackwood Hall. Cavendish, Calthorpe, Greville, and the housemaster abused and tormented me, Jamie, and Toby. There were others, but those were the ones who seemed hell-bent on bullying us.

The look in his eyes told her his scars from that time ran deep. Evie's heart ached for the young boy who had suffered and the man who still carried the pain, but she didn't speak. He needed to tell her the whole of it if they were to make a life together.

"My aunts saved us. One day when they visited, I broke down and told them everything that was going on. So they confronted our housemaster and told him they would return every week from that day onward. If their nephew and his friends suffered anymore, there would be hell to pay."

"How lucky you were to have them," Evie said. "They must love you very much to do what they did."

"I would do anything for them. The years preceding that had been the worst of my life."

He stood there solemn-faced, no hat, amber eyes locked on her, and she could do nothing to stop the flood of love she felt for this man.

"I have nightmares, Evie. That was what happened last night."

"I understand," she said.

He closed the space between them and took her hands in his. "Can you forgive me for what I said after we made love? I reacted and hurt you, something I will never forgive myself for."

"Thank you for telling me why."

This time it was he who exhaled. "I thought I suffered back then, but knowing you were out there somewhere and I could not reach you has been the worst day of my life, Evie. I realized that if I did not find you, I would spend my life in hell."

She found a smile at that. "Perhaps that's a little dramatic—"

"It's not," he said, matching her smile, "because I love you, Miss Evangeline Spencer, to the depths of my soul."

"Really?" She could do nothing to halt the tears now.

"Really. I love your determination. I love your fiery nature, but most of all I just love you."

"I have to be honest and warn you that my managing ways may annoy you, Anthony."

"Possibly, but I will never stop loving you, Evie."

"I love you so much too, Anthony."

His smile grew, and then she was in his arms exactly where she wanted to be.

"Be my wife, sweetheart."

"Yes, but I'm not letting you win at archery just because it bruises your ego when I do."

He snorted into her hair. "God, woman, I love you. And now we need to return to your family and allay their fears."

"Which I could have done with Mr. Greggor's lovely voice accompanying me, but now I must do so on your uncomfortable horse, clasped in your arms."

"Exactly."

CHAPTER THIRTY-FIVE

ANTHONY HAD WANTED to make a run for Gretna Green and marry Evie immediately. Her family and his, however, had other ideas.

Things apparently needed to be done properly, his Aunt Petunia had said when he'd returned to the house party to find all their families there, worrying together.

The issue of when they would wed was discussed loudly, and eventually after he'd said he was not waiting more than two months, he'd got his way.

Evie had been too tired and hungry to argue with anyone on the matter and spent her time during the discussion eating and yawning after she'd bathed and changed.

Two months to the day later, he was now standing awaiting his beloved's arrival in the church his aunts had chosen. St. Georges Church in Hanover Square.

Looking down the aisle as the guests all took their seats, he thought he would have married her anywhere. She'd changed him. He was no longer cold and empty because she'd filled all the places inside him with her love.

Life would not be easy with Evangeline Spencer, as he'd once thought it would be when he took a wife, because she challenged him. Both were strong-willed, and he saw many arguments in their future, which he was looking forward to.

"I'm sure a groom is meant to be pale and nervous. You,

however, appear the exact opposite," Toby said from beside him.

"Exactly. Look a little pathetic at least," Jamie added.

Anthony turned down the sides of his mouth and lowered his eyes.

"Much better," Jamie said.

"She is the perfect woman for you, my friend," Toby said. "Had you not married her, I may have."

"And yet, like me, you have no wish to marry," Jamie added.

"There is that."

"Besides, I would have killed you had you tried," Anthony said. "And as we are friends, I would rather not do that."

"Fair point," Toby said. Then a breath hissed out of his mouth.

"What?" Jamie and Anthony asked him.

"That woman is here. Why would you invite her?"

"There are many 'hers' in the church. Care to elaborate?" Anthony asked.

"Talbot's daughter," Toby snapped. "She's rude and opinionated. For a duke's daughter she has the manners of a hoyden."

"You've never told us why she is now your enemy, when you grew up together," Anthony said. "One drunken night you even admitted to her once being your closest friend."

"She's no longer a friend," Toby gritted out.

"But she was," Anthony persisted.

"I am not discussing this further with either of you."

"I quite like Lady Liberty Talbot," Jamie said. "She's forthright, and that's refreshing."

"She's remarkably like my future wife actually," Anthony added.

They looked at Lady Liberty Talbot. She nodded to Anthony and Jamie, but her eyes chilled when they met Toby's.

"She and Evie have become friends lately. I'm not sure how I feel about that," Anthony added, waving to his aunts. Who all waved back from the front pew, looking happy.

"You need to stop that friendship at once," Toby said looking like a thundercloud.

"Close your eyes, Anthony," Jamie said suddenly.

"What? Why?"

"Don't argue. Just do it."

He did as his friend told him.

"Open them," Jamie whispered.

And there she was. Evie stood at the beginning of the aisle on her father's arm, stunning in a soft shade of rose. She wore a circlet of flowers, and a veil fell down her back.

"Take a breath, Anthony, before you faint."

"Very amusing," he said to Toby, not taking his eyes off the woman that today would become his wife. She'd move into his house, and he could wake with her in his arms and hold her whenever he wished.

The music carried her down the aisle to him behind her sister and his, both in pale blue, until finally there she was, beside him.

"Hello," he said.

"Hello," she replied in a firm voice that told him she was not nervous either. "I'll be glad when this is done," she added. "I have a pin jabbing me in the scalp."

He laughed and drew the eyes of those closest.

"I shall remove it shortly. For now, how about we get married?"

"What a lovely idea," she whispered.

"I love you," he said out of the side of his mouth.

"I love you, too."

And nothing else mattered, Anthony realized, because he now had his champion at his side, and she had hers.

Forever and always.

The End

About the Author

Wendy Vella is a *USA Today* and Amazon bestselling author of historical romances filled with romance, intrigue, unconventional heroines, and dashing heroes.

An incurable romantic, Wendy found writing romance a natural fit. Born and raised in a rural area in the North Island of New Zealand, she shares her life with one adorable husband, two delightful adult children and their partners, four delicious grandchildren, and her pup Tilly.

Wendy also writes small town contemporary romances under the name Lani Blake.

wendyvella.com/index.html